Hero's Welcome
Copyright ©2013 by Rosalind Foley
Fiction
ISBN trade paperback: 978-0-9886226-0-9

Printed in the U.S.A.

Additional copies are available from:
www.rosalindfoleyauthor.com
$14.99 plus s/h fees

Hero's Welcome

by
Rosalind Foley

For those who remembered
and all who believed

Chapter One

Jacques Viator woke up in his own bed for the first time in two years, three months and eight days. He had counted, out of habit, before falling asleep the night before.

His waking was instantaneous, a spasm of consciousness with all his senses rushing to report at once. You learned that fast in the Army, or else. It would be a hard habit to break. At ease, he told himself. You're home.

This was the moment he'd dreamed of since the day he left for boot camp. In every crowded barracks, every lousy foxhole, he had dreamed of waking up at home. The dream became his only sure ration of sanity. It got him through the dry heaves on the troop ship, a merciful alternative to the U-boat nightmares from which he awoke in a cold sweat.

Jacques imagined he had dreamed it even during the days he couldn't remember after the Nazi shrapnel had torn up his leg. For a while there had been no days or nights, nothing but a fiery universe swarming with Technicolor planets, like when you were a kid and rubbed your eyes in the noon sun, only add the pain. The godawful tearing pain.

Now, lying in his own bed, his eyes closed, Jacques smiled. The dream had come true. No other place in the world had quite that same soursweet smell, a south Louisiana autumn morning smell, something that came from the way fog squatted over the fallow rice fields. In an hour or so, a fat white sun would burn it away, but come nightfall it would be back, as sure as the little creatures from the swamp would sneak in to scavenge. The swamp let you know it was waiting, waiting for you to get tired and give its land back.

Jacques smelled sausage curing in the smokehouse, and the chrysanthemums, which, over his protests, Adele had planted under their window. Just one more thing to mow around, but he didn't really mind. They were part of Adele and her city ways.

He'd known from the start that she'd never be a typical farmer's wife, not like his best friend, Carl's wife, but she was the only wife for him. Hannah didn't mess with flowerbeds. Hannah planted beans and peppers. Still, she and Adele had taken to each other right off.

Jacques had missed the couples' Saturday night card games. It's going to be like old times, he thought.

He heard the clink of dishes and Adele's alto voice singing "It Had to Be You." He'd have to get up soon.

Christophe, he supposed, would be out in the barn. Damn, the boy had grown. He was tall for eleven, tan and straight with the unmistakable Viator walk.

Jacques turned his head and saw the indentation where Adele had slept. Tracing it lightly with his fingertips, he sighed. This was luxury, not like the hospital sheets that rubbed you raw. He put his face in Adele's pillow. It smelled of her shampoo and good country air. He could picture her on tiptoe, mouth full of clothespins, hanging the laundry on the line.

Stretching, he studied the room. He hoped no one had heard the springs creak. He wanted to be alone a little longer to get used to it all.

What his dream hadn't included were the changes. Here in their bedroom the cabbage roses on the wallpaper were covered with fresh paint and Adele had put up silly criss-cross curtains not good for anything but catching dust. Lord knew they had plenty of that.

At least she'd left the furniture alone. He made a fond inventory of it; the second-hand five-dollar bedroom suite they'd bought as newlyweds, her cedar hope chest, the rocker with its rice motif Papa had carved for Adele when Chris was born.

He raised up on his elbows to look at her dressing table across the room where the light was best. On a scarf embroidered with pansies lay her tortoise shell brush and comb, a pink and white cold cream jar, and the blue bottle of Evening in Paris he'd mailed from the PX last Christmas. On one side stood the picture of him taken after boot camp – before the two stripes and the Purple Heart. The photo, like the mirror, showed the fan lines of a farmer's squint, but the reflected image had new creases, souvenirs of a jaw too long clenched, of too many nights peering in the dark for the enemy.

Jacques shrugged and lay back to think. He was weaker than he expected to be, and the leg ached.

What a scene it had been at the train station, the night before. They'd all been there to meet him: Carl and Hannah herding their bunch of tow-headed kids, Father Sebastian in the rusty black suit that was vintage World War I, Aunt Eudolie under one of her floppy, flowered hats, waving a huge Stars and Stripes to the peril of friends and relatives standing near.

How his heart had pounded when he saw Adele and Chris on the front row scanning the slowing passenger cars. Papa stood behind them like a guardian angel, an arm around Jeanette.

Funny, how you never expected your kid sister to grow up. Jeannete looked rounder to him, thicker in waist and hips. "Don't baby her," they warned him at the Institute when Papa sent Jacques with her to learn Sign. He tried not to, but he worried. It didn't surprise him that Jeanette had been the first to know he was back. She always could feel the train's vibrations before the rest of them heard it coming.

There had been pandemonium at the station, everyone talking at once, and then a caravan to the farm with more horn blowing than you'd have at a wedding. Somebody, Aunt Eudolie probably, had festooned the whole house with red, white and blue crepe paper. Jacques had to duck to get inside.

They'd set up a chair of honor for him in the parlor and made him sit there with his leg on a footstool. It made him feel conspicuous and foolish, and he was soon giddy from all the greetings. He hated being treated like a hero and dreaded the questions plastered across their faces. They wanted to talk about the war, the one thing he didn't want to talk about. Not yet. Maybe not ever.

Before long he'd begun to get a headache and wished desperately that he could escape outside, go for a walk. People meant well, but what he needed was to pick up a handful of soil, to hear the cattle shuffle and low, to sit on the fence and listen till it all got real again. He cursed the leg for trapping him.

Things got a little easier when Tee Broos brought out his accordion. Carl and Uncle Alcide tuned up their fiddles and right away launched into a squeaking, wheezy version of Jolie Blonde. As people began to dance Jeanette made her way among them carrying a tray of beer and the homemade sausage called boudin. Jacques had been aware of her all evening, watching him in that darting, sparrow-like way of hers. He caught her eye and made the Sign for 'I'm glad to be back'. His fingers stuttered, out of practice, but she'd understood and nodded, beaming. He'd loosened up after that. Things would get better, once the newness was over.

Jacques touched Adele's pillow again. He remembered how she looked, when they were finally alone, and flushed. She'd come to him soft and sweet smelling, a little bashfully, in a cloud of nightgown. He was embarrassed, letting her see the leg and explaining. They'd waited so long. It wasn't fair.

She'd laid her hand over his mouth and said it didn't matter, that nothing mattered except being together. She said they'd work it out.

She'd kissed him till he stopped apologizing. Her hair brushed feather light across his chest and he was shaken with gladness. Gently, he sat her up and lifted the gown over her head. It seemed a miracle that she was just as he remembered. He pulled her to him and they made love like newlyweds, working it out the way she said they would, in spite of his leg. She'd gone to sleep in his arms and he'd slept fitfully, then, but without dreaming.

Jacques stretched. Breakfast must be about ready. His shorts were stiff and uncomfortable and he began maneuvering his body to get up when he heard a truck crunch to a stop in the oyster shell driveway. In the still Louisiana morning the husky voices carried clearly.

"Wuenseht sie diese Erde im Gemuesgarten?" (Does she want this dirt in her vegetable garden?)

"Ja, Rolf. Dorthin."

Ex-corporal Jacques Viator, wounded at St. Lô soon after D-Day, covered his ears and fell back screaming.

Chapter 2

Adele jerked, dropping the biscuits she was taking out of the oven. The baking sheet clattered to the floor and the biscuits rattled around on the linoleum. For an instant she stood paralyzed in the blast of the stove. The holy medal around her neck began to brand her, but she had never felt more chilled in her life. The screams came again, high gargled howls like those that sometimes came from the woods at night, but undeniably human.

"Oh my God!" she cried and fled down the hall.

He was rigid against the bedstead. One knee was drawn up. The bad leg, uncovered, twisted outward leaving it mercilessly exposed, its inflamed ridges with the purple pockmarks lining the scars like eyelets. Later, she remembered thinking how pathetically thin the mutilated limb was, next to the hairy, healthy one.

She gasped. Jacques had a pillow clamped over his ears so hard the veins in his hands stood out. His eyes looked like dead coals. They reminded her of an engraving in her prayer book of the souls in Purgatory. Adele had never seen a real person look that way.

Before she could get to him he began to scream again.

"Jacques!" she threw herself on him. "Jacques, don't. What's wrong?"

His whole body was like marble, but she held him as tightly as she could, so tightly her arms ached. It was probably only seconds, but it seemed like forever before she felt him go slack. She couldn't tell whether it was his heart she heard pounding or hers. Neither of them spoke.

When she could stand to look at him the wildness was gone from his face, but in its place a vacancy which was worse. He let her lower his arms, obeying dumbly. She took the pillow and eased it behind him, murmuring, kissing his forehead, automatically straightening the chaotic bed. Then she sat beside him and took his hand. His wedding ring had worn so thin it moved loosely on the long finger. She raised his palm to her cheek and whispered, "What's wrong?"

He stared at her, out of reach, the way he had after their little girl was stillborn. When he finally did speak, his deep voice came out strangled, as if the screaming had broken parts of his voice.

"I'm losing my mind, Adele. God help me, I'm going to end up like the rest of them after all."

"Jacques, you're not! Don't say that. What are you talking about?"

He pulled away from her and said fiercely, "You don't know!"

Stunned, she put her hands in her lap and studied them, praying for guidance.

"No, love, I don't. Not unless you tell me."

"I did! I'm HEARING things. Shell-shocked, cuckoo, buggy, whatever you want to call it! For God's sake, Adele, I'm not a hero. I'm just another crazy cripple!"

"Don't...don't..."

But he went on, talking hard and fast. "You should have seen them, woman. You want me to tell you? What do you want to hear? Which freak do you want me to tell you about? About the college professor who used to dive under the table whenever somebody in the chow hall dropped a spoon? How about the plumber from Minneapolis who sits around rocking on the floor all day, jabbering baby talk?"

"Jacques, stop!" Adele had seen men like that in a movie once. "You're not like that. You're home, and..."

Before she could finish, there were men's voices outside and Jacques was in a frenzy again, screaming and yelling, "Get down, Adele. Get the guns! The Nazis are here!"

Oh, God, she thought, and suddenly understood what was happening. The Germans. Dear Jesus, why hadn't she told him when there was time to explain?

"Listen to me, Jacques...listen! It's all right. You're not shell-shocked. You heard the POWs." But he was too agitated to comprehend.

The screen door whanged and Chris bounded into the room. "What's wrong, Mama? I heard..." At the sight of Jacques he froze. Adele moved quickly to block his view.

"It'll be all right, son. The POWs scared Daddy. Go call Papa and tell him to come right away. Quick!" Chris looked uncertain. "Run call your grandfather," she said, turning him and pushing him into motion.

Jacques was in a daze, but the leg had been covered and he was sitting up straight. He kept staring at the crucifix on the wall, their wedding present from his cousin, a nun in Mobile. He would not look at Adele.

She began to raise the window shades, taking pains to hang them evenly as if achieving that symmetry might correct what was wrong in the room. At the last window she stood and fiddled with the organdy curtain. A breeze swept sunlight across the floor. It steadied her a little. Absently, she shuttled hair pins back in place.

She sat down, very straight, on the edge of the bed, nervously pleating her apron.

"Jacques, did you understand? The voices are real, but we aren't in any danger. You just heard the prisoners."

"The WHAT?"

"The POWs. They're German." Jesus, Mary and Joseph, what was taking Papa so long?

"German...prisoners...here?"

He grabbed her and spun her so violently her hair tumbled completely loose, falling over her shoulders. He kept shaking her with his strong arms, shaking her and whipping her with his words.

"What do you mean? Has the whole world gone mad? What are they doing here? Answer me! What are those goddamn Nazis doing on my land?"

"Please, Jacques, don't," she sobbed. He'd never laid a hand on her until now, never. "Please," she begged, but he continued shaking her until a deeper voice roared, "For God's sake, man, have you lost your mind? Turn her loose!"

Jacques let go.

Neither of them had heard Papa come in nor seen Jeanette and Chris clinging to each other in the doorway. Adele buried her face in her hands. She couldn't stop crying.

Turning on his father, Jacques yelled, "All right, YOU tell me. What the hell are those sonofabitches doing on my land?"

The older man's ruddy face darkened and he clenched his fists. "That enough, you. Think of the women and the boy."

"Think of the women and the boy?" Jacques sneered. "What the hell do you think I got shot up for? Who do you think mangled my leg, some bloody Englishman? It was those bastards out there!" He shook his fist at the window.

Adele gasped and for a minute nobody spoke. There wasn't a sound anywhere except for some sparrows outside in the bushes.

Then Papa, twisting his sweat-stained straw hat in his hands, sucked in his breath and said, "I understand how you feel, son. We should have told you before..."

"You're damn right you should have told me, you two-legged Cajun. You let those sonofabitches on my land? Like hell you understand!"

Etienne Viator would have struck his son if Adele hadn't jumped between them.

"No, Papa, don't! He doesn't mean it. Sit down," she pleaded, pulling her father-in-law to the rocker. "Christophe, bring some coffee. Get Jeanette to help fix it. Hurry!"

Jeanette followed her nephew reluctantly, looking back over her shoulder with a stricken expression. Jacques watched as if they were strangers.

"Sit, Papa, please! It's just a misunderstanding." Adele began to talk in a rush, trying to break through the armor of Jacques' anger. The work had become too much, she explained...the government needed more rice, more beef...it was for the troops...for victory, and all the workers were gone...if the service didn't take them, the factories did...

"You're telling me they work here?" Jacques stopped her. "You hired them to take my place?"

"I thought you'd understand."

He looked scathingly at her, at Papa and back to her again. "And which of you geniuses came up with that brilliant solution?"

Before Papa could respond, Adele said, "Be reasonable, Jacques! The sugar cane farmers were using them, so the rice farmers applied for some, too. We were desperate for help."

"Oh, so you aren't the only traitors."

"Don't be an ass!" Papa barked, "We pick them up first thing in the morning, they work good, don't give us no trouble, we take them back to camp at five. What would you have done, you?"

"Starved!"

That was too much for Papa. His boots banged the floor as he stood and crammed on his hat. "Pooyie!" he spat out. "When he gets some sense in his head, Adele, you let me know. I done wasted enough time already. Me and my men're fixin' that old irrigation pump."

She nodded, her throat tight, and watched him go. They were so much alike, her Jacques and his Papa, good honest men, sturdy as oaks, but they could be wooden-headed, too.

Jacques was raising himself by the bedpost when she turned around.

"Whether you believe it or not," she said, "we were going to explain about the POWs after breakfast. It was my idea to wait. I didn't want anything to worry you or spoil your first night home."

He hobbled to the bathroom. "Heil Hitler," he said and slammed the door.

Chapter 3

His anger reverberated through the house. In shock, Adele listened to it echo in the flush of the toilet, the clink of the bathroom stopper he was fumbling with and the grating faucets that sent water gagging and coughing up the creaky pipes. Finally, she fled.

When at last he came to the kitchen she was sitting on the back steps in the sun, regaining her composure. She heard him getting coffee.

"Here, I'll fix that," she said, going in.

"I'm not helpless."

"Oh, Jacques, for heaven's sake!"

She was surprised to see he'd put his uniform back on. In his last letter he'd said he couldn't wait to get back in his own clothes. He brushed past her, but at least he went straight to his old place by the east window. Out of the corner of her eye she saw him lift the red and white checkered curtain. The so-familiar gesture made her choke up again. That curtain. How many times had she starched and ironed it, trying to flatten the spot he pulled aside every morning to check the weather? No amount of laundering had fazed that crimp. It was the little things like that, when he was away, that had made her cry.

"Where's Chris?" he asked gruffly.

"Under the cistern, playing with Caspar."

She'd found him earlier, nuzzled up to the old dog, stroking its wrinkled side. Under the cistern, with its big wooden barrel standing on a platform, was Chris's playhouse. It was also where he went to think.

"I'll call him in, in a minute," she said. She couldn't face them together yet.

Her hands shook as she removed eggs from a large crock and cracked them with a sharp tap on the edge of the bowl. Twice she had to stop and pick out shell, and she chattered nervously the whole time.

"I thought you'd want some fresh yard eggs. The hens have been laying up a storm. I guess they're patriotic, too." Over the whir of the rotary beater she went on, "Chris has been dying to show you his new pirogue paddle and his model airplanes. Wait till you see his matchbook collection. He loved the ones you sent." She reached for the skillet. "Did you know his war bond poster won first place? We were so proud of him! I think he was more excited about his Dick Tracy badge, though. Remember I told you how we had to eat six boxes of corn flakes to get it? Well, the first thing he said when it came was, 'When Daddy gets home...'"

Just as she was taking out a fresh batch of biscuits, Jacques stopped her with a flat, "Where do the Nazis stay?". Her heart sank and she almost dropped the pan again. She had so hoped the questions would wait, at least till they'd had a little time together, just the three of them.

"At the old C.C.C. camp," she said with a resigned sigh, and set his plate in front of him.

Before Jacques could say anything else, she hurried to call Chris, but he was just coming in, cupping a blue jay's nest in his hands.

"Look what I found," he offered cautiously. His eyes were wary, measuring the situation and them. "It fell out of a pine tree."

Adele squatted to inspect the tangle of straw.

"Look," she said, "the tiny feathers And there, isn't that a string from your basketball net?"

"I'll be darned," the boy exclaimed. "It sure is. Look, Daddy!"

But Jacques gave an irritable shake of his head.

"Your breakfast's getting cold. Get rid of that and wash your hands."

Chris's chin fell. His wiry young body seemed to shrink inside his overalls and he shuffled off, looking as dejected as the cornfield scarecrow. His "yes, sir" was barely audible.

"Oh, Jacques, did you have to do that?"

"Adele, will you quit 'oh, Jacques-ing' me for God's sake and eat?"

She sat as if she'd been pushed, causing the chair cushion to make a little whooshing noise. She could feel her face redden. He didn't look up; just went on eating grits like it was a chore he had to get done with. When Chris returned, damp and red-faced, he said a hasty grace and proceeded to eat as silently and desultorily as Jacques. Adele picked at her own food, feeling miserable.

"Salt, please," Jacques said, coldly polite.

"More eggs?" she asked.

"No thanks."

She offered to hand Chris the molasses, but he turned it down and asked to be excused. Jacques kept on eating indifferently, so she nodded yes. She wished she'd sent Chris to school. It had seemed only right to keep him home for Jacques' first day back, but now what?

"Why don't you check your traps, son?" she suggested. "The muskrats are bad this year, Jacques. They're really tearing up the levees. Papa's paying Chris a quarter apiece."

Jacques only grunted, but Chris brightened and went off, his relief obvious.

After she rinsed their cups, Adele refilled them from the chipped white enamel pot that that sat all day in a bubbling pot of water on the stove. She noticed with surprise that Jacques took two spoons of sugar, one more than he used to. She watched as he poured cream and stirred it in deliberately, almost hypnotically. Then he began to talk, and for a moment he sounded like the old Jacques.

"I used to think, boy, what I wouldn't give for a cup of your coffee," he said.

Adele relaxed a little.

"The stuff they give you in the army's like dishwater, and Yankee coffee's got no taste at all. You could read a newspaper through it." He cradled the cup and got a faraway look. "When we found out we were going to France, I told the boys, 'at least we'll get a decent cup of coffee'. You know how they were always riding me about my Cajun accent and calling me Frenchy."

Adele's smile was short-lived.

"Well, the joke was on me, all right," Jacques said. "By the time we got to France, the people over there were boiling roots to drink. We were lucky to have K-rations." He frowned and his face hardened again. "Except at headquarters, of course. Nothing but the best at headquarters, nice and cozy behind the lines while the rest of us poor bastards were out there getting our asses blown off."

Adele shivered. His rancor shocked her. It was so unlike him. She'd expected some change, and she was prepared for his handicap but not this. Not such bitterness. She stared at her husband and wondered what had become of the man she knew.

He took a pack of Camels from his shirt pocket. She hurried to get him an ash tray, praying as she did for the right words.

In a voice tight with strain she said, "I'm sorry, Jacques. Sorry for all you've been through, sorry you're upset about the prisoners, sorry we didn't consult you first. But please! Try to understand. We were only trying to help."

"I don't understand anything any more," he said. "I don't even understand myself." Shaking his head, he added, "I didn't mean to snarl at Chris."

She reached across the table for his hand. "I know," she said softly. "Oh, Jacques, what are we going to do?"

He stiffened and pulled away.

"We're going to get rid of the goddam Gestapo, to start with!"

Adele was aghast. "We can't do that, Jacques. We've got a contract!"

"What do you mean, a contract? What are you talking about?"

"That's how it works. You apply to the government and if you get clearance you sign a contract."

"Are you trying to tell me we pay to have those devils here?" He looked as though he wanted to shake her again.

"Well, not exactly - we pay the army. It's a dollar twenty a day per hand. I think the army gives them eighty cents of that in coupons to spend in their canteen or save. It's a rule. Geneva Convention, or something."

"To hell with the Geneva Convention!" He banged the table, making the dishes dance. "Why should we observe it when they don't?"

She stood up and yanked off her apron. "You listen to me, Jacques Viator, I didn't start the war and I don't make the rules! Papa and I are breaking our backs to keep both farms going. Even with you home we'll still need help, and there isn't anybody but the POWs, so you'd better get used to the idea!"

One day home and we're fighting, she thought. It made her sick. They'd never fought before the war. Argued, sometimes, but never like this.

"How much longer?" he growled.

"How much longer what?"

"The contract."

She sighed. "I just renewed it for three months. We need the POWs, Jacques. America needs the rice, isn't that important, too? The war will be over soon, you said so, yourself."

She could tell he wasn't moved. Maybe she could appeal to his business sense.

"Do you have any idea how much money we're making? Why, you can build your new barn, and we won't have to worry about Chris's college. Papa's investing Jeanette's share in case anything happens to him. Here," she said, rising, "let me get the account book and show you."

He glared at her in disgust. "So now the end justifies the means, does it? Don't bother. You seem to be doing fine without me."

In his hurry to push away from the table he lost his footing and had to grab for a chair. When she'd waxed the floors she hadn't thought about them being slippery. Oh, God, she thought, help me to help him.

She followed him down the hall, protesting, "But I'm not doing just fine. I can't be, till you are."

"Don't hold your breath," came the terse answer.

Back in their bedroom he leaned on his cane and pushed aside the civilian clothes she'd laid out for him. He grabbed his wrinkled army jacket and hobbled to the back porch where he jerked the truck key from a nail.

"You aren't going to drive yet!" she cried.

"No? Watch me. Is it gassed up?"

"Yes, but...where are you going?"

"To see if my sister still makes sense. Or is she a collaborator, too?"

He let the door slam.

Adele wheeled around. She spotted a biscuit next to the clawed foot of the stove and kicked it across the room. When she heard the truck rumble over the cattle guard and turn onto the road, she leaned against the refrigerator and burst into tears.

Chapter 4

Jacques tore off so fast he left a half-mile trail of white dust along either side of the shell road.

To hell with them, he thought.

He shifted gears. Gradually, his breathing slowed and he began to relax. It felt good to be driving the old red Ford again. He eased up on the pedal and loosened his grip on the sweat-soaked leather steering wheel cover. Slowing to twenty, he ran a critical eye over the fields. They were in better shape than he expected, but here and there a levee - the dirt ridge designed to act as a dam - needed rebuilding. That one to the south would never hold.

You had to know every rise and soft spot of your land to get the drainage right. If you didn't control the water, you might as well forget rice. Jacques couldn't explain to his Ag teacher how he knew about irrigation or when he'd learned. Maybe it was instinct. Maybe you were born with it. You could show a man how to plow and plant and thresh and bind, but if he couldn't get the water in and out just right he'd be better off raising cattle. Papa had a French saying about it: Feed the rice water and the rice will feed you. The old Cajuns had a saying for everything.

Jacques changed positions to take the pressure off his leg.

The winter glare made him squint. As far as he could see, the low fields of beige and brown stubble lay still and idle except for the busy pecking of ducks. The sight of a mallard, its green head shining in the sunlight, made him smile. He'd forgotten what pretty creatures they were. They made his mouth water for the taste of some good gumbo. He'd ask Jeanette to make him some.

Without water around them, the levees wandered like a maze, like the tunnels he and Jeanette used to build when Papa took them to Turtle Beach. The dark green scrub growing wild on top of the far levee was thicker than ever, and the contrast with the rest of the sepia, mottled landscape reminded Jacques of camouflage.

Ahead was the huge oak that everyone called, simply, The Tree. Moss hung from its arthritic branches like old gray rags. The Tree had been planted two generations back as a boundary between Viator land and the Kaufmanns'. Since Jacques had built his house on the acreage he and Jeanette had inherited from their mother, the Kaufmann place was sandwiched between Viator farms.

No telling how many times he and Carl had said, "meet me at The Tree", even after they were grown men. They'd torn their overalls on it and broken their pocket knives trying to carve their initials in its alligator-hide bark. Jacques wondered if Chris had tried that. The thought made him wince. He wished he hadn't been so hard on the boy. If it weren't for the damn Nazis, everything would be just fine. Damn! He thought. How could Adele be so stupid?

Carl's house, coming up on his left, looked the same as ever, solid and square as the old Kraut who built it. But it wasn't the same, and never would be, Jacques realized with a shock, without the old man on the porch. No more chewed up cigar stubs, no more magic whittling, no more yarns about the Old Country. Jacques remembered the thin blue airmail letter from Adele saying, "Sad news, honey. Mr. Max's heart gave out yesterday. We buried him this morning. He was listening to Edward R. Murrow on the radio like he always did and just keeled over. Dr. Del says he died instantly, so that part was merciful..." Sure, Adele had told him, only it wasn't real till he caught sight of the empty rocker.

He cursed and sped past, but as soon as the house dropped from view he stopped and rested his head against the steering wheel. Pain rang through his leg like a bell bonging, like the bell that had tolled for Mr. Max, the bell he and Carl had raced to get to pull when they were altar boys and Mr. Max was the number one rice grower in the state.

Jacques' head throbbed, too. He tried to stop remembering, but couldn't. As fast as he fought back one memory, another one attacked. He began to pant, and had to roll down the window for air. He gulped. Smoke from a grass fire made his nostrils twitch, and the smell took him back to France, back to the booming and hissing, the crackling and screaming of battle...

Seconds or minutes later - he wasn't sure which - he began to recover. He blinked. His hands were clammy against his temples. This wasn't St. Lô. The screaming wasn't in his head. A calf was bawling across the road, its shoulders stuck in the fence. Jacques got down and stumbled over to it.

"Okay, okay, I'm coming. Easy, girl."

He worked the bloody hide loose with trembling fingers, trying to concentrate, trying desperately not to think of the other barbed wire, great rolls of it, stretched over the French countryside, arced with corpses, the bodies of his buddies. He broke out in a sweat. The calf got free, shuddered, and lurched off toward the pond.

Jacques climbed gingerly back into the truck. Looking for something to wipe his hands on, he found a paisley scarf of Adele's in the glove compartment. It still held her scent. The thought of Adele hurt worse than his leg. He was tempted to turn around and go home, to say he was sorry, anything. That's what I'll do, he said to himself, I'll make peace with Adele and Chris. We'll figure out a way out of his mess - as soon as I check on Jeanette.

Fate was crazy. Jeanette was the one who'd always wanted to travel, while he'd had no yen whatsoever to leave Junction Bayou. He could still see her poring over the Richard Halliburton books, wanting to show Papa some sphinx or pygmy village or something. She'd be chewing on a pigtail and her face would be lit up like a birthday cake. Poor Jeanette. He remembered how she used to wait by the road for the postman, hours at a time, when the National Geographic was due to come.

She was sure to be waiting now, for him to tell her what he'd seen over there. He scowled at the thought. Let her keep her picture postcard notions. She'd been cheated out of enough dreams.

Noticing that the mailbox by the driveway was faded, Jacques made a mental note to paint it. The first sight of the old house made his eyes sting. Its white frame sat on brick posts hidden by azalea bushes, nondescript and dust covered except during their few days of glory in the spring. The house itself was L-shaped, with a porch wrapping two sides. Gingerbread followed the roof like ivy, a concession Jacques' grandfather had made to his bride and to vogue.

The yard was small, with just enough room for the necessary clothes line and out buildings. No sense wasting good rice land. Ruts in the driveway were freshly filled with oyster shell.

Jacques parked around back, as always. The wind raking the shriveled fields was chilly and he hurried up the steps to the back porch. He yanked impatiently on the window blind hanging over the door so Jeanette would know he was there. He could see her at the sink washing butternut squash, making a godawful racket. He'd forgotten how noisy she was, how it used to drive him crazy, at the Institute, the way deaf people would stomp to get each other's attention or chunk something in a metal wastebasket, oblivious to the racket it made.

The flickering light finally caught her attention. She ran to let him in. She was flustered and kept drying her hands on her apron.

He leaned on his cane and embraced her with his free arm. To his distress she dissolved in tears. She cried in terrible high wailing sounds that tore him up. He kissed her forehead and fumbled for his handkerchief. She was upset about the scene with Adele, he knew.

"Got some coffee for your favorite brother?" he asked her in Sign.

The old joke brought a weak smile. "I'll make some," she said. Her voice was high and twangy. It had become more of a monotone as time went by, the way the doctors said it would, now that she couldn't hear. "Be glad she learned to talk first," they'd said.

While she was busy at the stove, Jacques wandered around studying photographs, stroking the backs of chairs, pausing in front of Jeanette's high school diploma and his B.S. in Agriculture. The degree was hanging crooked. He straightened it, then picked up a seashell from a mahogany what-not and held it to his ear. It was the one their mother had found that last summer at the beach before she and Jeanette got sick. Long after the grass had grown over their mother's grave, Jeanette kept trying to hear that shell. For quite a while they'd all kept hoping, even though the doctors said it was no use.

A foldout map from Life magazine was thumbtacked to the wall in between the old blackboard and the telephone. It had a tear going toward Australia. Czechoslovakia and Denmark were faded to a pinkish orange. Scattered across the map were colored stars, the kind your teacher put on your papers if you made good grades. Jacques saw that a star marked every place he'd been.

"Did you do this?"

Dishes clinked.

"Jeanette, did you..." God, you forgot in a hurry. Her back was turned. He went over to her, touched her arm, and pointed. "Who did the map?"

"I did. Do you like it?"

She was so damned eager to please.

"Every night Papa would have me read the paper to him, and when we got your letters I'd figure out where you were. I hated it when you couldn't tell."

He started to explain, but she kept talking in the steady pitch kids use when they're learning to read. He wished she would stop. He didn't want to talk about Normandy, he wanted to forget it. The kettle began to sing, but Jeanette was going on and on about what a hard time she had finding St. Lô.

"...so I got the lady at the library to look it up for me, Mrs. Castille. You remember Mrs. Castille at the library, don't you?"

The noise from the tea kettle got more and more shrill.

"For god's sake, turn that thing off!" he shouted without thinking.

Confusion and panic flickered across her face. Limping, Jacques brushed past her and fumbled to turn off the fire himself. Then he flopped in his father's easy chair and closed his eyes.

He heard Jeanette sniffle and blow her nose.

She brought his coffee and stood staring at him.

"Don't," he said.

"Don't what?"

"Don't look at me like that."

"I can't help it. You're different. I'm scared."

"So am I."

She took the wadded handkerchief out of her pocket and blew her nose again. He felt a rush of pity. Poor kid. It wasn't her fault. He was the one she confided in, the only one she'd ever talked to about the sickness and how frightening it was to come out of the delirium deaf. Her teachers told him she'd feel left out and showed him how to help her be as normal as possible. He'd coaxed her through high school, with Papa pushing them both. Jacques could still hear Papa bragging to his poker club: "Mes amis, my Jacques and my Jeanette, they ain't going to be like us, non. They going to be educate!"

He picked at the frayed arm of Papa's chair.

"How is he?" he asked.

His sister looked quizzical.

"Papa. How's Papa?"

She frowned. "He's mad. Is Adele mad, too? What did you say to them?"

"Nothing they didn't deserve. They shouldn't have let those prisoners come here."

"Why? Why not?"

He couldn't believe it, not from her. Had they all lost their minds? He got so agitated he could hardly sign.

"Why not? Because they're Nazis!" He had to spell Nazis one letter at a time which increased his frustration. "You said you read the papers every day. You ought to know. They're murdering butchers, that's why!"

"They're not!" Her hand flew to her mouth. "I mean, some aren't." Emotion made her voice crackle more than usual.

Now she was the stranger, and he saw her as if from a great distance. Something was different about her, some new confidence in the way she spoke. Like a Viator, he would have said, if he hadn't been so angry.

"How would you know?" he demanded.

"I just know."

"I asked you HOW!"

"Because Werner's not a murderer and he's not a Nazi, either."

"What are you talking about?"

"Werner. He told me he wasn't. When he brought the squash he even asked me how you were doing."

"Who," he said through clenched teeth, "is Werner?"

She cringed, but defied him nonetheless. "I won't tell you. Not till you act like my brother again."

Chapter 5

"Who the hell is Werner?"

Adele and Chris were putting away the last of the party dishes when Jacques stormed in.

Oh, Jesus, Adele thought. Not that, too. Not already.

Chris froze on the middle rung of the ladder, gawking at his father. She handed up the punch bowl. "That's got it, son." She turned to Jacques and answered quietly, "Werner's just a boy. Only seventeen."

"A POW?"

"Yes."

"A goose-stepping wonder kid, huh? You think that doesn't make him a killer?"

Chris jumped down between them, crying, "He's not! He's not!"

Jacques pushed the boy aside, but Chris kept on.

"You're wrong, Daddy. He's not a killer, honest. Werner's my friend, and Jeanette's, too!"

"Mon dieu," Adele said under her breath.

The veins in Jacques' neck pulsed.

"Go, Christophe," he ordered. "I want to talk to your mother."

The boy looked from his father to his mother. Adele nodded.

"Go ahead," she said. "Why don't you see if there's a cabbage ready to pick."

Chris bit his lip and went out.

Meeting Jacques' steely glare, Adele explained about Werner as

simply as she could, how Papa had found the boy crying one morning in the field, off to himself where the others wouldn't see.

"Papa asked him what was the matter, and Werner said he
didn't know if his family was dead or alive because he hadn't heard
from them since he got captured. Werner speaks good English for
a foreigner, and a little French, too. He wanted to be a doctor, but
he got drafted."

Jacques gave a little snort. Adele ignored it and went on.

"Well, anyway, Papa went through the Red Cross and found out
Werner's folks are all right." She decided to leave out the part about
Carl and Father Sebastian writing letters to help. "You can imagine
what a relief it was. The boy's so grateful he can't do enough for us.
You'd like him, Jacques. Why, he's almost like one of the..."

In her nervousness she'd gone too far.

Disgust rippled across Jacques' face. "Win one, lose one," he
sneered.

"Jacques, don't say that! You know what I mean. I'm telling
you Werner and the men at the camp here aren't at all what you'd
expect. They're not hateful or arrogant like some you hear about.
Most of them got drafted and had to go, just like you."

"Sure. You really believe that crap, don't you? You think they
were just a bunch of Boy Scouts playing soldier. Well, kiddo, let me
tell you something. I was there with them, remember? And believe
you me, we played for keeps."

She shivered. She couldn't let herself think about what Jacques
might have had to do. He'd always been a peaceful man who never
killed anything for sport, hadn't even enjoyed hunting the way Papa
and most of the Junction men did.

"Please," she begged him. "I know it's terrible over there and
I can't even imagine how awful it is, but this is here, Jacques. Now.
The war is over for you and for them."

"For them, maybe." He rubbed his bad leg. "But not for me."

The reminder was like a slap. Her protests stuck in her throat.
How could she make him understand? She hadn't liked the idea of
the POWs at first, either. Papa had been just as wary, until he saw
how well it turned out. To look at them, you'd have thought they
were Americans except for the 'P's and 'W's stenciled on their shirts
and their pants legs. The Germans were friendly in a polite, formal
kind of way, and they liked to keep busy. By now they'd come to
seem like any other hands.

The American soldiers hung around to keep an eye on things, of course, but half the time the guards who were supposed to be watching the men spread out in the shade and went to sleep, leaving the prisoners to themselves.

If we hadn't been so used to them, Adele thought, we'd have realized how they'd affect Jacques. Past arguing, she waited for him to speak.

When he did, finally, he was like a judge passing sentence, cold and impersonal.

"All right, Adele, you win. I don't like it a damn bit, but if you signed a contract, I'll abide by it. But get this - and get it good! - after that there won't be any more Nazis on my land. You hear? And don't you let any of those sonofabitches within a hundred yards of this house. If they come any closer, so help me, I'll shoot. You tell them I'll shoot, you hear me, woman?"

"Yes, Jacques, I hear."

He called for Chris, and the boy couldn't have been far, he got there so fast. Chris started to mumble an apology, but Jacques cut him short.

"You're a good boy," Jacques told him, "but you've got a lot to learn. Now listen to me," Jacques went on, "I don't want you having anything to do with that Werner guy or any of the other Nazis ever again, do you understand? Don't talk to them, don't listen to them, and you be damn sure they stay away from your Aunt Jeanette. I told you to look after her!"

"But Daddy…" Chris had blanched, and his voice came out in a squeak.

"No buts. That's how it has to be."

Chris gave Adele an imploring look, but there was nothing she could do. She could see there was no use trying to reason with Jacques till he cooled off. Whatever he'd been through over there must have been horrible, to change him like that.

To buy time, she got Papa to reassign the work details and told him to caution the Germans about keeping their distance. Papa grumbled about it, but Jeanette was downright indignant.

"That's not fair!" she exclaimed. "Werner never did him anything. Werner's good. You know he's good."

It was true. She and Papa were so busy running the two farms that more and more they had come to depend on Werner to look after Jeanette and Chris. Adele remembered how Jeanette would sit, mesmerized, watching Werner's lips, getting him to tell her about Europe. Sometimes he would take a pencil stub and draw pictures to explain, crude sketches which Jeanette collected and pasted in her scrapbook. Since last summer, Werner had handled all the work around the house, relieving Papa to be in the fields. Not having him there would be a hardship on them all, but especially Jeanette.

"I'll ask Werner to speak to Jacques," Jeanette said to Adele, frowning, "that's what I'll do."

"No, no. Don't do that, please, Jeanette! Don't talk to Werner whatever you do. We have to give Jacques time to get over this. He's been through so much. We have to be patient. You want Jacques to be all right, don't you?"

"Well," Jeanette said, her bottom lip quivering, "okay. If that's what it takes. I guess so."

Chris was the hardest to convince, but he gave in, too, after she said he could write a letter to Werner, explaining. Papa delivered the letter and said Werner took the news pretty hard but sent word not to worry. "Tell Chris I understand," Werner told Papa. "When the war gets inside a man, it has a hard time to get out."

The rest of the week they tried to get back to normal. The natural rhythm of the farm helped, but not much. Jacques made things too difficult. She was nervous when he was around, but she worried if he went out.

She would wake up before dawn and hear him on the front porch. The glider squeaked, and every ten minutes or so she heard the click and scrape of his cigarette lighter. The minute the truck with the POWs came down the road, Jacques would return to the bedroom and stay there, emerging only for meals. All day long he'd read and smoke or lie across the bed, staring into space. As soon as the prisoners were gone he left the house, going immediately to see what they'd done and check the equipment for sabotage. He went all day, sometimes, without speaking.

Adele took to getting dressed while he wasn't around and cleaning their bedroom in the evening, after he left. She'd find his fatigues dumped in a corner, ashes on the bedside table, mud from his combat boots on the throw rugs. He'd never been thoughtless before. She alternated between being hurt and angry.

Chris was practically invisible, taking hours over his chores. The eggs were washed spotless when he brought them in, and there was more butter than she could use. He quit complaining about being the first on and last off the school bus. Concerned about his daydreaming, his teacher sent home a note from school. Adele didn't know what to do. She overheard him fibbing to a friend that Jacques had taken him hunting and though she should have scolded him, she didn't have the heart.

Evenings were the worst. She began to dread sundown. In the old days, she'd played piano for them or they'd talked or had lively games of Monopoly, each of them vying for Boardwalk and Park Place. Now, as soon as supper was over, Jacques turned on the radio. No matter what was on, whether it was President Roosevelt or "Amos 'n Andy", he just sat in his chair rocking, devoid of expression. There were times when she thought shouting would be easier to take.

When she ran out of mending, she started a quilt for Jeanette. On the floor beside her Chris would dawdle over homework or make balsa wood airplanes till eight. Then he'd say goodnight and go to bed without being told, as mechanical as the cuckoo that announced the hour. It was unnatural, the way they were living. Soon after Chris left, Jacques would get out the big flashlight, make rounds outside and lock up. He went to bed before Adele did, and barricaded her with his back. Not since he first came home had they made love.

Adele thought she couldn't bear it.

Saturday night, when Jacques had turned in, Adele fixed herself a cup of cocoa and started reading the new Cronin novel. She simply couldn't keep her thoughts collected, and when she found herself reading the same page for the third time, she gave up. Putting out the lights, she got undressed and knelt for a long time on the cold floor. Then she edged carefully into bed and lay there, trying to think what she could do to make things right again.

Chapter 6

It never occurred to Adele that Jacques wouldn't go to Mass. She got up early Sunday morning to make pecan pies. When she had those in the oven she prepared vegetables and set the dining room table, humming Hit Parade tunes. The POWs didn't come on Sundays. Jacques had gone toward Carl's in the truck. He'll feel better, she thought, when he gets around people again. She took her kitchen shears outside and picked yellow mums to put in her grandmother's vase, feeling lighter than she had in days. There was nothing like a fresh bouquet to make a house more cheerful.

A little later, when she rang the iron bell, Jacques and Chris appeared from different directions. Chris went after his french toast with gusto, but Jacques was as indifferent to food as he was to everything else. Despite her earlier optimism, the conversation was polite and perfunctory, the way it had been all week. She sighed, disappointed. She'd thought it would be different, with the Germans gone for the day.

Chris took his dishes to the sink.

"That was good, Mom. Are you sure it's my turn to serve Mass?"

"Yes. I checked the schedule. We'd better leave about ten thirty. Did you polish your shoes?"

"Not yet, but I will."

"Don't forget to comb your hair."

"Okay," he said, grinning. It was their little joke. Conceding the battle with his cowlick, she'd broken down that week and let him get a crewcut like his dad's.

While she and Chris were talking, Jacques headed for the back door.

"Where are you going?" she said. "We need to get ready for church."

"Don't let me stop you," he said from the steps.

"But Jacques..."

"I'm not going, Adele."

"Not going to Mass? You're not serious! That's a sin."

"Oh, come off it, Adele. What difference does it make?"

"You don't mean that."

"Don't I, though."

"But what...what will I tell everybody?"

"Anything you like, cher. Anything you like."

She was glad Chris was too worried about remembering his Latin to give anything else much thought. She had to listen to him practice the Confiteor five times on the way to church. It gave her less time to brood over Jacques, at least.

Adele managed to get through the ordeal somehow. She stayed close to Jeanette and Papa after Mass, avoiding the gossipy Boudreaux sisters. Most people, knowing he'd been wounded, took it for granted Jacques was laid up. A number inquired of him and said they hoped he'd get his strength back soon. She thanked them as graciously as she could and pretended not to notice the surprised look on Father Sebastian's face.

While Papa hung around with his friends outside to smoke, she and Jeanette steered their way to the church hall where the altar society was serving coffee and doughnuts.

"Let us help," Adele said to Clothilde Bergeron.

"Gladly," Miss Clothilde said and handed them each an apron.

"Let Jeanette give you a hand," Adele said, "and I'll start washing up."

Staying busy shielded her from so many people asking questions, although the Boudreaux sisters managed to catch up with her in the kitchen.

"Where's that handsome hero of yours?" the younger one, Miss Bertha, asked. "He's not sick, is he?"

"No, not exactly. He just isn't up to getting out yet."

Father Sebastian came to her rescue.

"Hello, ladies. I was looking for you."

"Hello, Father," the sisters purred.

"I notice some of the altar boys' surplices are torn," he said. "I wonder if you good ladies would go through the lot and fix them for me."

"Of course, Father," Lucy Boudreaux said. "I was just telling Bertha the other day that some of those boys were looking down-right ratty, wasn't I, Bertha? You'd think their mothers would have more pride. I said to Bertha, 'It's a disgrace, the way some people don't care how their children look on the altar...'"

Adele twisted the hot water faucet so violently it sent a cascade of suds over the side of the sink, making the priest and the sisters duck. Miss Lucy gave her a dirty look.

"We'll go look through the sacristy closet right now, Father. While we're at it, Bertha, we might as well replace some of that tacky lace. I tell you, some people have no taste, no taste at all."

They huffed off, full of their own importance.

Father Sebastian waited for Adele to mop the floor.

"What's wrong with Jacques?"

Adele looked away.

"He's not himself. I guess he isn't feeling very well."

"That's strange; I thought I saw him in his pickup one evening."

Adele blushed. "It's probably hard for him to get used to things," she said lamely.

"Well, tell him to come by. I've got a new radio I want to show him. He won't believe the stations I can pick up."

Father Sebastian and his radios were legendary. Repairing them was his hobby, and the more complicated, the better. He'd tinker with them for hours. It kept him sane, he said, when there was so much else in the world he couldn't fix.

"I'll tell him," Adele said, drying her hands. "Did Chris get his Latin right? I was in the back and couldn't hear."

"Just about perfect," Father Sebastian said. I think he's bucking for the Server of the Year award."

"And the silver dollar that goes with it," Adele added with a smile.

The following weeks were pretty much the same, depressingly so.

Sometimes she would stand looking out the glass front door at the frostbitten yard where the ash blonde plumes swayed softly on the shocks of Pampas grass and wonder if she had imagined the past. She began to think in terms of before and after Jacques came home, and the good times, the dreams they'd had got harder and harder to remember.

Jacques did seem to feel better. He wouldn't talk about his leg, but he seldom used his cane any more. Adele couldn't get used to the sight of him limping; it dismayed her every time.

The Sunday after Thanksgiving she was just putting the good dishes away when Carl and Hannah dropped by.

"Are y'all busy?" Hannah called from the back steps. "It was such a pretty day we decided to take a ride."

Adele's spirits lifted. She'd been dreading the long afternoon. "Come on in!"

The six Kaufmann kids, already piling out of the car, barely paused to give her a hug. "Where's Chris, Miss Adele? Where's Chris?"

"Look in the tree house," she told them, but they had already scampered off.

Carl was leaning up against the dusty Chevy, elbows propped on the roof of the car. As fair complexioned as Jacques was dark, he had Mr. Max's hearty way about him. What was left of his hair was the color of ripe rice. His eyes were a mischievous bright blue.

"Where's the man of the house?" he drawled.

Adele looked down at the ground. "Painting the barn, I think."

"On Sunday?" He clucked in mock disapproval. "My, my. I shall have to go speak to the sinner."

She and Hannah went in the kitchen, exchanging small talk while Adele made a pitcher of Koolade and a fresh pot of coffee. Handing the cookie jar to Hannah, Adele said, "Put some of these on a plate, will you? I'll slice some pound cake."

"Sure," Hannah said, adding nonchalantly, "What's wrong with Jacques?" Bulls eye. That was Hannah. Goodhearted as she could be, but direct to the point of bluntness. Adele bit her lip and shrugged.

Hannah put an arm around her. "Is there anything we can do to help?"

"Not that I know of, but thanks." Adele cleared her throat.

"Let's take these out to the kids."

She saw the men cut through the yard to the front porch, so she got out two bottles of beer and set a bowl of cracklins between them.

Hannah wanted to copy Adele's pecan tart recipe. Back in the kitchen, Adele got her the tin recipe box and some index cards.

"While we're at it," Hannah said, "How about giving me the one for hamburger stroganoff too, and that lemon Jello cake you made for Chris's birthday party?"

"Take whatever you want," Adele said. "Here, I'll help."

They sat at the table, writing. Every so often Adele would check on the kids playing Red Rover in the yard. She half-listened to Hannah, chatting and scribbling away, and half-heard the men. At first the talk was about football. Then their voices fell and they started laughing. It was the first time she'd heard Jacques laugh, she realized, since the night he got home.

"Do you chop the pecans or put them in whole?" Hannah was saying.

"What? Oh, chopped."

The children, with red Koolade mustaches, wandered in to use the bathroom. It always amused Adele the way Hannah would reach over without missing a syllable to fasten a gripper, tuck in a shirt or tie a passing child's hair ribbon. Hannah was cooped up with the kids so much, when she got with grownups she talked a mile a minute.

But when Carl's voice rose and the men started arguing, Hannah stopped what she was doing and looked up.

"Bull!" they heard Carl say. "You're just making excuses. You've hibernated long enough. I thought you'd at least have respect for Dad's memory."

"Okay, okay, we'll go! Are you satisfied? Now, get off my back, will you?"

Carl came whooping through the house. "I won, Han. I told you he'd come! You owe me three back rubs."

Hannah smirked. "I was hoping you would."

"Will somebody tell me what's going on?" Adele said.

In a rusty baritone, Carl warbled, "Jol-lee old Saint Nick-o-laaas.."

"You sound like our billy goat, Abner," groused Jacques, after following Carl to the kitchen.

Carl laughed. "I'd forgotten about old Abner. Remember the time I was over here playing and Abner ate our shoes while we were down at the pond swimming?"

"We're giving a St. Nicholas party," Hannah told Adele, "like Mr. Max used to do."

Serious for a moment, Carl said, "I thought we ought to try to pass on some traditions, now that Dad's gone."

"I'm glad," Adele told him. "What are you going to do?"

"Oh, you know," Carl said, "I'll dress up like St. Nick and scare the kids into being good. Ask them a few catechism questions, give them candy if they answer right or switches if they don't." He made the latter sound ominous.

"How are you going to know the difference?" Jacques asked dryly. He was leaning against the counter, almost relaxed. Hope climbed inside Adele.

"Better make the questions real easy," Hannah said.

"All right, you wise guys. I ask you, Adele, is that any way for them to treat a saint?"

"Ha!" hooted Jacques and Hannah at the same time.

"You wouldn't really give out switches, would you, Carl?" Adele asked him.

"Shh…" he said. The kids were coming in.

Adele turned to Hannah. "What shall I bring, and when do you want us?"

"Not a thing, but I'll borrow some folding chairs if you don't mind."

"Sure, but why don't you let me make the punch or something."

"No, really," Hannah said. "I'm all set. I'll pick up the chairs tomorrow on my way home from town. Y'all be there Tuesday at seven."

Little Kurt Kaufmann, who idolized Chris, came panting in. "Can Chris come to the party, Daddy? Huh, can he?" Chris shot Jacques an apprehensive look. Carl swung Kurt piggyback, saying, "Of course he's coming," at which Chris and the others jumped up and down.

"Come on, kids," Carl said, leading a parade to the car. "Load up. We have to go cut our switches."

Hannah rolled her eyes. "It ain't easy, being married to a saint. Thanks for the recipes and refreshments, Adele. See y'all Tuesday!"

Chapter 7

The night of the party the thermometer nailed to the post on the back porch read thirty-six degrees. Jacques stayed out after dark wrapping pipes that might freeze. Adele went back and forth from the bedroom mirror to the kitchen stove, taking turns checking her looks and stirring Jacques' supper. She changed dresses twice before deciding to wear the powder blue sweater set and plaid skirt. Jacques had always preferred her in blue.

She began to wonder if he'd changed his mind about going. They were due at Hannah and Carl's in five minutes. Chris fidgeted, watching the clock. Adele was on the verge of calling Hannah to say they'd be late when Jacques came in, blowing into his hands.

"Dress warmly," he said matter-of-factly. "I'll be ready in a minute."

"Your supper's hot. I'll serve up."

"Never mind. I'll eat when we get back."

He doesn't intend to stay very long, Adele thought.

She huddled between Jacques and Chris in the truck, wrapping her skirt around her legs to keep warm, unable to think of much to say. It felt strange, the three of them going out together again.

Chris wrote on the steamed up window with his finger and watched the letters drip. Adele peered out the corner of her eye at Jacques, stiff in his dress uniform. He had on his campaign ribbon, but not the Purple Heart. She wished he would start wearing his own clothes.

There were pickups and cars all over the Kaufmanns' yard. It

looked like auction day at the cattle barn. Jacques found a spot to
squeeze into, and the minute they parked they were swarmed by a
bunch of boys so bundled up you could hardly tell who was who.

"Chris is here!" somebody yelled.

"Hey, Chris!"

"Come on, Chris…"

"Come see St. Nicholas. Come see!"

Chris took off running.

"Put your cap on," Adele called after him.

"Let him go," Jacques said. "He's too excited to be cold."

He held the door open for her the way he used to. She smiled
and tucked her hand in his arm and together they walked toward
the house.

Squeals and laughter split the thin, crisp air as silhouettes moved
in a kaleidoscope behind the lighted windows and the leaded glass
front door.

Adele and Jacques slipped in the back way so as not to draw attention, and stood watching from the kitchen doorway. The cream
colored french doors between Kaufmanns' dining room and the
double parlors had been opened, but at that there was none too
much room. Older couples like the Zimmers and the Theriots observed from chairs along the wall, craning to see through the crowd.
There must have been half a dozen baby carriages and strollers, and
dodging the grownups everywhere you looked, at least twice that
many giggling little girls.

Carl was playing his role to the hilt, hamming it up. He was
dressed exactly like a bishop, pointed hat, staff and everything.
Adele recognized some of the old vestments the altar society had
finally persuaded Father Sebastian to abandon in favor of newer,
more reputable ones. It was a standing joke among the parishioners
how the priest hated to give up anything that was broken in. Just
when it was getting comfortable, he'd complain. Ragged, was more
like it.

"Where do you suppose they got the hat?" Adele whispered to
Jacques.

"Corn flakes," he said, with a trace of his old smile.

Carl's voice boomed, "Have you been a very, very good boy?"
He was interrogating the Schuller child who looked pleadingly to
his parents for support. Frank and Gert Schuller nodded yes.

"And is he obedient?"

"Most of the time, Saint Nicholas."

"Good. Does he remember to say his prayers?"

"Every night," Gert said. The little fellow nodded vigorously.

"No switches for this one, then." Carl waved to someone dressed like Black Peter, carrying the fateful sack. Adele couldn't figure out who it was.

"Give John here some candy," Carl directed.

Young John almost collapsed with relief.

"Next?" Carl shouted. "Who's next?"

"Wouldn't Mr. Max have loved it?" Adele asked Jacques.

"Yeah," Jacques said and squeezed her hand.

She hadn't been so happy in weeks.

Carl had confronted a freckle faced girl whose cheeks matched her pink pinafore.

"What about you, Anna Lou? Do you know where Jesus was born?"

"In a thable," the little girl lisped, "with thome cows and horthes and thome thmelly old theep."

It brought the house down and the little girl's cheeks got pinker still.

After Anna Lou came Shirley and Ursula and Irwin. Carl kept it up till he had all the children convinced that he would be hiding in their attics, waiting to give them presents on Christmas morning if they were good. Big-eyed, they sucked on their candy, and the smell of peppermint permeated the house.

From outdoors came bursts of yiping and hollering as the men from the church choir chased the older boys who wanted, at all cost, to avoid a public accounting to St. Nick. Chris and Kurt, after hours of deliberation, were sure they had figured out a sure-fire hiding place, they'd told Adele.

She and Jacques had barely moved past the kitchen when some of the neighbors made a beeline for Jacques.

"By gosh, it's good to see you up and about," Mr. Ohlenforst said, throwing an arm around Jacques. "We sure have missed you, boy."

"We sure have," the Jeansonnes added in unison. They were an older couple who lived on the Gantz place and raised cattle. When Jacques learned they hadn't any family to speak of, he'd made it a point to check on them now and then, and he always helped when it was time to vaccinate the cows. Mrs. Jeansonne wrapped him in a hug.

About that time the whooping in the yard reached a new pitch.

Adele had just asked Jacques, "Do you think they've found the boys?" when footsteps clattered on the porch and the front door blew open. Carl's brother from town strode through in triumph with Kurt under one arm and Chris under the other.

"Better luck next year, fellas," he twitted.

Even Jacques laughed.

When all the young people had been found, people began to mill about, and Hannah pulled Jacques and Adele into the crowd.

"Look who's here, everybody. Let's sing carols. You'll play, won't you?" Hannah asked Adele.

"Yeah, Adele," Carl said, "play us some carols. Just spare me any more scales or "Chopsticks". Hey, Jacques, help me get out of this rig, old pal. This beard's driving me nuts. I feel like I've got fleas."

While Adele played she had a view of almost everyone there, thanks to the gilt-framed mirror over the piano. It hung suspended by silk ropes from a tassel attached to the ceiling molding, and like everything in the Kaufmann house, was large and heavy. Mr. Max used to love to tell how his father had ordered the massive furniture made to order from green wood by the finest craftsmen in Germany, shipped to New Orleans and then up the bayou. By the time the pieces got to Junction Bayou and the Kaufmann house, they were dry and solid as could be and never had cracked, not even in the hottest summer, the way other furniture did.

Playing carols didn't require Adele's concentration. She smiled at people and kept glancing in the mirror, wondering how Jacques was doing. It was wonderful, having him there, just like the old days. Several times she got up to join him, but each time, one of the carolers around the piano made another request. Hannah brought a tray with egg nog. The dusky scent of candle wax mingled with nutmeg and the smell of old Mr. Guidry's pipe. It made Adele think of other Christmas Eves the Kaufmanns and Viators had spent together.

"How about 'O Holy Night'" Mrs. Theriot suggested when Adele paused to drink some egg nog.

"'The First Noel' next,'" called someone in the other room.

She played on, happy to stay there and observe Jacques among his friends. About nine, while the carolers were in the middle of a

second chorus of "Jingle Bells", the singing suddenly trailed off and
she heard arguing. Her hands froze on the keys, stopping the music
as abruptly as if someone had lifted a phonograph needle.

What she saw left her stunned. Jacques and Carl, tense and bel-
ligerent, were poised by the dining room table, both of them red-
faced with anger. Jacques held a painting of some kind, a picture of
a chalet and some mountains, as far as she could tell. Carl jerked it
away.

"And why shouldn't I take a present from the POWs?" he bel-
lowed. "It's St. Nicholas Day, damn it!"

"You've got them working for you, too?"

"What of it!"

"Why didn't you tell me?"

"Why should I? It's none of your cotton pickin' business what
I do on my farm."

"Oh, yeah? Well I damn near got killed so you could keep it!"

"And the rest of us were here working our butts off, so don't
come back like a little tin hero tellin' us what to do!"

"I'll tell you what you can do, you can take your farm and shove
it up your ass!"

"Jacques!" Adele cried in dismay, but nobody noticed.

"I ought to throw you out the door," roared Carl. "Who the
hell do you think you are, anyway?"

"Just an all-American guy," Jacques sneered. "I'd forgotten
you were one of the Kaiser's boys."

They lunged for each other.

"Stop them!" Hannah yelled.

Frank Schuller and Carl's brother moved to break it up.

"You go to hell!" Carl shouted over their heads at Jacques.

"I already did," Jacques responded, and flung Frank Schuller
against the sideboard.

Before Adele could get through the crowd, Jacques had roared
off into the night.

Chapter 8

Jacques had to get out of there. He didn't know how it had happened, but they were all against him. He needed a drink. He floorboarded the accelerator and headed for Jo Jo's. Everything else would be closed, probably, except Jo Jo's. Most people around there went to bed with the chickens.

Sure enough, the old green sign was on - Jo Jo's Bar and Grille. That old tightwad Jo Jo never had fixed it so it lit right. One 'o' and the 'G' had been burnt out for years, long before Jacques' eighteenth birthday when, with Carl for an audience, he had bellied up to the bar and ordered, "Gimme a beer" in his best James Cagney growl.

An old jalopy, a jeep and a muddy pickup were parked in front.

As soon as he pushed open the red leather door he was bathed by the stink of ashtrays and stale beer.

"Home sweet home," Jacques muttered under his breath.

Some gal he didn't know had taken Al's place behind the bar. She was squeezed into a shiny black dress two sizes too small, and had on enough jewelry to fill a store counter. The penciled arches that were supposed to be eyebrows went up like window shades when Jacques walked in, but the bright red mouth didn't miss a chew of gum.

"Bourbon and water," Jacques said. "Where's Al?"

"Alphonse's in the Navy, him. Pacific. Been gone."

"Oh."

"You from around here, soldier?" she said.

"The Junction," he muttered and paid her.

Seeing he wasn't going to chat, she shrugged, licked her thumb and resumed flipping the pages of a dog-eared movie magazine.

He couldn't get comfortable on a bar stool, so he moved to a corner table, the top of which was tattooed with water marks and cigarette burns. He leaned back on the hind legs of a beat-up chair and loosened his tie, letting his eyes adjust.

Some things didn't change after all, for all the fat lot of comfort that was. He could hear 'Tee Broos' Broussard and the old faithfuls playing dominos in the back room. There was no one in the bar, though, that he knew. Several G.I.s and a couple of young kids had looked up when he came in, but the kids were playing a pin ball machine and the soldiers had gone right back to shooting the bull.

The old Budweiser clock read ten after ten. Jacques downed his drink. Garish pink roses on the sign over the bar blinked off and on, off and on, shooting ripples of color over a row of upended glasses and a gallon jar of pickled quail eggs.

The sergeant with the Texas accent kept feeding the jukebox. After he'd played "Don't Fence Me In" half a dozen times, his buddies complained, so he switched to "That's What I Like About the South".

"Ain't that Phil Harris somethin'?" the sarge asked no one in particular.

Jacques got himself another drink. His eyes were used to the dark now and he could see a man passed out on a table by the wall.

"John Parker Landry?" he asked the barmaid.

"Mais yeah," she said with a pop of her gum. "Guess it's about time to send him home."

She fished a nickel from the register and called the cops.

As long as Jacques could remember the cops had been putting John Parker to bed. It got so that was just part of the job. You joined the police force, you figured on hauling John Parker Landry. Nobody seemed to mind. Everybody felt sorry for John Parker's mother. Miss Nell was the kind of elderly gentlewoman southerners took pride in, genteel all the way from her snowy hair to her gloved fingertips. She didn't deserve a son like John Parker.

There are lot of things folks don't deserve, brooded Jacques.

Like coming back and finding your loved ones chummy with the ones who tried to do you in! How could they be so stupid? It was a miracle they hadn't all had their throats cut.

The more he thought about what happened at Carl's, the madder he got. Carl, of all people, on top of Adele and Papa, a traitor! And by damn, he muttered, if I don't end up the villain!

"Give me a shot of Southern Comfort," he told the barmaid.

Tee Broos came out to use the john. He saw Jacques and waved.

"Hey, Jacques! Comment ca va?"

"Bien merci, Tee Broos," he lied.

"You wanna get in the game?"

"No thanks, Tee Broos. Some other time."

The wiry little man nodded.

"Okay. Do me a favor, huh? Tell your papa I bring him the bull Saturday, yeah. For sure this Saturday."

"All right, Tee Broos."

Assuming it was the barmaid who had come up while he and Tee Broos were chatting, Jacques was surprised to find a tall girl in a fuzzy short-sleeved sweater giving him a big glad-to-see-you smile. She was a good looking gal, a real pin-up type, and the sweater made a lot of promises. Her hair, shiny and silvery blonde, was done up in one of those net things, snoods they called them, like a Hollywood star's. Something familiar about her face teased at Jacques' memory, but for the life of him he couldn't come up with her name.

"Remember me?" she was saying. "Good old Courville High?"

He racked his brain a moment before the dawn broke.

"Betty? Betty Whittington! I'll be damned. How have you been?"

"I get by. How about you?"

No wonder he hadn't recognized her. She was quite an improvement over the old Betty, and besides, she wasn't the kind you'd expect to see at Jo Jo's.

"Well, uh, how's Armand?" he said, still flabbergasted. "You did marry Armand Hebert, didn't you?"

"Armand?" she said in a tone that made him shiver. "Armand's dead. Kaput. The Nazis got him at Anzio. Can I sit down?"

"Oh...sure." He scrambled to help with her chair. "I didn't...

Jesus, Betty, I'm sorry."

"It's okay. You get used to it. I heard you were back safe. I'm glad."

"Yeah, well, more or less."

"Yes, I heard. Your leg. Is it bad?"

"Not too bad. Buy you a drink?"

"If you want to. I'll take a Tom Collins."

They drank and made small talk. It felt good. They griped about the cold weather and agreed that war was hell. Betty gave him a rundown on their classmates. He didn't know Linda Sue Dore had joined the WACs.

"Do you remember the time she came to school with her teeth blacked out?" he said. "She and Billy Langlinais were going steady and he nearly had a fit."

Betty nodded, laughing.

"Whatever happened to Billy?" he asked.

"I don't know. His dad got a political job in Baton Rouge. I guess the war caught up with Billy, too."

No matter what you talked about, it seemed like you always came back to the same thing.

Betty asked if he knew that Inky and Angelle had twins.

"No kidding."

"Twin girls. Cute as they can be. Angelle keeps them dressed like little dolls."

"How about you?" Jacques said. "Any kids?"

"No. No such luck." She picked at the cherry in her drink. "Y'all just have one boy, don't you? I see him around sometimes with Adele and your dad. Walks just like you."

Jacques let that pass.

"Chris is eleven now," he said, "growing up too fast." He paused and added, "We lost a little girl."

They were quiet for a moment. Jacques noticed the time and wondered if Adele had gone home yet. The thought of what happened at Carl's was like a new wound.

"Imagine you with an eleven year old kid," Betty said. "Time sure flies, doesn't it?"

Jacques took a swallow of his drink and asked her about some of their teachers to keep the conversation going. Betty was good company and he didn't feel like being alone.

"What about old Miss Webre? Boy, was she a tyrant! Do you

ever see her around?"

"Oh yes, and she still tells me to hold my shoulders back. But you have to hand it to the old battle-ax, she pounded those logarithms in our heads, didn't she?"

They reminisced that way for an hour or so. Jacques lost track of the time and the drinks.

"You know what?" he said to Betty. "You're the first person since I've been home who's made any sense."

"Really?" she said. "I guess that's a compliment." She toyed with her swizzle stick. "I had a terrible crush on you when we were seniors. You didn't know that, did you?"

Jacques was dumbfounded. "You're kidding."

"No, honest. But you went off to college and found Adele, so I went back to Cary Grant."

She turned serious. "How is Adele?"

"Hot under the collar, probably. I walked out on a party. They won't miss me."

"Oh, so that's it."

She stood, and he thought she was going to leave, but instead she said, "Got a nickel? I can't take any more Phil Harris."

Jacques handed her his change. She went to the jukebox and punched "Tuxedo Junction". When she walked her skirt swung like the metronome on Adele's piano. One of the soldiers asked her to dance. She had good legs and moved lightly on high heels. Jacques couldn't get over her. She must have lost twenty pounds since they graduated.

"You've changed," he said when the number was over and she came back.

"Sure. Haven't you?"

"I guess so. Who're the doughboys, friends of yours?"

"I see them around," she said. "They're guards at the POW camp."

Jacques frowned. "Shit."

"What's the matter?"

"I'm just sick of hearing about the goddam POWs, that's all. Why'd they have to come here?"

"Don't ask me. They make me want to spit."

"Well, hallelujah, a kindred soul. My family feels sorry for them, can you beat that?"

Betty shook her head in disgust.

"Lots of people do. You ought to see the way they wave when the Nazis pass through town. You'd think it was a parade."

"I don't get it. Whose side are people on?"

"Sometimes you wonder." She twisted in her chair and called out, "Hey, Tex, what'd you guys do with that Nazi you caught yesterday?"

"Aw shoot, Betty. He ain't goin' no place. We got him in the pigpen gettin' his bread and water on the ground right there in front of God and ever'body, and no roof over him, neither. Reckon five days of that'll cure his itch to travel?"

"Oink, oink," one of the soldiers snorted, tickling the heck out of the kids at the pinball machine.

"Where'd you find him?" Betty asked.

"Know that train station out at Robicheaux? Back of there. Damfool was walkin' the tracks. You ever see them coupons the POWs get to buy cigarettes and stuff at their canteen? That joker had his pockets stuffed with them things. Thought they was United States money!"

Tex's buddies guffawed and Betty and Jacques laughed, too.

"Buy you another drink?" Jacques asked.

She stretched.

"No thanks. I'd better call it a night."

She rearranged a strand of pearls. It came to rest in the hollow of her neck.

"We working girls need our beauty sleep."

He didn't want her to leave.

"Where are you working?"

"I'm running the insurance agency till Armand's brother gets out of the service. He's got a desk job in Washington."

"You live with your folks?"

"My, aren't you full of questions. No. They moved to Arkansas last year. You know how it is in the oil business. I stayed here to wait for Armand." She paused. "Then I just stayed."

She pulled on a pair of kid gloves slowly, one finger at a time, as if trying to make up her mind about something.

"I've got a garage apartment on Tenth Street, back of Chatelain's house," she said.

"Here." Jacques moved to help her with her coat, but her perfume made him dizzy, or maybe it was the booze. He wasn't used to drinking much. He broke out in a sweat.

"I'll walk you to your car," he said once he'd steadied himself.

"You'd better be getting back to your party," Betty told him.

"For what? My wife and my best friend think I'm nuts. You don't think I'm nuts, do you, Betty? Tell me the truth. Do I act like a crazy man to you?"

"No, friend, but I suspect you're a little bit drunk. Take care of yourself."

She unlocked a gray Studebaker and said goodnight. He watched her drive off. She went only a couple of blocks before she made a U-turn and came back.

Rolling down the window, she said, "You'd better come to my place and sober up."

He followed her coupe, keeping his lights on dim, and parked where she showed him, on the grass. She put a finger to her lips. They tiptoed up some worn wooden steps to a landing with a rickety rail. In the front window, hanging crooked, was one of the little blue satin flags with the gold star on it the government presented to mothers of dead veterans.

"Armand's mother gave it to me," Betty said, tight lipped. "As if I'd forget."

Jacques thought she'd never get the door open. He rushed inside the minute she did, found the bathroom and puked.

Chapter 9

About two in the morning he woke up, completely disorient-
ed. Wrong bed. Wrong room. He blinked. Across the room in the
moonlight he could see Betty curled up in an armchair by the window. Wrong woman! She'd put on a long red robe edged in lace
like a Valentine. Her hair hung loose and one curl lay on her breast.
Jacques shook his head to see if he was dreaming.

"Oh, shit," he groaned. "What have I done?"

She heard him.

"Nothing to worry about," she said.

Untucking her feet, she slid into some slippers with fur pom
poms on top.

"Wash up. I'll get the coffee."

She closed the venetian blinds and turned on a floor lamp.

He eased himself up, feeling foolish that he was in his socks and
relieved that he had on the rest of his clothes. How the hell had
he got there? His boots were standing at attention beside the bed.
When he bent to put them on, his head, already throbbing, began
to swim. He cursed himself for overdoing the booze.

He went to the bathroom and rinsed his mouth. The wavy
pattern of the chenille bedspread had left marks on his face. He
splashed himself with cold water and turned away from the mirror
to towel off.

Betty was waiting for him in the breakfast nook, looking amused.
Dammit, she was pretty, but this was no time to be funny.

Embarrassed and sheepish, he lowered himself to the yellow bench across from her.

"Feeling better?" she asked.

"Ugh," he said. "Lousy."

"Drink your coffee."

He cleared his throat.

"I...uh...I don't know how to say this, Betty, but I never did anything like this before."

"I didn't figure you had," she said impishly. "Not Jacques Viator, the pride of Courville High."

"Cut it out, Betty. I don't know what got into me. I shouldn't have come here."

"Whose reputation are you worried about, yours, or mine?"

He decided he'd better ignore that. Every time he thought things couldn't get worse, they did.

"Sometimes I wish I'd never come back."

"What's that supposed to mean?" she said. Her eyes threw sparks. "You wanted to be like Armand?"

"Oh, god, Betty, I didn't mean. I wasn't thinking."

He put his head in his hands.

Betty said, "I don't know what's eating you, friend, but you sure aren't your old self. I can't figure you out."

"It's the Germans," he said. "The POWs. Nobody warned me. Can you beat that? I just woke up and heard them jabbering outside my house. Thought I was shell-shocked, honest to God. And you know what they were doing? They were dumping a load of shit in my vegetable garden. Nazis, dumping a goddam load of shit in my own back yard!"

She whistled softly. "No wonder."

"What?"

"I said no wonder you're so hot under the collar."

"Wouldn't you be?"

"I guess I would. What a rotten thing to come home to. I'd heard there were some working at the Aucoin farm and out at Carl's, but I didn't know y'all had them, too."

"You knew about Carl? How about that. I just don't get it. You'd think he'd appreciate what this country has done for him. You'd think people would be more loyal, wouldn't you?"

"Well, what did Adele say?"

"She's the one who signed the contract."

"Adele? But why?"

"For victory, isn't that a laugh? That's what she tells me. Enemies all over my land. Some goddam victory, excuse my language."

"I'm a big girl."

"She says the government's after us to produce and there aren't enough hands."

"Well, that's true. They say farmers all over are short of help, but if the government didn't pamper their precious POWs so much, there'd be more food for the rest of us."

"What's that supposed to mean?"

"Oh, I just see red at some of the things I hear. It makes me mad to have to count every little ration stamp before I go to the grocery store when the guards say sometimes the POWs eat better than we do. Not just anything, either. Did you know Hitler's boys turn their noses up at grits? According to them anything from corn is pig food. Maybe if they got hungry enough they wouldn't be so picky."

"Maybe we should have shot them to begin with."

She leaned forward.

"Did you take any prisoners?"

Jacques tapped his spoon on the table. "A few," he said. "We trapped a squad right outside St. Lô, the day before I got hit."

He could still see their faces, tired, dirty, hostile, scared. The leader, a Prussian who inched out from behind a hedgerow with a white handkerchief tied to his bayonet, managed to look arrogant even in defeat. The others, though, were shaking with fear. While Jacques collected their weapons, the soldier with him, a cowboy from Montana, tore the swastika off one of the captives and ground it into the dirt. The Germans were as furtive as rabbits when Jacques and the cowboy herded them behind the lines to the makeshift holding compound. It was a damn headache to have to take prisoners with the battle still going on, and after the D-Day carnage they'd have preferred to shoot every Wehrmacht uniform in sight, but they had their orders. Too many Americans in enemy stalags might be done in, in reprisal.

Jacques tamped out a cigarette with more force than necessary.

Betty refilled his cup. As she bent over, her robe came open a little, revealing a matching nightgown. She closed it with a modest gesture and tightened the sash.

"What happened," she asked him, "when you found out about the POWs?"

He didn't like to think about it.

"Oh, I blew my stack. Cussed out my old man and raised hell with everybody, even my boy, Chris. They've all gone soft in the head over one of the POWs, some guy they call Werner. He must have given them a snow job that wouldn't quit."

"I don't get it," Betty said, shaking her head.

"That makes two of us, honey."

He realized, suddenly, how tired and pale she was. There were smudges under her eyes.

"Gee, Betty, I'm sorry. I didn't mean to keep you up all night."

"That's okay."

"I'd better go and let you get some sleep."

He got up and stretched. He was stiff all over.

"Thanks for everything," he said. "Sorry I made such an ass of myself. I shouldn't have unloaded like this on you, either."

"Any time, Corporal, any time."

He was on his way out when she said, "Jacques?"

She was biting her bottom lip. "Will you come back?"

He studied his boots. "I don't know. I'm not sure I should."

"No strings..." she said.

He hadn't realized how blue her eyes were.

"You sure you want me to?"

"I'm sure."

He just nodded and slipped out, making sure the door locked behind him.

The streets were empty at that hour. He was glad he didn't see anybody on his way out of town. Once he got past the city limits he drove slowly, cracking the little side window to let in some cold air. He needed to think. How was he going to explain to the family about Carl's? Hell, they wouldn't listen to his side, anyhow.

A whiff of skunk hit him and he rolled the window shut. He wished he'd asked Betty for some aspirin or an Alka Seltzer or something. His head felt about three sizes and ten pounds too big, and his stomach wasn't any too sympathetic. Boy, was he in for a hangover. All because of those sonofabitch POWs.

All right, he decided, I'll bide my time till the contract's up. Adele would see, they'd all see who was right and who was wrong.

At least there was one person on his side. Betty understood. Her image flashed through his head and left him aroused. Betty in the soft pink sweater, laughing at Tex. Betty curled up in the armchair like a lace trimmed valentine.

Forgetting his sore knuckles, he brought his fist down hard on the steering wheel.

"Dammit, Viator," he ordered himself, "cut it out. You know she's off limits."

It was just that he felt so damned alone.

He concentrated on driving. Every few feet fog rolled off the fields, cloaking the road. In the clearings the inky silhouettes of pine and oak trees made him think of the pictures his pal Boogie used to draw in the hospital. Jacques wondered how Boogie and the other guys were doing. He sure missed Boogie. Boogie would know what to do about a mess like this, or if he didn't, he'd have you laughing about it.

When Jacques got home, the house was dark except for a light in the kitchen. What if Adele was still up?

He was in luck, though. She was in bed asleep.

He went to check on Chris, trying not to clomp on the wood floor. Jesus, things were loud here at night, just like in the trenches. He straightened the boy's quilt. Damn, the kid snored. Sounded like a freight train. Maybe they ought to see about getting his tonsils out. A rush of tenderness went through Jacques. He'd missed two whole years of the boy's childhood. They had a lot of catching up to do.

Chris's jacket had fallen off the end of the bed. When Jacques bent to pick it up, one of Carl's candy canes fell out.

"Oh, shit," Jacques mumbled, and went to bed.

Chapter 10

Why Adele pretended to be asleep she wasn't quite sure.

It took every bit of her will power to do it. Partly, she didn't want Chris to wake up to a scene, and partly, after agonizing all night, she was weak with relief that Jacques was home and safe. Then, when he came in their room radiating smoke and whiskey fumes, she was too furious to speak. She lay motionless, biting the corner of her pillow case, until his breathing slowed and became steady.

Sleep was out of the question. She couldn't stop thinking, much as thinking hurt. Nowadays even memories hurt. She was beginning to wonder if she and Jacques had ever been happy, or if she'd made it all up. Their wonderful life together seemed like a fairy tale. She tried praying her rosary, but the repetitious prayers didn't comfort her or make her drowsy as they usually did.

At daybreak she got out of bed and dressed without bothering to be quiet. Not that it mattered; Jacques slept till almost noon.

She was at the stove making a roux when he finally appeared. She kept on stirring, but stepped aside so he could reach the coffee pot.

When he didn't speak, she took a deep breath and said, "Well?"

He lifted a pot lid and sniffed.

"Well, what?"

"Stop it, Jacques!"

She threw down the spoon and whirled around.

"We've got to talk!"

"What about?"

"You could at least say you're sorry."

"You want me to lie to you? I haven't done anything to be sorry for."

"Jacques, how can you? It wasn't wrong to spoil Carl and Hannah's party? Chris and Jeanette were embarrassed to death and I was nearly out of my mind worrying all night."

"Whoa, there. You're the one who wanted to go to the blasted thing and you knew all along Carl was hiring Nazis."

The roux started to smoke and throw off an acrid burnt smell. Adele grabbed a potholder and shoved the iron pot off the burner. Now she'd have to start all over. Nothing was going right any more. Her voice shook.

"They aren't Nazis, I keep telling you. I mean ours aren't. The Nazis are locked up in a special camp somewhere, I think it's Oklahoma."

"Don't be naïve, Adele. If their filthy Fuhrer was winning, you'd see how fast they'd salute."

She shook her head in resignation.

"It's no use, is it? You aren't going to forgive us for hiring them."

He turned his back on her and looked out the window.

"Where'd you go?" She hadn't meant to ask, she wasn't sure she wanted to know, but she couldn't help herself.

"When?"

"Oh, stop playing games. You know very well when. When you walked out and left us stranded last night."

"Town," was all he said.

He stuck his hands in his pockets and looked her straight in the eye, daring her to continue.

She swallowed hard, retrieved the spoon and took it to the sink to rinse it. Jesus, Mary and Joseph, she said to herself, help me to stay calm. She had to say it.

"Will you apologize to Carl?"

"Not while he has them working for him. Maybe he likes them better, anyway. Maybe they speak his language."

"Oh, Jacques, how can you say that? You've known Carl all your life."

"You think you know a lot of things, Adele. And do you want me to talk, or don't you? Make up your mind."

"I want you to talk sense!"

"Then you talk sense for a change!" he yelled back. "If you'd talked to me about the POWs this never would have happened, would it? You want me to put up with this crap, okay, but dammit, Adele, quit trying to make me like it. And get off my back about talking until you get rid of the damn Nazis, you hear?"

She turned off the burners and untied her apron.

"Your dinner's on the stove," she said tersely. "I'm going to Papa's."

After the cold night, the day was crisp and beautiful. Some of the POWs were cleaning ditches beside the road, chopping in rhythm with machetes at cat tails and wild grass. Their blonde heads and the yellow PWs stenciled on their clothes were bright in the sun. Heavy-hearted and feeling a little guilty, Adele waved. She wondered if any of them hated Jacques the way he hated them. Was it possible they truly were Nazis and as evil as Jacques said? Werner wasn't, she was sure of that much. Werner had told her about the other camps where, when the Americans weren't watching, the un-converted Nazis would beat up any of their comrades who spoke against Hitler or even suggested that Germany might lose the war.

But Jacques was so suspicious, constantly on the lookout for sabotage. He checked every single piece of machinery the men used. She thought he was almost disappointed when he couldn't find anything wrong. He even counted the tools every evening although the guards did that, and nothing had been missing yet. She'd heard stories about prisoners taking things to escape with, but their men never had. Once, when a wood carver asked Papa for a broken knife, Papa had given it to him, and a screwdriver to chisel with. Jacques would be furious if he knew.

The drive took only a few minutes, but it made her feel better. She found Papa and Jeanette in the kitchen, eating. Jeanette wanted to fix her a bowl of gumbo.

"No thanks, Jeanette. I'm not hungry."

"Are you sure?"

"Really. You go ahead. I didn't mean to interrupt your dinner."

She poured herself a cup of coffee and took the place opposite Jeanette.

The night's anxiety showed on her in-laws' faces. They probably hadn't got much sleep, either, after taking Chris and her home from Kaufmanns'.

"My boy still acting the fool?" Papa grumbled between bites. He blew on the gumbo to cool it.

Adele stirred her coffee without answering.

"What did Jacques say about last night?" asked Jeanette, her high voice even shriller from strain.

Poor dear, Adele thought. Things Jeanette didn't understand unnerved her, made her feel helpless, especially if she had trouble reading their lips. She looked worried all the time, now, even worse than when Jacques was overseas.

"Not much," Adele had to tell her. "He feels betrayed."

"By us?" Jeanette cried.

Papa choked, spraying gumbo on the oilcloth covering the table.

"We didn't do him nothin'," he sputtered. "All we done was hire us some farm hands."

"I know, Papa, but I'm trying to look at it through Jacques' eyes. It's true, isn't it, the Germans would have killed him? And they are always getting us into wars, you can't deny that. Jacques honestly believes the men are dangerous."

Nobody spoke. Bleating from the sheep pen out back cut the winter stillness. Adele could hear the teapot-shaped clock on the wall over the refrigerator, too, and somewhere a gate that flapped on creaky hinges.

"Papa..." she said hesitantly. "Are you sure we're doing the right thing? I mean we really couldn't get along without the POWs, could we?"

"Mais, Adele," he said with more than a trace of exasperation. "We just cleared twenty more acres; who we gonna get to plow? Bob, he's in the Marines, L.J. and Credeur's boys is in the army. Celestines and them other nigras, they gone work for the shipyard, them. So who we gonna get? What I'm gonna tell the government - I can't plant, my boy hates Germans?"

What could she say?

"I know, Papa. You're right. It's just that Jacques is so sure. He goes behind everything they do at our place, looking for trouble."

"Pooyie! Tell that boy to do a day's work and cut out the spy stuff."

"Papa! He's hurt!"

Papa cut his eyes at her and took a long time with a pouch of

Bull Durham, rolling a cigarette before he spoke.

"You think I don't know that? What you think it does me to see him walk hippety-hop?"

Adele wanted to cry. Jeanette looked back and forth at Papa and her, trying to follow.

"Lemme tell you, cher," he went on, "Jacques won't get over it actin' like that, non. He's just makin' it worse. I know."

He pointed a thumb at Jeanette.

"When her and her mama took sick and her mama passed away, I stayed mad at ever'body. I was mad at the doctors. I was mad at myself. Most, I was mad at God for letting it happen. And you know what? I didn't get over bein' mad till I quit thinkin' about what I'd lost. You got to concentrate on what you got. I know Jacques is hurtin', but I thank le bon Dieu, me, he got back alive."

Papa turned aside and wiped his eyes. It was the first time Adele had ever heard him refer to his wife's death. She rose and laid a hand on his shoulder.

"It'll be all right, Papa," she said. "We'll manage. The war will be over soon. It has to be!"

Jacques stayed in the bedroom the rest of that day. The following morning, though, he was up as usual and they all pretended nothing had happened. I guess it's best that way, Adele told herself.

She kept busy as the week crawled forward, trying to forget. She aired all the winter clothes and woolen blankets to get out the mothball smell. She shelled five quarts of pecans, without minding, in the long hours between supper and bedtime. Ordinarily, she hated that chore for leaving her hands nicked and stained, but now it gave her something to do while listening to the radio. She made a red flannelette gown for Jeanette for Christmas and let out the hem of Chris's Sunday pants, musing that the boy was growing faster than a swamp weed.

Determined to act normal, Adele took Jeanette to altar society meeting as usual, and offered to help decorate the church for midnight Mass.

Friday was the women's day to go to the American Legion hall to work for the Red Cross, putting together afghans for wounded soldiers.

Adele and Jeanette's arrival produced an awkward silence. It

seemed to Adele the room was full of knitting needles in mid-air.
She saw Bertha Boudreaux whisper something to her sister.

Hannah, God bless her, came to meet them.

"Hey, y'all," she waved, making room at the table where she
was working. "Come on over by us."

Bernadette Dupre, a fat, likable woman with a penchant for
polka dot dresses gathered at the bosom by a dime store brooch,
waddled over to Jeanette with a stack of blocked, brightly colored
squares.

"You start on these, honey. You match them better than anyone."

Pleased, Jeanette took out her crochet hook and set to work.
Adele picked up a skein of variegated wool and began winding it
in a ball.

The women's chatter bounced off the walls. A bare frame building on a concrete slab, the hall had been built after the First World
War, the one that was supposed to be the last. Before Pearl Harbor,
the roll of honor plaque had collected cobwebs, but these days,
names were added regularly. The plaque was flanked on either side
by gold fringed flags with vigilant brass eagles atop the poles.

In the old days, before Chris was born, when Adele and Jacques
used to attend the Saturday night dances there, Adele had tried to
figure out who the people in the fly-specked photographs were.
The only one she recognized was President Roosevelt, younger and
jauntier then.

Would she and Jacques ever dance again, she wondered.

A memory swept over her of a magical summer night when the
other dancers had cleared the floor just to watch them waltz. They
were that good together, in perfect step, and not only dancing.
Everyone said so.

Adele had to wind faster to choke back tears.

With Jeanette on one side and Hannah on the other, Adele
wasn't expected to contribute much to the conversation, and she
was thankful. Before Jacques came home, she'd looked forward to
Red Cross days, taking satisfaction in the thought that someone
else's husband might be more comfortable as the result of their
labors. Today it was a penance, but she made the best of it.

Hannah had gone several tables over to show Clarisse Le Blanc's
daughter, a young bride, how to count stitches. When she returned,
while the other women were arguing about Stella Dallas's radio

romances, Hannah whispered under her breath, "Are you okay? Is Jacques still mad?"

The yarn was sticky in Adele's hands. She shook it and her head at the same time. Hannah reached under the table and gave her a quick pat.

"Come on. Let's see who wants Cokes."

It was a relief to move around. The women who'd been at the party didn't act any differently, but Adele was self-conscious, nevertheless. What did people think? By now, everyone in Courville must have heard about Jacques.

It was a long, trying afternoon.

Otherwise, the days were as short as the nights seemed endless. She did the shopping for both farms, kept all their accounts, dealt with banks and mills, with equipment dealers and the county agent, handling as much of the business as she could to take the load off Papa, but there was no catching up.

"When is Jacques going to farm again?" asked Jeanette one day while she and Adele canned pumpkin.

"I don't know, honey," Adele sighed. "It looks like we'll have to manage without him a while longer."

Chapter 11

Jacques had made up his mind he wouldn't go back to Betty's and he wouldn't have, he told himself, if it hadn't been for the argument with Papa and the call from Boogie.

It happened the week before Christmas. Papa came by that evening while Jacques was examining a swollen hoof on Chris's pony, Silver.

"Lost a shoe?" Papa asked.

"Yeah. He's limping pretty bad. Easy does it, boy."

"Need some help?"

"No thanks."

"Come on in, Papa," Adele called out the window. "I'm baking oatmeal cookies."

"Can't stay, Adele. Thanks anyway. Jeanette'll be lookin' for me. I just passed on my way home to see if y'all want to come over. I got us a sack of oysters from that Breaux kid. What you say, Jacques, you want to shuck and go halves?"

Jacques hadn't meant to pick a fight. The words just jumped out before he thought twice.

"Why don't you let your Nazis do it?"

Papa stiffened.

"They don't know how," he said. "You want half or not? Or maybe you lost your stren'th wherever your manners is at."

Adele started to intervene, but Jacques stopped her.

"There's nothing the matter with my arms. I'll be over as soon as I finish here."

"C'est bon," Papa said. "Adele, y'all come eat supper with us. Where's Christophe? Okay if he rides with me?"

At first Jacques thought it was kind of fun, like old times when he and Papa used to race.

Jeanette had newspaper on the kitchen floor. He and Papa put the gunny sack between them. After a few tries, Jacques began to get the knack again, and before long he was keeping up with Papa, oyster for oyster. Chris wanted to try. They showed him how to stick the knife in just so and twist, but all the boy got for his struggle was blisters.

"Don't worry," Papa told him, "Your daddy like to never got the hang of it, either, and look at him now. You run fetch us a empty sack for the shells."

They worked in a steady rhythm, prying and scraping the oysters with a plop into the pan.

"Mailbox needs painting," Jacques remarked, deciding to make a stab at conversation.

"Uh huh. House, too. Looks like we stay so busy in the fields, ain't time to keep up. That hot sauce ready yet, Adele? We got any crackers?"

"Coming," she told him.

"Price of fertilizer gone up much?" Jacques said.

"'bout twenty per cent. Not as bad as gasoline."

"Any trouble getting gas?"

"Some. Them tractors eats it up in a hurry."

"Did you get the big tractor fixed?" Jeanette asked Papa.

"Not yet." Papa frowned at her.

"What's wrong with the big tractor?"

"Magneto went out."

"Jacques jabbed the oyster in his hand so hard the knife slipped. He almost cut his hand.

"I knew it! Sabotage. What'd they do to it?"

Papa gave him a disgusted look. "Nobody didn't do nothin' to it. Damn thing just wore out."

"You sure?"

"Sure, I'm sure."

"You want me to take it to the shop tomorrow?"

"Already did."

"Didn't they fix it?"

"Can't. Don't have the parts. Take two or three months."

"Bull. I'll go talk to Jim."

"Never mind."

"What do you mean, never mind? You can't operate without your tractor, can you?"

Papa laid down his knife and rinsed his hands.

"Johann says he can fix it."

"Who? Oh, no, don't tell me. One of the POWs!"

"Magnetos was his trade before the war."

"And you believe him?"

"He's good with his hands, him. I've watched him work."

"You're really going to let a Nazi mess with your best tractor?" Jacques couldn't believe the stupidity of it.

Papa wouldn't answer. His jaw was set stubbornly and he kept on opening oysters without missing a lick. Jacques felt like knocking him off his chair.

"There's no fool like an old fool," Jacques said, throwing down his knife. "Come on, Adele. Chris. Let's go!"

They didn't say a word in the truck and neither did he. Adele sat way over, practically in Chris's lap, all the way home.

They'd been back only a minute when the phone rang, breaking the thick silence. It rang so seldom any more that he was startled.

"For you, Jacques," Adele said tersely. "It's long distance."

"Hello?"

"Mr. Viator?" The operator pronounced it like theater.

"Yes?"

"Hold the line for long distance, please." There were several nasal-voiced exchanges punctuated by clicks and bursts of static before the operator announced, "Go ahead, sir. Your party's on the line."

"Hey, Frenchy! That you? It's me, Boogie."

"Boogie, you crazy fool! How're you doing?"

"How the hell do you think I'm doing? I'm going home!"

"No kidding! Damn, that's great. That's just great. When are you getting out of there?"

"Doc says Friday or Saturday next week - soon as they get my paper work done."

"Going home in time for Christmas dinner, huh, Boogie?"

"You know it. My old lady's already cooking."

"That's great, buddy, no bull. How's your back?"

"Pretty good. I'm getting a new corset, just like my Aunt Maggie's."

"A corset!"

"Well, hell, man. It's better than a brassiere. Didn't you ever hear of money belts? Mine's going to be a real custom made job."

"Yours would be. How are the rest of the guys?"

"So so," Boogie said. "Tony had to have another operation on his foot and Shorty's all torn up. Got a dear John letter from his wife."

"Oh, shit. That's all he needed."

"Yeah, I know. They all said to tell you hi. We sure do miss you around here. That red headed nurse asked me the other day if I'd heard from you. How's civilian life?"

"It's okay, I guess. What are you going to do when you get out?"

"I dunno. Get a job. Go back to art school. I still haven't decided. First, I'm going to eat the biggest steaks I can find and drink a case of beer and sleep till noon. I dare anybody to come near me with a thermometer!"

"I'll send your mom a record with Reveille on it so she can play it for you on the Victrola."

"You do and I'll get your discharge revoked."

"Why don't you come down here and let me show you God's country?"

The operator broke in.

"I'm sorry, sir; your three minutes are up."

"I might do that," Boogie said. "Let me see how things go at home. Good talkin' to you, Frenchy!"

"Glad you called, Boogie. Let me know how you get along. Merry Christmas."

"You, too. So long."

Grinning and shaking his head, Jacques put back the receiver. He couldn't get over Boogie calling all the way from Maryland. So Boogie was going home. That called for a celebration. In his excitement, Jacques forgot all about the ugliness at Papa's. He went to tell Adele the good news, but she was in the bathroom running water in the tub, and Chris was already in bed.

Too keyed up to listen to the radio or read, Jacques paced the house thinking of Boogie and the guys in Ward D. Adele was taking her sweet time in the bathroom. He knocked on the door.

"Yes?" she answered with icicles in her voice.

"I'm going to town to get some more books. Do we need anything from the drug store?"

Either she didn't hear or she was ignoring him. Let her pout, then. He grabbed his Ike jacket and took off for Courville.

On Main Street the window of Ortigue's Pharmacy and Soda Fountain was scalloped with a threadbare rope of tinsel that framed a red and green crayon lettered sign saying 'OPEN EVERY NIGHT TILL XMAS'. Inside, a young couple was trying to pick out a doll. A bell tinkled as Jacques walked in, and the couple looked up. They smiled half smiles like people do if they aren't sure they know you, and went back to their argument.

"She isn't old enough for that one, George. It's bigger than she is."

"You just don't want one that wets," he said.

Mr. Ortigue was counting pills behind the prescription counter.

"Be with you in a minute," he called.

A radio played "Silent Night". Jacques thumbed through the paperback rack, picking out Ellery Queen and Nero Wolfe murder mysteries, good for passing the time. He scanned the lending library for something else. They didn't have Look Homeward Angel; it must be checked out. Boogie said it was good. Jacques spotted a new Du Maurier novel and got that for Jeanette. She liked those English stories.

He scowled, remembering Jeanette, all set to fry oysters in the big iron skillet, and Papa, and the latest quarrel.

"Jacques!" Mr. Ortigue boomed. "I didn't know it was you. Comme sa va? Welcome home!"

Rene Ortigue and Papa were old friends.

"Thanks, Mr. Ortigue. How've you been?"

"Not bad for an old Cajun. And you? I heard about your leg. That's sure too bad."

"Yeah, well, these things happen. Business doing all right?"

"Could be better. The shortages like to drive me crazy, but folks has to make do when there's a war on. What can I do for you tonight?" He leaned over the counter and said to the young couple, "You folks need any help there?"

"No sir," the young woman answered. She tightened the knot

of her plaid head scarf. "We're still trying to make up our minds. It's our little girl's first Christmas."

The young husband turned red.

"You don't have to tell people everything you know," he whispered.

"I'll take these, Jacques said, handing Mr. Ortigue the books.

After ringing up the sale, Mr. Ortigue beckoned Jacques to come closer and said in a confidential voice, "How about a box of chocolates?"

From under the counter he brought out a Whitman Sampler and wrapped it quickly in paper covered with pine cones.

"Candy's real scarce, you know. We don't get much. But you bein' a hero and all..."

"Thanks," was all Jacques could think of to say. "How much do I owe you?"

"Not a thing. It's on the house."

"Well, thanks a lot."

"Sure thing. Least I can do after what you done for us. Hope you and the wife enjoy it."

That wasn't quite what Jacques had in mind. He looked away and hurried out.

On his way to Tenth Street, he stopped at Wally's liquor joint. Wally's wife, Dorothy, was tending the store.

"Hey, Jacques!" she said. "Long time no see. Glad you're back. Must have been pretty gruesome over there, huh?"

"Hi, Dot. Where's your old man?"

"Aw, phooey. He had another draft board meeting tonight. I swear, if it ain't the draft board, it's the air patrol. Any old excuse to leave me stuck here."

"He probably wants to show off what a pretty wife he has."

"Sure. Tell me another."

Everyone in Courville knew how lazy Wally Devereaux was.

"Business pretty slow?"

He'd seen her polishing her nails when he came in.

"Slow ain't the word for it. 'Cept for the soldiers out at the camp we'd have had to close up a long time ago. Them and John Parker Landry."

"Yeah, I saw the old lush at Jo Jo's the other night. Still going strong, huh?"

"And you know, my kid brother says John Parker used to be

smart as a whip. They was in school together. Myron, that's my
brother, he says everybody thought John Parker would be a senator
or something, maybe even president. It just goes to show you."

Jacques looked around, half listening. Dot would go on for
hours if you let her.

"Don't you have any champagne?"

"Champagne! Are you kidding? Ask me something easy. There's
a war on, you know."

"So I heard," Jacques said. "Give me a pint of Southern Comfort, then."

"Wally ought to be back before long," Dot said. "Why don't
you stick around?"

"Some other time, Dot. I've got to get going. Tell Wally I'll be
seeing him."

"All right," she said. "Don't take any wooden nickels."

He faltered before getting out at Betty's, although her car was
in the garage and her lights were on. It's just a friendly gesture, he
told himself. He owed her something, didn't he, for taking care
of him a couple of weeks back? He didn't like to admit how much
she'd been on his mind. If only he could talk to his family without
getting into some damfool argument. He hadn't seen Carl since the
night of the fight. A guy had to have somebody to talk to.

Betty looked surprised.

"Hi," he said. "I'm celebrating."

"Three cheers for you. What's the occasion?"

"May I come in and tell you about it? I'm sober this time."

She hesitated, giving him a long look. "I see you are," she said
and moved aside.

He handed her the box of candy.

"Here. Put this under your tree. Where's your Christmas
tree?"

"No tree," she said, "but thanks, anyway."

She felt the box and held it to her nose. "Is this what I think it
is? I didn't know they still made the stuff. Mmmm."

"You've got to have a tree. It wouldn't be Christmas. I'll cut
you one tomorrow. How tall? Five feet? Six?"

"Thanks, Jacques, but don't. I don't want a tree."

"Betty," he said gently. "It's been almost a year. Armand
wouldn't want you to stop living."

"It's not Armand," she said with an expression of such pure

pain he winced. "Don't you know where Christmas trees started? The POWs even have one in their camp. Them and their peace on earth. I don't want any part of their hypocritical customs!"

Her voice cracked and her eyes glistened.

Before Jacques had time to think, he'd taken her in his arms.

Chapter 12

Although she longed to see them, Adele was thankful her parents had not been able to come for the holidays. She didn't want them burdened with her problems. They had enough to worry about already, what with merchandise being so hard to get and help almost impossible to find. She thought it a miracle they didn't both have ulcers. Her mother had started working for her dad at the dry goods store on Poydras Street after half his staff had gone to war. Adele found it hard to imagine her mother in business, dressing windows and checking invoices instead of playing bridge at the club, but then her parents couldn't get over their only daughter being a farm wife. Life certainly was full of surprises.

Hoping for a letter, Adele hurried to finish ironing Chris's overalls when she heard the postman's truck, and was elated to spot her mother's lavender stationery among the feed bills and magazines. Without waiting to get to the house for a proper opener, she tore the envelope and read as she walked back to the house.

'Often as not,' her mother wrote, 'your dad and I have to clean the restrooms and sweep the store. The darkies have all gone to work for the shipyard or the refinery, and the school kids, too. You can't blame them. They make a lot more than we can pay.'

'We finally got that shipment from St. Louis,' Adele read. 'Everything takes longer now because the troop trains get priority. That's as it must be, but we do find it hard to sell summer sandals in January!'

The letter ended by asking how Jacques was and when they were coming. Adele put it in her pocket with a rueful sigh, more lonesome than before.

When her parents couldn't come for Christmas, Jacques had urged her to take Chris and go to New Orleans, but she wouldn't think of it without him, even as miserable as they all were. Not after they'd been apart two Christmases already. Nor would he consider going to the city, much as he'd once enjoyed it. In the early years of their marriage, they'd driven there several times a year. Jacques loved to go to the Quarter to listen to Dixieland and then walk through the French Market in the early morning while the water-front was still misty and the hucksters bantered, unloading sacks of crabs and fresh produce.

One night at dinner, thinking Jacques might weaken, she made a point of telling Chris how you could get a huge stalk of bananas just off a ship from South America, how the stalls were decorated with garlic and red pepper braids and how pyramids of artichokes filled the backs of pickup trucks.

"Remember how we used to eat beignets at Café du Monde, Jacques, and I'd get powdered sugar all over my black coat?"

Nothing worked. Jacques was adamant.

"You and Chris go on," he said. "I'm no good to you, anyhow. I'll stay and keep an eye on the Nazis."

She hadn't argued. She merely wrote, trying not to show her disappointment, and told her family he wasn't up to traveling yet. Maybe Mardi Gras or Easter, she told them, depending on how much vacation Chris got.

She was glad when the holidays were over and Chris was back in school. It was too much of a strain, trying to keep a cheerful front. Every day she woke up praying something would change, but between the war news and Jacques' coldness, she was often close to tears.

And here it was February. Adele plumped pillows and routed lint from under the beds, brooding. She'd turned the calendar page that morning. Mardi Gras was just around the corner.

Jacques did seem a little better lately. Not as tense. He didn't use his cane as much and he'd started plowing the field next to the house when the POWs were working Papa's land. He and Papa hadn't fought any more that she knew of. She should have felt re-lieved, but she didn't, and she didn't know why.

When Jacques wasn't aware, she studied him the way he studied the weather, looking for storm warnings, trying to foresee what was coming next. Once upon a time she would have known exactly what he was thinking. They'd understood each other so well they could finish the other's sentences. Nowadays the extent of their conversation was 'Pass the salt' or 'Is it cold?' She hated it. At least when he was gone there'd been letters, good, long, loving letters. To have him with her and still not have him was torture.

In the middle of folding a quilt Adele paused to ponder the situation. Jacques had taken to going off several nights a week and coming back late. He never explained, and she was determined not to ask again where he'd been. He hadn't come home drunk but that once, after the fiasco at Carl's.

She kept telling herself she trusted him completely. It was just that she couldn't get used to being left out of his life. Maybe, she thought, he's playing bourree at the pool hall. That didn't seem likely, though, without Carl, and most of Jacques' other friends were in the service. From checking the gas gauge in the pickup she decided he must be going to town or else just riding around listening to the radio. He used to like to do that, too.

"Oh, what's the use?" she said out loud and gave the quilt a vigorous shake.

The door to their bedroom was closed. That was something else he'd begun to do lately, close their door. Rather than argue, she used the hall entrance to the bathroom and left him alone. Some nights she considered moving to the sofa to sleep, but she balked at that. Let him move, darn it, if he didn't want to sleep with her!

After she finished cleaning Chris's room she went to the back door to shake the dust mop. The north wind yanked the screen right out of her hand. It cut through her cotton house dress, adding to her restlessness. She took the clothespin apron and went to bring in the wash, but the clothes were still damp, so she left them on the line. The POWs were gone. She hadn't noticed when the hammering stopped. There'd been a crew in the pasture, earlier, repairing the fence. It made her nervous to have them that close to the house. She never knew what Jacques might do. She shivered, went back in to get a sweater and some things to take to Papa.

She found him giving orders to some men cleaning his barn. Johann, the spokesman for the POWs, relayed the instructions in German. The men were all attentive except for the one named Rolf.

He stood apart from the others, leaning on a shovel. Something about Rolf bothered Adele, though there'd never been anything specific she could fault him for. She got the feeling he wasn't popular among his comrades, either.

Papa strode over to her with a big smile of welcome, wiping his hands on a faded blue and white bandanna.

"Comme ca va, cher?"

Adele leaned out the window.

"Pretty good, Papa."

She handed him a sheaf of papers and a fountain pen.

"The ones on top are the new gasoline and tire forms. We have to turn those in once a month from now on."

"Some more? Damn politicians," he grumbled. "That all them fancypants in Washington got to do, think up papers to fill out? How they expect us to do our farmin'?"

"Don't ask me, Papa. Just sign where I put the red check marks, will you?"

He got in beside her to use the dashboard, and laboriously wrote his name, muttering all the while the pen scratched.

"There," he said when he'd worked his way through the stack. "What else you got?"

"The rest are for Captain Bentley. I was wondering if you could drop them off at the camp this afternoon."

"Mais yeah."

He folded the papers to fit his pocket.

"How's Jacques?" he said.

"All right, I suppose."

"Still in his shell like a turtle?"

"Yes sir."

"That him I been hearin' out late at night?"

Adele nodded and looked away.

Papa grunted. "Don't drive like no turtle. How's he act?"

She wished Papa wouldn't ask so many questions.

"About the same," she told him. "Better, in some ways. He doesn't stay in the bedroom all day like he did, only when there are POWs in sight. I don't understand it, Papa. Some days he acts almost normal, but it seems like we just get farther and farther apart."

Her eyes were beginning to water. Darn it, she didn't want to cry. She turned the key in the ignition.

"Tell Captain Bentley I'll get the rest of those reports to him next week," she said.

But Papa was giving her his weighing-real-hard look that meant there was something on his mind. He laid a work-hardened palm on her arm.

"You didn't stop at the house, did you?"

"No, why?"

"Werner's there. I got him building that pantry Jeanette's been after me about."

Adele cut the engine.

"But Papa, you know what Jacques said!"

"'Course I know what he said," Papa snapped, "but Jacques ain't the boss on this farm."

Adele took a deep breath.

"But Jeanette...she promised."

"Phooey! Promises don't mean nothin' to Jacques. He promised Jeanette he'd be over Friday night to play Monopoly and he ain't got there yet. How come he don't have to keep promises and we do?"

Adele was too shocked to protest. When Chris came down with a stomach ache Friday night she'd told Jacques to go on to Papa's without them It never occurred to her he might not have.

"I mean it, Adele," Papa was saying, "I'm fed up. I been patient long enough. I'm tired seein' Jeanette hang a lip and sniffle all the time."

"You're right, Papa," she said heavily. "It wasn't fair. Just try to keep him out of Jacques' way, will you?"

God help us, she thought, if Jacques finds out.

She was about to leave when Werner eased down the steps carrying a two by four. Papa called him over.

"I was just telling Miss Adele about the pantry."

"Hallo, Frau Viator. It won't cause trouble, I hope?"

His eyes were anxious, too old for a face that barely needed shaving. Werner was unfailingly polite, and eager as a puppy to please, but he seldom smiled. Adele had come upon him once when he was describing the Munich Opera to Jeanette. You could almost see the chandeliers and the red velvet curtains. Having to search for the right words in English, he spoke slowly and carefully, making it easy for Jeanette to lip-read. Only once had Adele heard him laugh. That was over Chris cutting up on the old tire swing, playing circus.

She simply couldn't think of Werner as an enemy after that.

"I hope not, Werner," she answered his question. "You do whatever Papa says." He looked so relieved she added, "We've missed you. How have you been?"

"Well, danke. I mean, thank you."

Werner got his 'v's and 'w's mixed up, and sometimes his words were in odd sequences, but it was amazing, really, how well he spoke. According to Papa, his French wasn't bad, either, once he got used to the Cajun dialect.

"How are your parents and your little sister?" Adele asked him.

She knew he scoured the paper every day to see where the bombing was.

"I have not a letter from them since Weinachten - Christmas," he said, "but there is a new fellow in the camp the name of Franz from the village next to mine. Franz says the S.S. came and took way the school teacher - that's my Vater - for not making the children salute der Fuhrer's picture, but after three days they let him go. The S.S. was packing to leave before the coming of the Russians. Franz says the Russians will any day now be there."

Papa made a clucking noise.

"Oh, Werner," Adele said.

"My father takes the family to my grandfather's farm, I think."

"C'est bon," Papa said.

Adele could tell Werner was not pleased.

"They'll be safe there, won't they?" she asked.

"I wish it was the Americans or the English," he said.

"I don't understand," Adele told him. "What difference does it make as long as they're out from under Hitler?"

"My Vater has no trust for the Russians, either," Werner explained. "They want to make us all Communists, he says."

"Oh," said Adele, perplexed.

"I think the Russians will be glad to see us crushed. They do not like us Germans. We are not, how you say, good neighbors."

"Well," Papa declared, getting out of the truck, anybody's got to be better than those lunatics in Berlin. How's that pantry comin', boy? You got enough lumber?"

Adele told them goodbye.

"Oh, Papa, I almost forgot. Mother and Dad want me to go for Carnival. I don't like leaving Jacques, but I hate to disappoint them again. Do you think you could manage if Chris and I go to the city for a few days? We wouldn't stay long."

"Sure. Go and pass you a good time. Don't worry none about us. We'll be okay."

"Thanks, Papa. I haven't made up my mind for sure. I'll let you know."

To her surprise, Jacques was pacing the driveway when she got back, waiting for the truck. He looked disheveled and upset. As fast as she got out, he got in and left, mumbling something about business in town. The POWs were gone, so she knew it wasn't that. Puzzled, she watched the truck till it was out of sight.

Chris was home soon after and she sat with him while he had his snack.

"Where's Dad going?" he asked. "He passed us, going the other way."

"Don't gobble, son. He said he had something to do."

"Then can I ride Silver a little while before I do my chores?"

"I guess so. Don't stay too long, though."

She decided to finish cleaning before time to start supper. At the door to their room she stopped, aghast at the mess. The rumpled bed was covered with bright bits of colored paper. Balls of paper were wadded up and thrown on the floor, too, nowhere near the wastebasket.

"What on earth did he do that for?" she said aloud.

On the other side of the hope chest, lying on the rag rug, she found what was left of a Life magazine, the one that had come several days ago with the weird Dali painting on the cover. She hadn't had time to look at it yet.

Gathering up the scraps, she began painstakingly smoothing them out and piecing them together on her dresser.

By the time she had reconstructed the torn pages, the sun was setting. In the darkening amber light she sat staring at ragged pictures of the ravaged buildings, the tangle of power lines and the cratered cobblestones that were the remains of the Square of St. Lô. A fifteen foot crucifix from which telephone wires had been strung stood in the center of a courtyard. Beyond it, two G.I.s were leading away captured Germans, all of them choking from the smoke and dust which lasted, Life said, for days after the battle was over.

Chapter 13

Jacques hesitated when he got to Courville. Betty worked till five, but he had a key to her apartment hidden in his billfold, behind his driver's license. He could let himself in, play solitaire, read magazines. There was beer in the refrigerator. He didn't feel like being cooped up alone, though, and he sure as hell didn't want to see any more magazines.

On impulse, he took a right at Eighth Street, turned off on Willow, and drove out to where it stopped being a boulevard and ran into the highway north of town. About a mile down the road, just over the tracks, he came to the POW compound. Across the way was a boarded-up honky-tonk, the old Stardust Lounge. Weeds, waist high, had taken over the parking lot, all but obscuring a faded FOR SALE sign. Jacques pulled in there and parked so that he was half-hidden, with the camp in full view.

The old C.C.C. buildings had been spruced up, all right. Last time he'd seen the place a bunch of windows were shot out and crab grass was taking over. Now everything was neat, trim as a G.I. haircut.

High above the camp in an unpainted wooden tower a yawning guard shifted his rifle from shoulder to shoulder. Jacques would have bet money the soldier had tied one on the night before.

The damn fence was a joke, just a couple of flimsy strands of barbed wire hitched to a post every few yards. Wouldn't keep a calf in. Who was the army kidding?

He looked over the empty parade grounds and playing fields. Out by the pecan grove two guys were tinkering under the hood of an olive drab truck, and way in back a couple more were burning trash in rusty barrels.

Of the three main buildings, only the middle one showed much activity. It appeared to be a combination mess hall and office. A jeep sat out in front. When nobody went in or out of the barracks on the left, Jacques decided that must be where the POWs bunked. Lucky sonofabitches. He'd heard of other camps with just tents, even so a helluva lot better at that than the lousy Stalags the Krauts had our boys penned up in.

Some G.I.s were lounging on the steps of the other barracks wisecracking with a red-faced cook who came out every so often to dump a pan of water. Jacques could catch most of what they said.

"Hey, Sarge!" one guy yelled. "What's for supper, fee-lay me-yone?"

The cook gave him a dirty look. "Wait and see, Smart Ass."

"Better watch your mouth, Willie," his buddy said, "or you won't get no seconds."

Willie laughed.

Jacques shifted positions and lit a cigarette.

The first to bring his POWs back to camp that afternoon was Emile Ardoin from the rice mill in town. A guard Jacques remembered from Jo Jo's came to open the gate, not that anything was protected except maybe somebody's neck if a colonel who went by the book showed up.

Coming and going in each other's dust, one by one the farmers returned their crews.

When Jacques recognized his dad's truck down the road his hands started to sweat like when he was a kid, scared Papa would catch him smoking. There was a guard in the cab with Papa, and another sitting in the back riding shotgun. The POWs, eight of them, rode on wooden benches and came in singing. Hell, why not? Jacques thought. They'd probably never had it so good. He watched them jump down while a guard with a clipboard checked them off.

As far as appearances went, they looked pretty much like soldiers anywhere, agile, with all the fat burnt off. Jacques studied their faces. He wished he knew which one was Werner. Adele had said he was young, but at least three of them could have passed for school kids if you didn't know any better. You sure couldn't go by looks. Give 'em regular clothes and they'd pass for Americans.

Papa went in the front door of the main building. Jacques squinted to make out a sign. 'Capt. L. J. Bentley, CO' it said. He wondered what Captain Bentley had done to deserve a two-bit command like this. Maybe the captain wanted a safe, cushy place to sit out the fighting. Some guys were like that.

Whatever Papa was doing didn't take long. He left without even looking over where Jacques was.

"C'est bon," Jacques said under his breath and settled back to watch the rest of the column of trucks. A few of the farmers hung around chewing tobacco and shooting the breeze, but most left right after they dropped off the men, probably in a hurry to get back to work.

By now the camp grounds were crawling with POWs jabbering their godawful gibberish. "You know what they sound like?" Jacques had said once to Boogie. "A flock of turkeys at feeding time."

The sun was slipping off the horizon and floodlights came on in every corner of the compound. Jacques was as jumpy as when he'd had battle nerves. He lit one cigarette from the butt of another without bothering to use his battered Zippo. The possibility occurred to him that some of the POWs across the road might be men he'd captured. He strained to get a better look, and wished he had the binoculars Adele kept in the kitchen to watch birds.

A radio blared over the rest of the noise. Some gal making like Carmen Miranda was singing the Chiquita banana jingle.

Most of the POWs, as soon as they jumped off the trucks, headed for the playing fields. They were nuts over soccer, those Germans. One team played without shirts. They kept in shape, all right, Jacques observed, watching them weave in and out kicking a black and white ball. Fighting shape, he thought darkly.

What he was scouting for he didn't know, but he continued to scrutinize the camp. He noted two men sitting on the steps sharing a newspaper, and off to the side, a little guy doing chinups on a piece of pipe lodged between pine trees.

"Siebzehn, achtzehn, neunzehn," his buddies chanted, keeping count.

A few of the POWs wore white armbands. That meant they spoke English, Betty had said.

Jacques smelled cabbage and realized Adele would be fixing supper. So what, he thought. What did she care if he showed up or not?

A skinny cook came out to have a smoke. Boogie was suspicious of skinny cooks. He claimed to have made a survey. "If they don't like their own food," he used to warn, "you'd better watch out."

While Jacques was thinking about Boogie, a bugler in the camp blew "Come and Get Your Chow, Boys", and damned if those Nazis didn't line themselves up in two perfect rows so fast it made you blink. No lingering, no last-minute plays, just snap! And there they were, marching in. A couple of G.I.s stood watch outside. The rest went around to their own mess.

Shifting positions, Jacques wished he'd brought something to drink. There wouldn't be anything to see during chow time. Except for the language, the sounds that carried across the road, the clink of utensils on metal trays, the banging of pots and pans, could have come from any army camp anywhere. Jacques swung his bum leg around on the seat. When he sat still for long, especially in a cramped position, it ached. He leaned against the door until the handle jabbing his back became uncomfortable.

Right before the men went in for chow, Jacques thought the guards were going to tell him to leave. He saw the gate guard climb the east watch tower and point in his direction to the sentry. Jacques waved. The guy from Jo Jo's scratched his head, shrugged and went back to duty. They were probably used to sightseers.

In winter the sun went down fast, orange and purple like a bad bruise. Jacques would be glad for the slow sunsets of summer. Oh well, he reasoned, you had them when you needed them for the rice. He thought about the land, his land, tilled and ready to seed.

Before long the POWs trickled out of the mess hall. They looked satisfied and cheerful. Jacques sat up again to watch and listen.

Someone plunked out "The Beer Barrel Polka" on an out of tune piano, and somebody else was practicing birdcalls. Several men lit cigarettes and strolled along the fence. The soccer game - or another one - resumed. Jacques spotted one of the POWs he'd seen plowing at Papa's, standing off to one side by himself, looking like he'd eaten green persimmons.

Near the gate, five POWs got into an argument, two against three, near as Jacques could tell. Guards moved in fast to break it up. Jacques was glad to see they were on their toes. There wasn't any resistance, but the separated groups kept yelling at each other. The maddest looking guy shouted "Sieg heil!" and waved his fist at the others. His buddy tried to shut him up but the M.P.s hauled him off. Sonofabitch Nazi. Outrage, thick as blood, rose in Jacques' throat. And Adele thinks they're harmless!

The bugle blew again and the Germans instantly, efficiently filed back into the mess hall. What now? A few minutes later the inside lights went off. Jacques heard clapping, and recognized the Lone Ranger's theme music.

"Oh crap," he said, "a movie."

He sprayed gravel getting out of there.

By the time he got to Betty's he'd cooled down a little, but not much.

"Where have you been all my life?" she greeted him. "Give me your jacket and come in the kitchen. You're just in time for some of that beautiful roast you brought me last time. All that meat and no ration coupons. I think I like being a kept woman."

"Don't call yourself that," he said, pulling her to him.

"My, aren't we manly tonight?" she teased. "What's going on?"

"Remember that soldier at Jo Jo's the other night, the one that ate all the peanuts? The guys call him Carver. He was on gate duty out at the camp. Looked like he was trying to figure out where he knew me from."

"You've been out at the camp?" Betty stopped tearing lettuce. "Why'd you want to do that?"

"Just reconnoitering. Guess what the bastards were doing when I left. Watching a shoot-em-up. Having their own damn picture show. Doesn't that take the cake?"

"At least I got them out of ours."

"What does that mean?"

Betty blew on a spoonful of gravy and tasted it. She added salt to the pot and some hot pepper before answering.

"Something that happened before you came home. When they first opened the camp they were letting the Germans go to the Bijou on Monday nights."

"You're kidding."

"Nope. Every Monday night. Captain Bentley said it helped prevent mischief. He likes to keep them as busy as possible. And you know old man Miguez, he wasn't about to pass up some money on the slowest night of the week."

"So what'd you do?"

"Threatened to write my Congressman and anybody else I could think of. Walter Winchell, if I had to. The very idea! How would you like your kid at the show with those killers?"

The mention of Chris made him squirm. His conscience gave him enough trouble without her prodding it. He checked to see if the blinds were closed. He knew it wasn't right, his being there, but he couldn't seem to stay away.

"You like kids, don't you?" he said when they were eating.

"Yeah, why?"

"Mind if I ask you something?"

"Shoot," she said. "Want some more salad?"

"No thanks. How come you and Armand never had any?"

She set her fork down and wiped her mouth on her napkin. Her expression made him sorry he'd asked.

"Forget it, babe," he said. "It's none of my business."

"No, it's okay," she told him. "Armand couldn't, that's all. The doctors tried to fix something, but it didn't work. He felt lousy about it, like he'd let me down or something."

"I'll bet. That's tough on a guy."

Jacques got up and gave her an awkward pat.

"Stay there and finish your coffee," he said. "My turn to do k.p."

"It's a deal." She stood and stretched. "I slaved over a hot type-writer all day, getting out the monthly bills."

After she'd drunk her coffee and smoked a cigarette, she excused herself. He cleaned up in the kitchen and went in the living room to lie on the sofa. In a little while Betty returned wearing some turquoise lounging pajamas that floated on her like water lapping the beach. She slid over the end of the sofa and put his head in her lap. Her perfume was strong, with a sort of powdery smell.

She reached over and turned on the radio on the end table. A creamy-voiced announcer informed them that tonight's music was coming to them from the Blue Room of the beautiful Roosevelt Hotel in downtown New Orleans.

Tired and full, Jacques dozed off, but when the band playing a conga came to an abrupt stop, he awoke with a start.

"Ladies and gentlemen, we interrupt this program to bring you a special bulletin."

Jacques stiffened and so did Betty. He felt her fingernails sharp on his shoulder.

"Reports continue to be confirmed of the mass extermination of Jews at the death camp in Auschwitz liberated by the Russian army on January twenty-sixth. According to reliable sources, of the fewer than three thousand survivors, many are women and children. Only a handful are expected..."

"Goddamn them!" Shaking, Jacques reached to cut off the radio. There had been rumors of such things, but it was too hideous to comprehend.

"Three thousand, Jacques! Good God, how many did they kill?" She was pummeling the arm of the sofa with her fist, moaning, "Women and children, Jacques. Women and children."

He stood and pulled her up by her wrists. She heaved with sobs and was becoming hysterical. He couldn't think what to do but hold her close. "Shh, now..." he kept saying over and over, kissing her hard till she gasped and grew quiet. He carried her gently to bed then, but the taste of her tears and perfume had aroused him, and rage became all mixed up with desire until Jacques forgot everything except the pounding, pounding need.

He woke up as the first tint of dawn brought the horizon in relief. He dressed quietly, without disturbing Betty. Now you've really got yourself in a fix, he thought.

Chapter 14

Adele and Chris were the only passengers to get on at the Courville station, which was a good thing. She'd never seen the Sunset Limited so crowded.

The train barely paused to let them board. Chris jumped on first and reached down to help her, then the conductor whisked up the metal stool and the train was rolling again before Chris had time to tug open the heavy coach door.

"Fine young fella you got there!" the conductor yelled. He smiled at them with rusty teeth.

"We're proud of him," Adele answered, although her reply was lost in the racket of the train.

The air inside the coach car, a heady mixture of smoke, onion breath and damp wool, made Adele cough. She and Chris stumbled their way along the cluttered aisle between the elbows of standing servicemen balancing themselves by gripping the overhead baggage rack. Disheveled children lounged on duffel bags, and an old man, folded up in his overcoat like an owl, perched on a peeling valise tied round and round with knotted rope. Travelers were jammed in everywhere; hatboxes, satchels, baskets and boxes piled at their feet.

A young Marine - Adele guessed he wasn't more than eighteen - got up and squeezed in ahead of her.

"Here, Ma'am," he said, offering her the seat.

"Oh no, please. You keep it."

"Naw," he insisted. "I been ridin' for two days. It'll do me good to stretch."

He acted so sincere that she accepted, grateful not to have to make the long trip on her feet. Her good shoes were designed for looks, not comfort. She settled into as small a space as she could, putting their lunch and her overnight case under the horsehair seat. She offered to let Chris sit on her lap, but the suggestion embarrassed him. He was busy making friends with the Marine.

"I'm okay, Mom. Honest."

He'd taken to calling her that, lately, instead of Mama. She wished he weren't in such a hurry to grow up.

The Marine's name was Dick. She heard him tell Chris he was on his way home from boot camp. Home, he mentioned, was Bay St. Louis, Mississippi.

"Do you know where that is, Mom?"

"I certainly do. Grandma and Grandpa had a summer place there when I was just about your age. I used to love to sit and watch the sea gulls on the Gulf."

"Sonofagun. Let me shake your hand, lady," Dick said. "You don't know how glad I am to find somebody who's heard of Bay St. Louis! You like to swim, kid?"

Adele leaned back and let them talk. The latest trouble with Jacques had been the last straw, and she was having a hard time thinking of anything else, much less acting normal. She wished she could wear a mask, one of those carnival masks, perpetually smiling.

In the seat in back of her a young mother jiggled a wailing baby. One of the soldiers lurched off in search of the diner to fetch some milk. There was a lot of joking and bantering throughout the coach. Someone up ahead was working a crossword puzzle.

"Anybody know a six letter word for a Russian carriage?" a New England voice called out.

Beside Adele, next to the window, a middle aged Master Sergeant snored, his slack head bouncing against the lowered green shade. He'd loosened his tie and shoelaces. The orange ticket sticking out of his pocket read Birmingham, and from the look of his uniform, he'd been traveling a long time.

His jacket fell on the floor. Adele brushed it off and laid it over him. He quivered and the snoring stopped, but to her relief, he didn't wake up. He might want to talk. Conversation was such an effort any more. She felt as if everyone could see how paralyzed she felt, as though the numbness stuck out all over. Not sleeping for two nights had left her even more wilted, and she was having to force herself to eat. All she could think about was what Jeanette had told her. Poor innocent Jeanette.

She became vaguely aware than Chris was getting acquainted with a little girl down the aisle.

"My dad's a hero," she heard him say. "He's got the Purple Heart and a sharpshooter medal and three ribbons. He got wounded in France."

"Oh," said the little girl. "That's too bad."

"That's why he couldn't come with me and my mom. We're going to my grandparents' house. Where are you going?"

The little girl said they were going to see her daddy before he went overseas.

Hearing that made Adele choke up. The last few days it seemed like everything anyone mentioned, everything she saw, touched a nerve. She closed her eyes and tried to pray.

She could hardly bear to look at the injured men on the train. There were several. One in an Air Force uniform wore a patch over his left eye, and another had bandages covering one whole side of his head. There was a sailor with his arm in a sling. The men had begun arguing good-naturedly among themselves about which service was doing the most to win the war.

"I just wish I could have stayed in to the end," Adele heard the pilot say.

Adele listened wearily to the counterpoint of their accents against the steady bass rhythm of the wheels, and tried to think. Every so often the train would let out a hair raising whistle. The locomotive would chug to a halt and then, after a flurry of maneuverings off and on, strain to get up speed once more.

She sat with her hands folded over a faille purse, her white cotton gloves already dingy. There was a handkerchief tucked in one palm, just in case. She wasn't a crier, but she couldn't trust herself any more. Everything made her think of Jacques. What would she tell her parents? They were sure to sense something was wrong.

Just past Bayou Verde the Master Sergeant woke up and straightened his legs. He yawned and raised the shade.

Dick had moved two rows down to talk to the sailor.

Adele fished awkwardly under the seat for the lunch box which had slid out of reach. By scrunching her knees, she could make room for Chris to perch on the corner of her seat.

"Do you mind if I move over just a little so my son can eat?" she asked the man next to her.

"Oh no, sure," the soldier said sleepily, and rearranged his legs to give them more room.

"Thanks. I'm Adele Viator. This is my son, Christophe."

"Mom, please! Call me Chris."

"Sergeant Martin, ma'am. Hector Martin. Glad to know you both."

"Would you like a chicken sandwich?" Adele asked him.

"That's all right. I can wait."

"No really, we have plenty, don't we, Chris? We made extra, just in case."

"Yes, sir," Chris confirmed, in a hurry to unwrap the waxed paper. "There's fried pie, too, and even some brownies."

The sergeant laughed. "Well, thanks a lot. I think I will. I haven't had an offer that good in a long time."

They managed, clumsily, to eat the lunch she'd packed, spilling only a few drops of milk from the thermos. She felt badly about the milk.

"The baby could have had some of ours," she said. "I don't know where my mind was."

Chris discovered the sergeant liked to fish, so they found lots to talk about and didn't require her attention. She went back to rehearsing explanations for her folks.

When the train approached the Huey P. Long bridge, Chris stood up to see. He squeezed her shoulder.

"There's Old Man River," he said with a smile.

The passengers all stooped or stretched to get the best view.

"Hot damn, it really is muddy!" Dick said.

A voice like raked gravel shouted, "Get a load of those boats. Cheez!"

"Ships, dummy, not boats."

"Boats, ships, what the hell."

"Send 'em after Tojo and let's get this thing over with," someone called.

"Must be twenty miles of docks..."

"How far down is it?"

"Where's the Gulf of Mexico? I can't see."

Adele smiled at their excitement and felt her own pulse

quicken. No matter how long she was away she was always exhilarated by the first sight of New Orleans. She loved the farm and their life at the Junction, but this was home. For a moment she forgot about Jacques.

They passed a shirt factory, some more warehouses, the sugar refinery. The railroad began to wind through the outskirts of the city, past baseball diamonds gone to seed and big barn-like factories, past night clubs and a Nazarene church, the Palmetto Golf Course and some Spanish style tourist courts with a No Vacancy sign. Nearer the city limits were clusters of houses, bungalows, mostly, frame or stucco, never very far from a church steeple.

The blocks rolled by faster than she could read the street signs. Houses and buildings were closer together until they seemed to rub sides, with barely any sidewalk in between, and the roofline looked like rickrack against the gray-blue sky. On the balconies clotheslines drooped, and in the tiny yards poinsettias and banana trees dejectedly waited to be revived. Nothing, Adele thought was more pleasant in the summer nor sorrier in the winter than banana trees, their frostbitten fronds drooping brown and slimy to the ground. They would shake off winter soon, though. Adele had loved the sound of the one by her bedroom when she was a little girl, loved the way its green fans whispered during those steamy afternoons she spent dreaming and resisting a nap.

Paint was peeling on many of the places they passed. A lot of the population was poor, but the war was to blame, too. The men were gone and paint was hard to get.

Now people on the train were pointing to the iron grille work decorating some of the houses. Some homeowners, hoping to have a part in a tank or some ammunition, had removed theirs to give to the scrap metal drives, a sacrifice for victory.

New Orleans, as always, was a city of contrasts. You saw a house with its window mouths stuffed with newspapers right next to a picture book cottage; the one with a chicken wire gate hanging like a broken wing and the other wearing a ruff of red and white azaleas.

Adele pointed to Murphy & Sons, telling Chris that was where Grandpa bought glassware to sell at his store. In the next block they watched men on a long wooden platform loading blocks of ice with giant tongs onto trucks waiting in line. The drivers stood around smoking, glad, probably, to get down and stretch.

A little farther on, they came to shotgun houses, weathered

gray, where colored children peeked through ragged screens and the mothers wiped faded aprons or straightened kerchiefs on their heads. Here and there one of them gave the passing train an idle wave.

"Those the southern mansions you-all brag about?" the sailor teased Dick.

Adele wondered why railroads invariably went through the most dismal part of town. It seemed a pity, but then, who'd want trains lumbering through their neighborhood at all hours?

The train groaned, braking for the station.

"Are we there, Mom?" Chris asked.

"Almost, honey."

The conductor shoved his way through, calling "N'walins! Next stop, N'walins!" till he was satisfied his passengers were awake; then he pushed on to the next car.

People gathered their luggage. Adele got out her compact and made a face when she saw herself in the mirror. It would take more than powder and lipstick to help.

Outside there was daylight only at the street corners, the taller buildings having attached themselves to each other like Siamese twins. The shorter ones had connecting gates that hid everything from sight except some palm leaves in the courtyard beyond. Closed shutters gave the streets a deceptively sleepy look. Behind that bland facade, Adele knew, men were making deals that would affect the stock exchange, and servants were scrubbing tile floors with Pine-Sol. There would be starch boiling on the stove and supper's cornbread baking in the oven. New Orleans had its own tempo, indolently industrious. Adele missed it. Guiltily, then painfully, she remembered Jacques, but she was distracted by Chris's calling her attention to a billboard.

"What's Lucky Strike green?" he asked. "It says, 'Lucky Strike green has gone to war'."

Adele didn't know. Sergeant Martin said it had something to do with the dye they used on the cigarette packaging.

A woman in front of them said, "What difference does it make whether they come in a green package or a white one if you can't get either one? I've been rolling my own so long I've forgotten what a real cigarette tastes like."

"Here, have one of mine," Dick told her. "Courtesy of Uncle Sam."

The friendly chatter tapered off and everyone quieted down, waiting to pull into the station. They watched the scenery go by in slow motion, five and six story buildings with iron fire escapes running down their sides like spines.

As the train sizzled to a stop, the passengers exchanged good-byes. The ones getting off worked their way to the door with a litany of "excuse me", "excuse me, please". Adele gripped Chris's hand in the swell on the packed platform.

Even the old high-ceilinged station was crowded, but at least there was room to breathe. Chris watched in fascination the way an elderly man spat an arc of tobacco juice into one of the brass spittoons that guarded the ends of the worn oak benches.

"I'll wait by the shoeshine stand," Adele told Chris, who needed to go to the bathroom. "See the men's room over there?"

"Why does the sign say 'Whites Only'?" he asked her when he returned.

"Shh..." she said, lowering her voice. "Because colored people have their own bathrooms."

"Why?"

"It's just the way it's done."

"When Lula Mae works for us she uses our bathroom."

"I know."

"She's colored."

"Never mind," Adele said, frowning. "Fix your zipper and let's get going."

Chapter 15

Too tired to fool with suitcases on the street car, Adele looked for a porter who could flag them a taxi. Redcaps, however, were in short supply, and those she saw were struggling to clear a path for already overloaded carts.

She didn't mind waiting. It meant she could postpone explanations a little while longer. Besides, Chris was having fun looking around. She let him have a nickel to buy some bubble gum at the concession stand. He was full of pent-up energy and questions.

Eventually, the crowd thinned out a bit and a grizzled Redcap came to their rescue with a smile as shiny as his bow tie. Black elastic garters secured his starched white shirtsleeves, the fraying cuffs of which were neatly trimmed.

"Help you, Miss?"

"Yes, please. Could you get us a taxi?"

"Yes'm. Right this way."

He scooped their luggage onto a dolly and plunged toward the entrance. They passed through swinging doors, exchanging, as they did, the marble echoes of the station for the street noises of Howard Avenue.

The cab stand was a bustle of loadings and unloadings, with a line of people waiting. Oblivious to all the honking and shouting, Chris entertained himself blowing bubbles. The Redcap, used to it all, leaned on the suitcases and whistled "Sweet Georgia Brown". He made Adele think of the man who danced with Shirley Temple in the movies.

After being in the country so long, Adele wasn't used to the excitement of the city and she felt a little light-headed. She shifted her weight from one foot to the other, wishing she'd worn more sensible shoes.

Finally, their turn came. A yellow cab pulled up to the curb. It had seen better days, but new ones were out of the question as long as the war went on. The Redcap put their things in the trunk with a flourish and Adele slipped two quarters in his casually extended palm.

"Thank you, ma'am," he said. "Y'all have you a good visit, now."

He picked up the tune where he'd left off and went whistling on his way.

The cab driver, a gaunt old fellow with a chicken skin neck, let Chris sit in front by the meter. He answered the boy's non-stop questions with good humor. Chris wanted to know everything from how far they were from the river to how fast the cab would go. He'd been too small to pay much attention the last time they'd been to New Orleans, but now he was taking it all in. Adele sank back to watch for familiar landmarks, glad to let the two of them chat.

The driver shouted at a kid on a tricycle to get back on the banquette.

"What's a banquette?" Chris asked.

"I guess you'd call it a sidewalk," the cabbie said.

"Oh."

Chris pointed to a statue they were just passing.

"Who's that?"

"Robert E. Lee. Know who he was?"

"I don't think so. A soldier, I guess."

"He was a general in the Civil War. A real brave soldier."

"So's my dad," Chris informed him. "What's loi...loi-ter-ing? That sign says NO LOITERING ON THE NEUTRAL GROUND."

"It means hanging around up to no good, something like that."

"What's a neutral ground?"

"Boy, you're a question box, you are. That's that island in the middle of the street where the street car runs. You planning to be a lawyer when you grow up?"

"Not me. No, sir. I'm going to be a rice farmer like my dad and my grandpa. Is there really a canal under Canal Street?"

He was still going strong when they pulled up at the white stucco house which, until she married Jacques, was the only home Adele had ever known.

Chris shook the cab driver's hand and bounded up the concrete steps into the ample arms of Weezie, the cook.

"Lawd, lawd, how that child done growed. Lemme look at you, boy. How you be doin', Miss Adele? You lookin' kinda peaked."

Adele gave her a hug, ignoring the question.

"Hi, Weezie. It's so good to see you! You and John been all right?"

"Yes'm, we fine. Sure is good to have you home. Your rooms is all ready and I'll have you a plate of seafood gumbo 'fore you can wash up. You' mama and daddy say for y'all to make you'selfs at home. They be back when the store close."

"All right, Weezie. We'll be right down."

Chris took her makeup kit and ran ahead. On the stairwell Adele stopped to look at her wedding picture hanging in the hall. She tried to remember what it was like to be that young bride with the pink camellia bouquet, another lifetime ago.

Chris did justice to Weezie's good gumbo, even if Adele couldn't. She kept thinking about all the times she and Jacques had come home together; the day she brought him to meet her folks, the Christmases before Chris was born, the time they treated Jeanette to Mardi Gras. It had been four years, she realized, since Jacques had been there with her, right before the war, when her grandmother died. The tears she'd been holding back stung her eyes.

"Excuse me, son. I'll be back in a minute. Ask Weezie to give you some more root beer."

Adele fled to the downstairs bathroom, willing herself not to cry. She ran cold water over her wrists and felt calmer.

"You all right, Miss Adele?" she heard Weezie's anxious voice through the door.

Mustering what she hoped was a normal sounding reply, she answered, "Yes, Weezie. I'll be out in a minute. Is there any coffee made?"

"Yes'm. And a piece of pecan pie?"

"Maybe for supper. I really can't, right now."

The coffee revived her. It wasn't quite three o'clock. She thought about surprising her parents at the store, but they might be busy. Chris was raring to go. She didn't think she could stand to stay in the house all afternoon, anyway.

"Why don't we take the streetcar to Audubon Park?" she suggested.

"Oh boy! Now?"

Chris loved the streetcar ride, and she began to feel better. There was something soothing about the tree lined boulevard with the graceful old mansions that had outlived several wars already. They were a testament to endurance and care.

Adele had always enjoyed observing people from the streetcar. It was something like watching a picture show with a lot of bit players.

At Jackson Avenue, a young woman in checkered pedal pushers leaned over the corner mailbox, adding a last p.s. to a serviceman husband, probably, and rocking a baby carriage with the toe of her saddle oxford at the same time. Adele knew what it was like to write that daily letter, trying to think up cheerful news to tell, and praying, praying, the next mail would bring one for you.

Chris laughed at the sight of two blue-haired grande dames in the next block promenading their poodles in front of a residential hotel.

"Look, Mom! They're twins!"

The frisky poodles, coifed to match, were giving their mistresses such a chase that the old ladies were hard put to keep their dignity intact.

A few shops on the way had Carnival window displays, and here and there on St. Charles Avenue you saw the traditional purple, green and gold bunting of Mardi Gras, but for the most part the Stars and Stripes remained dominant. People were waiting for the armistice to celebrate. Surely, Adele thought, it won't be long now.

They got off at the park, and she turned Chris loose. He was as frisky as those poodles from being cooped up all day. It's a good thing I changed shoes, Adele thought. She didn't want to dampen Chris's enthusiasm, but she had to almost run to keep up with him. It was worth it to see him having fun.

He headed for the seal pool first and the seals got so excited when he mimicked their bark that they flopped willy- nilly into the water, sending spray ten feet in the air.

She had to beg him to stop.

"You'll get us soaked! What did you say to them?" she asked him, laughing.

"Military secret," he grinned and gave one more bark before jumping down off the rail and bounding off to see the lions.

They wandered around after that, stopping to read the plaques on the cages. The leopard flexed its muscles and gave them the evil eye. Chris waxed enthusiastic over the reptiles which Adele found repulsive; all those beadily insolent iguanas and alligators. She wouldn't even go near the snakes, but waited for him outside. It made her nervous enough, the way he leaned over the reptile pit.

She bribed him away with cotton candy, and they bought peanuts to feed the elephants.

"Don't be scared, Mom. It tickles," Chris assured her.

They were at the monkey cage when closing time came.

"We have to go, son," she called.

"Aw, Mom. We didn't get to the birds yet. Can we just go see if they have an ostrich? I want to see if they really stick their heads in the ground."

Like me, Adele thought.

"I don't know about ostriches. I remember seeing peacocks. Maybe we can come back another time."

"Tomorrow? Can we come back tomorrow?"

"We'll see. We have to find out what Grandma and Grandpa's plans are, first. Okay?"

"Okay," he said, running ahead of her to a playground where some children were sliding.

His shirt tail was out and one shoe lace was untied, but Adele didn't mind. She hadn't seen him that carefree in ages. Not since Jacques got home, she realized, and the thought cast a shadow over the afternoon.

On the way back to her parents' house they treated themselves to nectar sodas at a glossy drugstore fountain. Adele let Chris twirl to his heart's content on the red leather stool.

"I wish we had a machine like that," he said when the girl who waited on them mixed a chocolate malt.

"Can I fix you something else?" the waitress asked.

"Oh, no," Adele told her. "It's almost supper time and he ought to be about to pop. You should see what he's eaten already today."

"Maybe tomorrow," Chris said, giving Adele a hopeful look.

They sipped their sodas to make them last.

A soldier sat down at the other end of the counter and Adele saw Chris's face grow solemn.

"I wish Daddy would have come with us," he said. "The old Daddy."

"I do too, Chris," Adele said, swallowing hard.

"He hasn't seen Grandma and Grandpa in a long time."

"I know, son."

"Well, why wouldn't he come?"

Adele was tired of making excuses for Jacques. "He still doesn't trust the POWs," she said. "He's afraid they'll do some damage to us or the farm."

Chris sucked on his straw, thinking it over.

"Is anything wrong, Mama?" he said, slipping back into his baby name for her. "I mean, anything new, besides Daddy and the POWs?"

She saw his worried face in the mirror, watching her over the rim of his glass. He kept sucking, slowly, waiting for an answer.

What should she say? Suppose Jeanette was mistaken? Maybe Jeanette misread Lucy Boudreaux's lips. But even...even if she hadn't, Adele couldn't tell Chris anyway.

"I'm just tired, honey. Drink your soda and let's go. Grandma and Grandpa ought to be home by now."

Chapter 16

Aunt Eudolie was at the house when Adele and Chris got there, and the neighbors came over after supper, so conversation was lively and Adele was relieved of much need to participate. All she had to do to keep Aunt Eudolie going was to nod once in a while and look interested.

War put a strain on everyone, but Adele was glad to see her mother and father were holding up well.

At nine, pleading fatigue, she kissed her parents goodnight and left them arguing with Aunt Eudolie about taxes. Adele and Chris went up to their rooms; Chris in the guest room across the hall from the bedroom they still called hers.

She was hoping a hot bubble bath would put her to sleep. It did relax her, but sleep wouldn't come. She lay on the white four poster, the chintz coverlet turned back, listening to the murmur of voices from the living room and the hall clock chiming the quarter hours.

Surrounded by souvenirs of her life before Jacques, her dolls, books and music awards, all she could think of, staring at the water spots on the ceiling wallpaper, was what Jeanette had said.

Adele turned off her lamp when she heard Aunt Eudolie leave so that the light under the door wouldn't seem like an invitation to talk when her mother came up to bed.

The four of them went to early Mass at the cathedral next morning, and afterwards, to Café du Monde where high-hatted cooks skimmed crusty beignets from vats of bubbling grease. Adele and her parents drank the strong chicory coffee while Chris devoured an incredible amount of the hot, sugar-dusted doughnuts.

On the way back to the car, he and her father walked ahead and Adele noticed the line on Chris's good pants where she'd let out the hem. It was one of those moments when she realized how grown up her son was getting. But he's still so young, she thought. Don't let him get hurt. Don't let him find out about Jacques.

Her parents were expecting Uncle Marvin and his family to drive in from Slidell for a late Sunday dinner. Adele thought she should stay to help prepare the meal, but her mother shooed her away.

"You go ahead. Weezie did most of the cooking yesterday. Your daddy wants to show you how he's rearranged the store. Y'all just be back by two."

Adele rode in the middle so Chris could look out the window. Before going to town they went by Tulane to show Chris the stadium. Adele's dad parked the car and let Chris run up and down the bleachers.

"When the war's over," he told Chris, "you'll be old enough to come by yourself and I'll get us some Sugar Bowl tickets."

"Honest, Grandpa? You mean it?"

"It's a promise."

"He'll love you forever," Adele said.

Her dad drove the old green Plymouth at a slow steady pace although there was hardly any traffic in the business section. Sitting right next to him like that Adele couldn't help noticing the way his age was showing. Somehow she always thought of her parents as they were in their forties, fixed in time.

The store did look different. Being so short handed, they'd moved the checkout booth to the front where the cashier could keep an eye on customers.

"How'd Miss Lavinia take that?" Adele asked.

The orange-haired widow had been their cashier for thirty years.

"She balked at the idea at first, but she got used to it. I think she likes being able to see the street. You know how she loves to know everything that's going on."

He showed them the counters he'd built from the scrap lumber of an old bar that had been torn down. He'd widened the aisles and installed new lighting, giving the place a brighter, more spacious look. There were less goods than usual, due to wartime scarcities and the loss of imports, but the merchandise they'd managed to get was artfully arranged. Adele detected her mother's fine touch.

Much to Chris's delight, they let him play with the cash register and operate the elevator, things Adele had grown up doing. It came to her how different her childhood had been from her son's.

When they had toured the store, her father took them to see the shipyards. Although it was Sunday, work was going on full blast.

"It's like this seven days a week, twenty four hours a day," he told them.

The noise was stupefying, even with the car windows rolled up. Chris put his fingers in his ears. From where they parked they could see several ships under construction, some only skeletons, some nearly finished. Welders and riveters wearing helmets did their jobs from scaffolding high off the ground.

"Wow." Chris was big-eyed. "Look at those guys!"

"Your daddy probably went to France on a ship like that," Adele told him.

"Gee!" Chris said.

Reminders of the war were everywhere you looked. Newsboys on street corners hawked the latest headlines. You could hardly go a block without seeing a billboard advertising liberty bonds or a poster urging you to conserve gasoline.

"Your mother and I take the streetcar to work," commented her father, "and save our gas coupons for Sunday visiting."

They drove out to Lake Ponchartrain after that, and walked along the beach. Her father and Chris squatted to observe a crab. A breeze ruffled the fringe of her dad's hair, blowing it over his bald spot. Chris was listening to him, spellbound. Adele wished she had her father's patience and her mother's energy.

As if reading her thoughts, her dad came and put an arm around her.

"How's my girl?" he asked with a squeeze.

"All right, Daddy." She did her best to smile.

Chris was out on a jetty waving to some sailboats.

"Did you ever see a child get such a kick out of life?" she said.

"He's a champ, all right."

They got back to the house just in time to change clothes and greet the relatives. Adele hadn't met Uncle Marvin's new wife, a pale fluttery little woman who didn't say much all afternoon. David and Marvin, Jr. seemed to get along with their stepmother all right, but David's wife, Marguerite, acted a little strained.

Naturally, they all wanted to know about Jacques. Adele told them his leg was better but he had too much to do on the farm. She got so tired of explaining and making excuses.

She helped serve dinner and listened to the discussion of how the war in the Pacific was going. David, whose football injuries made him 4-F, was full of admiration for General MacArthur.

"He's a little too cocky for my taste," said Marguerite. "You'd think he was doing the fighting himself the way he takes all the credit."

"Adele, I like your slacks," Marvin Jr.'s wife interrupted. "Pass the pickles, honey, would you?"

"Thanks, Gloria. Mother got them for me. I'm not used to wearing pants, but I think I'm going to enjoy them. You don't have to worry about bending over."

"Maybe you don't. Can you imagine what I'd look like, bent over in britches?"

Gloria's appetite was the family joke. She took a big helping of the ham Adele had brought from the farm and said, "Mmm, mmm! I'd almost forgotten what ham tastes like. You sure are lucky, Adele, not to have to worry about rationing."

"Not meat, maybe, or canned goods," Adele told her, "but you can't bake or make jelly without sugar. Jeanette and I are thinking of raising bees."

She had a sharp memory of Jeanette complaining about Jacques not showing up to eat a coconut cake that had taken the last of her sugar.

"Bees? You, Adele?" It struck Gloria funny. "You used to run if you saw a roach."

"You'd be surprised what I've learned to do in the country," Adele said. "When are you and Junior coming out to see us again?"

She regretted the question instantly. What if they came? How could she cover up at home? Gloria, of all people.

But Gloria was shaking her head.

"Not till things slow down at the shipyard. Junior's worked so much overtime since they got their last Liberty ship contract I almost forget what he looks like."

"Well, take a good look, baby," Junior told his wife, "because I go back on the night shift tonight."

Gloria groaned.

Adele's mother brought in a fig cake. "Who wants ice cream on top?" she asked.

"Skip me," Uncle Marvin said. "I don't have room. Chris, let's you and me go out in the alley and play some catch."

"Can I have my dessert later, Grandma?"

"Sure, honey. You go ahead."

The rest of them, too full to move, lingered at the table over demitasse cups. Adele wanted to hear all the family news, and her mother got out the photograph album to show Uncle Marvin's wife who was who. David and Adele's dad were wound up on baseball, speculating on what kind of season the Yankees and the Dodgers would have.

"How much did the merchants' association make on their spring fashion show?" Marguerite asked Adele's mother.

"We cleared two thousand dollars for the U.S.O. I was tickled pink. Those folks really work to keep up morale."

Sooner or later the conversation always reverted to the war.

"I heard they bring some big name entertainers to the veterans hospital."

"The canteen, too. Did you know Dorothy Lamour was in town with a U.S.O. troop this week? She grew up here, you know. Used to live around the corner from Uncle Edward."

"Speaking of hospitals," Marguerite said, "my cousin Clark is supposed to get out next month. He was burned real bad when his plane was shot down, but thank God he landed in allied territory."

After the company left, Adele started cleaning up. Her mother had put on a big apron over her jersey dress and was at the sink filling the dishpan with suds.

"Just clear the table if you want to," her mother said, "and leave the rest. Weezie can finish tomorrow. I just want to put away the crystal."

"I don't mind doing it, Mother. Weezie has enough to do."

From the dining room Adele could hear her dad and Chris playing checkers in the parlor. Chris was telling knock knock jokes, and the tap of her dad's pipe on the humidor was drowned out by laughter.

It was the first time Adele and her mother had to themselves.

"You look tired," her mother said. "You aren't expecting again, are you?"

Her mother made no secret of hoping for another grandchild, preferably a girl this time.

"Hardly!" Adele answered, so flustered she slammed the bread box door.

Her mother's eyebrows went up, but all she said was, "Oh."

To evade more questions, Adele said, "I'll put away the leaves to the dining room table."

Night had fallen when she stood on the back porch to shake the tablecloth, the lace one her mother saved for special occasions. Adele held it to her with a swift, sweet recollection of the way it looked by candlelight with her wedding cake on it, and of camellias the color of seashell linings, floating in wide silver bowls.

"Oh, Jacques," she whispered to the stars, "I did so love you!"

Her mother was scrubbing a skillet when Adele returned. From the other side of the swinging door came the sound of Jack Benny baiting Rochester. Adele leaned up against the cabinets, still clutching the tablecloth.

"Mother, did Daddy ever look at another woman?"

Her mother was startled, and replied with a puzzled expression.

"Why, no. I mean, I'm sure he looked, but that's all. All men look, don't they?" she added.

"What would you have done if he had, if there'd been someone else?"

"Adele, why don't you tell me what you're driving at?"

They faced each other. Adele couldn't hold back tears.

"I don't know what to do!" she cried out.

"Jacques?" her mother exclaimed. "Oh, Adele, surely you must be mistaken! Jacques wouldn't do that."

Her mother took the tablecloth and tossed it in a heap on the counter.

"Come on, let's go out on the gallery," she said.

They sat on the porch swing in the dark, talking. Adele told her mother how things had been all winter, about Jacques and the POWs, how angry he was at everyone and the way he would go off for hours at a time without ever saying where he went or when he'd be back.

"Oh, Mother, it's just been awful! And then..."

It hurt so much she could hardly tell it.

"And then the other day Jeanette asked if I knew a blonde haired lady named Betty."

"Betty who?" her mother asked with a frown.

"That's what I said. You know how Jeanette rattles on sometimes when she hasn't had anybody but Papa to talk to. We were plucking chickens, working away, discussing a little bit of everything. So I said, 'Betty? From around here or New Orleans?' and Jeanette said, 'Here, I guess. Miss Boudreaux - the one with the wart on her face - was talking at the altar society meeting about her and Jacques.' I just froze, Mother. It went all over me. All those nights he was out late, all those..."

She had to stop to blow her nose. Her voice quavered.

"I tried not to panic. I asked Jeanette what they said about Jacques and Betty. She said she thought it was supposed to be a secret, that Miss Boudreaux put a hand over her mouth close to Edna Mae Aucoin's ear, like she realized Jeanette was watching. Nasty old hag."

"Adele! That's not like you."

"Well, she's just a big mess maker, Mother. Why doesn't she leave us alone?"

The sobs came loose now. Her mother patted her knee.

"Go ahead, honey. Have your cry."

They rocked in the swing a long time without talking. Several street cars clanged by and Mr. Galatoire next door put out his milk bottles. After that, it was quiet except for the swish of the swing.

"Are you sure you aren't jumping to conclusions, dear?" her mother asked, finally.

"No, Mother. It's true. You know how sometimes you just know something, deep down, even though you try not to believe it because you don't want it to be true? I've lost him, Mother, and in the only way I never worried about. Isn't that crazy? I didn't lose him in the war; I lost him to Betty Hebert."

"Nonsense," her mother said briskly. "You haven't lost Jacques. Maybe he's lost his head, maybe not. Suppose it's true. He's still a good looking man and men are scarce these days, good looking or otherwise. Suppose some fluffy headed fool does have her claws in him? What are you going to do, hand him over on a platter?"

"That's just it," Adele said wearily. "Betty's not a fluffy headed fool, Mother, she's a really nice person."

"Hmm!"

"Really. She and Jacques went to school together. Her husband got killed in Italy. They say she's bitter. I'd probably be bitter, too, if Jacques hadn't come back."

"Maybe so, but that doesn't give her the right to your husband. You aren't going to just sit back and let her have him, are you?"

"What can I do?"

"Well, stick to your guns, for goodness sake! He still lives with you, doesn't he? He still sleeps with you, doesn't he?"

"Yes, but that's all he does, sleep! I get so tired of looking at his back I could scream. Oh, Mother, you don't know how scared I am when he's gone, not knowing if he'll come back or not."

Her mother thought a moment before she responded.

"Do you think Chris has any idea?"

"I don't think so," Adele said, suppressing a sob. "Dear God, I hope not! His feelings are already hurt over the way Jacques snaps at him. Jacques tries to make it up, but he can't seem to help it. And Chris is worried about me, as it is. He asked me yesterday if anything was wrong."

"Well, then," her mother said in a firm tone, "you know how the saying goes: you catch more flies with honey than with vinegar. You put that head up and put a smile on and go back and show those busybodies a thing or two. Papa and Jeanette are on your side, aren't they?"

"I don't know what I'd do without them."

"Then don't pay any attention to the gossips! What's that Betty got that you don't have?"

"Jacques, on Saturday nights," Adele said between sniffles.

They had to laugh.

"We'll have to see what we can do about that," her mother said. "Tell you what. What do you and Chris have planned for tomorrow?"

"We're supposed to go out to Chalmette to see Aunt Irene. Why?"

"Call Aunt Irene first thing in the morning. She wakes up the roosters. Tell her I need you at the store, or something.

Make some excuse. I'll get you an appointment at the beauty shop
and you can pick out some new clothes afterward, some things you
feel pretty in. There's nothing like a different hairdo and a new
outfit to make a man take notice. How about it? Weezie'll be glad
to keep an eye on Chris."

Adele felt hope rally and flutter like a moth inside her.

"Thanks, Mother."

She wanted to say more, but she was choking up again.

Chapter 17

Going home Ash Wednesday, the train wasn't quite so crowded, and they both got seats. Before they were out of the city, Chris was sound asleep.

Adele wondered if she looked as different as she felt. She kept fingering the curls on her neck. Some soldiers had whistled at her when she was boarding the train. It made her blush.

She stared out at the blurring landscape, rehearsing the plan, trying to remember her mother's good advice. Her wan face with the dark smudge of ashes on the forehead was reflected in the window. She felt as though Lent had lasted a long time already.

There wasn't time for brooding once she got home. She and Jeanette had to get busy canning. The yams stored in the barn were going bad, and on top of that, Papa came home with a crate of strawberries he bought off a truck from Hammond.

The two women worked easily together; one at the sink, the other at the stove. Before long, Adele was short of work space and her counters were a mass of gleaming Mason jars and paraffin topped jelly glasses.

Jeanette wanted to hear all about New Orleans. Adele did her best to describe the whole trip in detail, all but the conversations about Jacques.

"I wish I could go to another Mardi Gras," Jeanette said plaintively when they stopped for a Coke.

"You will. I promise. As soon as the war's over and they have the balls and parades again. This year we let the kids dress up, and Mother had some friends over, but it really wasn't anything all that special. It doesn't seem right to be frivolous while our men are still fighting overseas. Did I tell you Uncle Robert - Mother's baby brother - got a promotion? He's a major now."

Adele felt badly about leaving Jeanette behind, but under the circumstances it would have been too hard on Papa to have both of them gone.

"Where in the world am I going to put all these jars?" she said to change the subject.

She dampened a dish cloth to wipe the ones that were sticky.

"I can store as much as you want in my new pantry," Jeanette said. "I've got lots of room now."

Adele turned, out of habit, to get in Jeanette's line of vision.

"Did Werner finish?"

"Saturday," Jeanette nodded.

"I'll have to go see it. Aren't you glad? I'd love to have more storage space."

Lifting a full rack of jars from the steamer, she set it down cautiously and brushed some loose hair back from her face.

"How's Werner? Any news?"

"No, I don't think so. He's pretty worried."

"You read about Yalta, didn't you? It looks like Werner was right about the Russians taking over."

"I don't understand what's going on," Jeanette said.

"I'm not sure I do, either," said Adele, "but Daddy says the Allies are getting closer to victory every day."

"Do you know what Werner's hoping for?" Jeanette asked her. "He's hoping his family can come over here after the war. He wants to get a job and stay with his relatives in New Orleans till he can save up enough money to send for them."

"What relatives? I didn't know Werner had family in New Orleans! Why didn't he tell me? I could have phoned them while I was there."

"He didn't know that's where you're from, until I told him about your trip."

"That's amazing," Adele said. "Who are they? Do you remember their names?"

"Faber, I think. It's his aunt's brother, Werner said, his aunt by marriage. He's a baker. They wanted to come visit Werner, but they couldn't get permission. You have to be immediate family, the army said. They write and send him cookies, though."

Adele checked to see that all the lids were screwed on tightly.

"Isn't that something," she said. "Who knows, maybe he can come back some day."

"Why can't he just stay?"

"I don't know, Jeanette, but I don't think it's allowed."

A truck clattered over the cattle guard.

"Let's talk about something else," Adele said. "I hear Jacques coming."

She went back to the story of Chris and the seals at Audubon Park, although some of it was repetitious.

As if he were performing a duty, Jacques kissed them both on the cheek and straddled a chair to read the mail. He tossed the bills to her and handed Jeanette the new "Life" magazine. Just the sight of it made Adele cringe.

"Don't you want to see it first?" Jeanette asked him.

"No, you take it. Papa likes to look at the pictures."

Adele couldn't tell if he was being sarcastic or not. With his head bent over he made her think of an actor she'd seen once playing Hamlet. Jacques' crewcut had grown out just enough so the natural wave in his hair made it cup his head. She noticed some new gray at the temples.

He was reading a letter written in pencil on lined tablet paper. She didn't recognize the writing.

"It's from Boogie," Jacques said with a chuckle, as if reading her mind. "My buddy I told you about, remember? The draftsman. He called me that night. Says he might come see us sometime."

Adele had wondered about the long distance call, but Jacques hadn't said and they didn't often mention things that mattered any more.

"You'll never guess what that crazy fool did," Jacques said, looking up with a smile. "He had this long layover in Pittsburgh, see, so he got some red and blue colored pencils and went in the men's room and drew pictures all over himself. Says his mother nearly had a conniption when he took off his shirt. She thought he'd gotten drunk and gone and got himself tattooed."

For the first time in months the three of them laughed together.

"Wait," he said, "that's not the best part. Boogie goes to wash the stuff off and he can't. He didn't know the pencils were indelible!"

He was still grinning when he finished reading the letter, folded it and put it in his shirt pocket.

"That Boogie," he said. "What a character."

Adele and Jeanette had stopped working to listen. After the unexpected familiarity came an awkward silence. He became suddenly self conscious, filled his thermos and left.

Jeanette bit her lip.

"Do you suppose we'll ever have him back like that, all the time?"

With more conviction than she truly felt, Adele said, "Sure we will."

"He doesn't come to see Papa and me any more."

"Maybe it's just as well. That way he won't find out Werner's working there and he and Papa won't argue so much. You can come over here any time you want to. Just give me a call, and if I'm home, I'll come get you. You know how. Don't forget to count to five after you pick up the phone, then tell the operator the number. Count to five again and say, 'Come get me, Adele.' If I'm not there in ten minutes, you'll know I'm out. Okay?"

"All right. But I miss Jacques, Adele."

"So do I, honey. So do I. Come on, grab hold of that last sack and let's finish up the yams. What else happened while I was gone?"

"Well," Jeanette said, her deft hands busy again, "let's see. You know those curtains I ordered from Sears? They came in, but Papa didn't like the design, so I got him to send them back. He said they looked like chicken tracks."

"That's too bad," Adele sympathized.

"I guess I'll make some," Jeanette said and chattered on. "Carl and Hannah had a boucherie Saturday. Papa and I helped to make the sausage, but Jacques didn't go. I don't know if they asked him to or not." She reached deep down in the sack. "Did you hear Bubba Hofmeister got his deferment? He told Papa in town this morning."

"I'm so glad," Adele said. "His mother couldn't possibly have run that farm all by herself. Have they heard from Guy?"

"He's shipped out again. They got a postcard from Hawaii. Mrs. Hofmeister showed it to me after Mass, Sunday. Guy says Hawaii looks just like those jungle movies, real orchids and everything.

He even saw a volcano."

"That reminds me," Adele said. "There was a sailor on the streetcar in New Orleans with the tackiest tattoo on his arm, a hula girl without anything on but a grass skirt. He'd move his muscles to make the girl dance. Chris's eyes nearly popped out of his head. You don't suppose that's the kind Boogie drew, do you?"

Jeanette got the giggles, thinking about it.

They finished the last of the yams and began cleaning up the mess.

"I told Papa I'd cook this evening," Jeanette said, starting to hurry.

"Let me go to the bathroom and then I'll take you," Adele told her. "Chris ought to be here any minute. He can load the truck and help me finish up when we get back. Why don't you look at your magazine for a few minutes?"

With the water running, Adele didn't hear the school bus and she didn't realize Chris was home until she bumped into him in the hall. He ducked his head, but not before she saw his face. His left eye was swollen to the merest slit, and a red welt bulged from his forehead. She couldn't tell right away if the marks on his cheeks were scratches or streaks of dirt.

"What happened, son?"

"Aw, Mom."

"Aw, Mom, nothing."

"What happened?"

He scuffed a mud caked shoe. "Aw heck, Sister's gonna call you tonight anyhow." He heaved a big, disgruntled sigh.

"Me and Artie Hebert got in a fight."

Oh, God, Adele thought. What next? Betty Hebert's nephew. Betty, Betty, Betty.

"I thought you and Artie were pals," she said cautiously.

"Yeah, we were, but not any more."

Adele took a deep breath.

"How come, Chris?"

It was hard to tell if the boy was pouting or whether his lower lip was swollen.

"'cause he picks on Kurt. He calls Kurt names."

"Like what?"

"Like 'Sauerkraut' and 'Little Hitler' and stuff like that. Kurt was about to cry. I told Artie to lay off, Mom. I warned him!"

"Let's clean your eye and get some ice on it," Adele said, unable to think straight.

"Kurt ain't a Kraut, is he, Mom? You don't want me to let Artie pick on him, do you?"

"Isn't, son. Of course not. The Kaufmanns are just as American as we are."

"Then why do people talk bad about them? Ouch!" He flinched from the peroxide she dabbed on his face. "That stings!"

"I'm sorry. I'll be careful. We have to clean it, though, so it won't get infected."

"Okay. I got him good, Mom."

Adele took Chris by the shoulders. "Listen to me, son. People do crazy things, when they're scared or angry. They feel helpless about the war, and the Germans started it, you know."

She groped for a way to make him understand.

"Remember that time you wanted to camp out with Kurt but you hadn't fed the stock like you were supposed to, so I told you no and you got mad and kicked Caspar? Remember that?"

"Yes, ma'am. I felt bad, afterwards."

The ice bag hid half of his face. He thought a while and then studied her with his good eye.

"Is it kinda like what's wrong with Daddy? I mean, the way he's really mad at the Germans, but he takes it out on us?"

"Kind of," she said, and held him close.

She was sorry about Artie and Kurt, but she couldn't help being thankful the fight had nothing to do with Jacques and Betty.

While she was brushing the grass off Chris's back, the phone rang.

"Jeanette's in the living room waiting for us to take her home," she said, going to answer it. "Tell her I'll be ready in a minute. Hello?"

It was Hannah.

"Is Chris all right?"

"Yes. More or less. He'll have a blue ribbon shiner tomorrow."

"Uh oh. What did Jacques say?"

"He hasn't seen it yet."

"Kurt told us what happened. I'm really sorry, Adele. Carl says Chris should get a Purple Heart."

"How's Kurt?"

"He'll be okay. You'd think we'd get used to it."

"Has it been that bad?"

"Oh, just off and on. Somebody drew swastikas all over the pickup the other day while Carl was in the feed store. The concentration camps have people upset. Josephine says the kids call the Steiner boys 'the Gestapo'."

"Hannah, no!"

"It's just a few ignorant people, Adele. Can't let it get you down. Speaking of ignoramuses, how's your husband?"

Adele laughed. "All right, I guess."

"Oops," Hannah said. "Katie's crying. I've got to go. Do the kids have a piano lesson tomorrow?"

"Yes."

"We'll see you after school, then. Tell Chris thanks for looking after Kurt, but we really feel bad that he got hurt."

When they came the next day, the Kaufmanns brought a lemon meringue pie, Chris's favorite.

Chapter 18

Jacques wasn't getting much sleep. The war nightmares had let up a little, but he kept having an exhausting dream that he and Adele were in the middle of an ocean. There'd been a shipwreck and she was calling out to him, crying. Her hair floated on the water like a fan, and she was about to go under. He'd swim to her, frantic, and just when he'd be about to grab her wrist, a big wave would come along and she'd slip away. He woke up at that part every time. Reluctant to dream again, he would lie awake, thinking, until the rooster crowed.

The days were getting longer, and though it wasn't quite day-break, the dark had melted enough that he could see her outline and right foot, as always, on top of the covers. She whimpered in her sleep. He reached to pat her, but stopped in mid-air.

He tried to tell himself she didn't need, didn't love him any more. Actions spoke louder than words, didn't they? But that was just it; except for the damn Germans, there wasn't a single thing he could fault her for. She was by far the nicest woman he'd ever met, and still pretty, too. He liked the way her body had rounded out after Chris was born. It was all he could do sometimes to keep his hands off her. And sometimes, when she looked at him with those opalescent eyes, he felt like his heart had been cut right out of him.

What kind of lousy heel are you? he asked himself over and over. Did she know about Betty? He didn't think so, but he couldn't tell. She'd been extra sweet since she got back from New Orleans. Damn, life got complicated. He didn't want her to get hurt, or Betty, either.

He remembered how disgusted he used to get when married guys would brag about getting some on the side. Now look at you, he thought contemptuously. Nearly every night he made up his mind to end it with Betty, turn her loose. She ought to be out having a good time with some guy who could give her a future, give her the kids she wanted. Yet every time he got up the nerve to break it off, he weakened all over again.

When he turned on the lamp, Adele frowned in her sleep. There were circles under her eyes and she looked thin. He pulled the covers over her shoulder, wanting to tell her how sorry he was, that he wished it could be like it used to, but he got up instead and lit the heaters.

During the day he usually had too much to do to have any time left over for thinking, which suited him fine. A guy could go nuts, thinking all the time.

Waiting for the coffee to drip, he went outside to look around. He liked being the first one up, with the place all to himself. It gave him a chance to get a bead on things. Once he took the weather's measure he planned his day accordingly. The rain had put him behind schedule. Some of the fields were still too sloppy to harrow. Unless they dried out fast, it would be the end of next week before he could start planting.

Maybe it was just as well. He had to replace a third of the barn roof and he wanted to get that out of the way. They'd lost a bunch of hay before he discovered the leaks. He was glad winter was almost over. Patches of new growth had cropped up in the pastures, like little green islands. At least they wouldn't have to worry about running out of feed. He stretched and went to get some coffee before heading out to milk.

By the time there were trucks on the road Jacques was on top of the barn hammering. His leg made maneuvering difficult and progress was slow. He and Papa had always done jobs like that together, but Papa had stopped offering, and Jacques was damned if he'd ask the old man for help.

Irritated, he mulled the change in his family. Papa came over once a day and they said what they had to, but nothing more and nothing personal. On Sundays, when Papa and Jeanette came to dinner, the conversation was strained. Jacques got jumpy over the way Jeanette watched his every move. He was getting pretty good again with Sign but he couldn't think of much to say, at least nothing that was safe. Seemed like anything they talked about was liable to stir up a hornet's nest.

The hammer slipped. A blood blister bubbled up on his index finger.

"Dammit, Viator," he swore, "keep your mind on what you're doing!"

By midafternoon the roof felt like a hot plate and his leg was giving him such fits he had to give up. He climbed down carefully, pausing on every other rung of the ladder to wipe his hands on his pants and get his breath. On the ground, he tried to walk the cramps out. He'd have liked a Coke or something cold, but Hannah's car was at the house, so he got a drink from the pump. He ached all over.

He rummaged in the barn till he found a beat up tin of salve and took it to the pasture to tend to one of the cows that had gone and got her tit infected. She was wary of him and gave him a hard time.

"Ho, there, Bessie," he said. "Hold on. This'll make you feel better."

Over the racket the animals set up he could hear someone butchering a waltz on the old upright piano he'd bought for Adele their first wedding anniversary. He'd forgotten it was music lesson day. He didn't see how Adele could stand it. She sure had a lot of patience.

He heard Hannah yelling at the boys for teasing Josephine.

"Josie," she called. "You come on in, anyway. It's almost your turn."

That evening, when the Kaufmanns were gone and it was getting dark, he found Adele in the kitchen putting away the ironing board. The steam from something she was cooking with crab boil made him sneeze.

"Bless you," Adele said.

"Thanks. Where's Chris?"

"I let him go spend the night with Kurt."

"What for?"

"Nothing special," she said, going past him with an armload of clothes. "Kurt wants Chris to help him build a tree house like ours."

"I haven't seen the boy for two days," Jacques grumbled. "Either he's sleeping or gone. Did he burn those old shingles like I wanted him to?"

"Yes, and he scrubbed the milk cans. For heaven's sake, Jacques, take it easy on him. He's just a kid. If we had…"

She didn't finish.

"If we had what?"

"Oh, never mind, Jacques. Let's not argue."

"Hell's bells," he said, "It's like a damn minefield around here, trying to carry on a simple conversation. I'm going to go get some cigarettes."

It was Friday night, and on Friday nights Jo Jo's was jumping. Some kids had cleared a dusty strip of dance floor and were jitterbugging for all they were worth. They couldn't have been but fifteen or sixteen, and had no business there, but Jacques wasn't going to ask any questions. He watched them a few minutes while his eyes adjusted to the dim room. The kids were having such a good time it made him wish he were young again. In the old days, he and Adele had been like that, dancing every dance.

John Parker Landry was standing at the bar holding forth to the barmaid, Lila Mae, on his favorite subject, Huey Long.

"I'd be a judge today if they hadn't killed old Huey," John Parker insisted. "It's the God's truth, so help me. You don't believe me, do you?"

"Sure I do," Lila Mae told him, lackadaisically wiping the gallon jar of pickled eggs.

A middle aged couple Jacques didn't know sat on the bar stools with their coats on, holding hands.

The guards from the camp waved. By now they all knew who Jacques was, and they were glad to have somebody different to talk to. They acted like he was the Chamber of Commerce or something, always asking him stuff like where to find some good fishing spots or who'd give them the best deal on a brake job.

They pulled another chair over to the beat-up table and Carver offered to buy him a beer. Jacques thanked him and ordered a Dixie.

"Whatcha been up to, Viator?" Carver said. "Ain't seen you around lately."

"Not much. Waiting for my land to dry out so I can plant. Y'all been taking good care of the national security?"

"You betcha."

Jacques leaned back and listened to them shoot the bull. Tex was in rare form, telling Little Moron jokes, and the guys started razzing the youngest guard, a private, about some woman who kept calling the camp for him. Carver complained that the fish weren't biting at Miller Pond, and Jacques told him to try Petit Lac. He was giving Carver directions, drawing a diagram on a napkin, when the juke box got stuck on "String of Pearls", playing the same notes over and over.

"Hey, Lila Mae!" the private yelled. "Fix that damn thing, will ya?"

"Keep your shirt on, soldier. I only got two hands, me."

"Me too, Lila Mae." He leered, "Wanna see what I can do with mine?"

"Aw, shut up, you," she said, and dodged him, going by.

Jacques was hungry.

"How about bringing us some more popcorn, Lila Mae? Anybody else want some more popcorn?"

"Not me," Tex said. "I'm full as a tick. You ought to come chow down with us sometime, Viator. We got us a sho' 'nuff chef in our mess. Made us some apple dumplin's today that'd make your mama jealous."

"Times have sure changed," Jacques said dryly. "The cooks weren't earning any stars when I was in the army."

"Man, oh man, can that Kraut fix pork roast!" the private exclaimed.

Jacques brought the front legs of his chair down hard.

"You guys let the Nazis fool with your food?"

"Why sure, Viator. Shit, it beats the hell out of eatin' old Skinny Butt's cookin'," Carver said.

"You gotta be crazy. What if they poison you?"

"Naw, they wouldn't do that." Tex told him. They know the jig's up for Hitler. All they want to do now is get home and see their families."

"Bull shit," Jacques said.

"I'm telling you, pal, these boys have had their fill of fighting, too. Hell, like as not they'd have been killed, if they hadn't been captured. They know a good deal when they see one."

Jacques shrugged. "It's your funeral." He got up and threw some change on the table. He was tired of talking to the wind. "See you around," he said, and went his way.

He even started home. He got as far as the edge of town, past the old roller rink where the gang used to hang out when he was in junior high. Armand, poor devil, was better than any of them, all the time skating backwards and dazzling the girls.

"Oh hell," Jacques said and turned around at the next fork in the road.

At that, he circled Betty's apartment twice before he could make up his mind to go in.

He found her sitting sideways in the wing chair, reading. Her legs, in tweed pedal pushers, dangled over the side.

"I thought you'd gotten lost," she said. "It's been twelve days."

"I know. I've been sort of busy," he said, avoiding her eyes.

He got a beer from the refrigerator and sat on the sofa. She already had a Dr. Pepper. The beer spewed when he opened it, and when he went to wipe it up he realized his handkerchief was dirty.

"Sorry," he said. "I didn't take time to clean up."

"That's okay." She got him a towel.

"I wasn't planning to..." he started to say, but he stopped.

She sat Indian fashion now, watching him uncertainly like a little girl who'd been punished and was longing for a reprieve. He couldn't bring himself to say goodbye. He told her about Tex inviting him to eat with them.

"Well, you said you wanted to see the camp."

"Not any more. As soon as we take Berlin they can ship the bastards back. It won't be long now."

"Do you really think so?"

"No doubt about it. Then we can throw the book at Japan. MacArthur's boys are on Iwo Jima, and now that they've got the Philippines and Guam back, nothing can stop them. You wait. I wish I could have stayed in to see it!"

Betty got quiet.

"What's that?" he said, pointing to the mimeographed papers in her lap. "Homework?"

"No." She gave him a funny look. "It's the camp newspaper. The POWs put it out. It's part of the army's democratization program."

She handed him three legal size pages printed on both sides and stapled together. There was a German word for a masthead with the date, March 16,1945 over CAMP COURVILLE, LOUSIANA in big print.

"I'll be damned," Jacques said. "They do a little bit of everything, don't they?"

He flipped through the pages. They were covered with articles, sketches and cartoons, even a crossword puzzle. Below every line of German was a line of English, both neatly typed.

"I guess that's so they can learn to out-talk us," Betty commented tartly.

"Listen to this: 'Where do we go from here?'" Jacques read out loud. "'Soon we will return to the homeland. Let us prepare ourselves to be good, responsible citizens. Let us shoulder the tragic consequences of our error and in a manly way, labor diligently to recover our lost dignity as Germans. No more Hitlers! No more wars!'"

Jacques stared at the words. He rubbed his chin.

"Lost dignity, my foot!" Betty said. "Germans have war in their blood. They think it's their holy calling or something."

"I wonder if any of these men were at St. Lô," mused Jacques, barely hearing her. For some reason, the paper disturbed him.

Betty got up and shoved it in a drawer.

"Let's talk about something else," she said. "How about a sandwich?"

"No thanks."

Jacques finished his beer and got up.

"Can't you stay? You just got here?"

"I'm tired, and I want to get an early start tomorrow."

"Please?"

"You said no strings, remember?"

"So I did. Fool that I am."

On the drive home he put her out of his mind and thought about the next day's work. Chris would be home. Maybe between them they could finish up the roof. It sure was slow going, doing something like that alone. The soil of the virgin acreage he was tilling was full of rocks. It occurred to him they'd be ideal for the grotto Adele had always wanted him to build. Maybe he'd get to that next winter, when work was slow. He decided to haul a load to the orchard for now.

Papa's house was dark, but Carl's place was lit up as bright as the night of the St. Nicholas party and Doc Delahoussaye's car was in the driveway. Sweat broke out on Jacques' hands and he bit the inside of his cheek as his mind raced with possibilities. Doc

Delahoussaye didn't make social calls. The bad measles were going around. That could explain it. Of course, there was always the
danger of a tractor accident, but Carl was too careful for that. Mr.
Max had drilled it into them. Maybe something had happened to
Hannah or one of the kids. Jacques shivered, remembering the time
little Billy Cheramie drowned in the irrigation canal. He hesitated
for a second, then stepped on the gas.

"He told me to mind my own business," he muttered.

For once he was glad Adele was still up. He found her at the
dining room table, making out reports.

"You'd better go see if you can help," he told her. "I think
something's wrong at Kaufmanns'. Doc's car is there."

He walked the porch, waiting for her to get back, till the mosqui-
toes drove him in. They were worse than usual, with the wind blowing
off the Gulf. He didn't feel like reading, and there wasn't anything but
static on the radio. He wished to God he'd stopped to see what was
wrong. Maybe he could have done something.

He thought Adele would never get back. Several times he started to phone. Once he even had his hand on the receiver, but he told
himself she'd let him know as soon as she could.

It was after two when she came home. Her voice was weary and
her face pale.

"It was Carl," she said. "He broke his ankle, sawing a dead limb
off The Tree. A branch gave way. They didn't find him till after
dark. Dr. Del set it and gave him something for pain. He thinks it'll
be all right in a few weeks."

Jacques felt his knees buckle.

"Thank God!"

Adele gave him a pitying look.

He wanted to ask her the details, but she left him there without
even bothering to say good night.

Chapter 19

On Holy Thursday Adele cut all the flowers in the yard that would keep, and after arranging them into bouquets, drove over to church. Father Sebastian was in the sacristy when she got there. He moved several boxes of candles to make room for her vases.

"I'll come back tonight to help set up the altar," she said.

"Fine," the old priest said with a smile. "I was counting on Adele and her lilies."

"It's too bad wisteria doesn't last," she said. "It smells so heavenly."

"How are Jacques and Chris?"

His question took her by surprise. She removed some irises and trimmed the stems with quick snips of the scissors.

"Chris is fine."

"And Jacques?"

When she didn't answer, he took the scissors out of her hand and lifted her chin.

"Come over to the rectory," he said, leading her by the elbow. "We'll get Effie to fix us a cup of coffee. You haven't seen my office since I fixed it up."

Father Sebastian had been at St. Isidore's since Jacques was born. You couldn't imagine him anywhere else. He knew everyone for miles around, Catholic or not, and more about them, probably, than they knew themselves.

Ed Landry, a trustee, thought Father Sebastian should dress better and act more dignified, said it wasn't fitting for a man of God to look down at the heels. Father Sebastian just laughed at people like that. He didn't see anything wrong with shiny pants or yellowing Roman collars, and Effie, having despaired of changing his mind, dutifully patched and mended his antiquated wardrobe.

Adele and the priest had hit it off from the start. He understood how it was to be away from home, and he, too, was city born. The grandson of Alsatian immigrants, he'd been assigned to St. Isidore because he could hear the confessions of the old folks in either French or German. Aging people had a way of reverting to their mother tongue, even after speaking English most of their lives. Father Sebastian and Mr. Max had been great friends.

The office didn't look that different to Adele, but she admired it, anyway, to be polite. One whole wall was taken up by ponderous looking books with mostly Latin titles. By the north window, where it would get the best reception possible, stood the short wave radio that was Father Sebastian's pride and joy. It kept him from getting lonely, he said, and missing a wife. Under the glass desk top were dozens of snapshots and studio portraits; pictures of school kids, combed slick and smiling stiffly, pictures of baptisms, weddings, graduations, confirmations, a little bit of everything. Father Sebastian's own ordination picture hung on the wall alongside a portrait painted by his sister of their parents. Adele had to look down the cassocked rows twice before she spotted him in the group of solemn, baby-faced priests. She was used to him wrinkled and sagging, like the easy chairs next to his desk.

"Thank you, Effie," Adele said when the housekeeper brought their coffee. "How's that grandbaby of yours?"

"You ought to see the little rascal, Adele. He's gained two pounds already, him, and he's good, yeah. Sleeps all night."

Effie went out, then, with unaccustomed tact, and Father Sebastian closed the door.

Out the window, as far as Adele could see, were the neighboring fields, the young rice in them a mantle of downy chartreuse. A mockingbird strutted on the path to the church.

Settling himself, Father Sebastian said, "Is there anything I can do to help?"

To her dismay, Adele found herself trembling. The cup and saucer rattled in her hands like chattering teeth. Tears rushed to the surface and she ended up telling him the whole story in fits and starts, from Jacques' first night home until this morning, when a song he heard the POWs singing got him mad all over again.

"You know how they're always singing, Father, but Jacques has it in his head they're goading him."

Father Sebastian listened attentively, nodding, scratching his bald head, asking an occasional question.

"The rumors about Betty Hebert. Did you ask Jacques if they're true?"

"Oh, no, Father. I can't do that."

"Why not? Wouldn't it be better to have it out in the open?"

"Maybe," she said, but there was doubt in her voice. "Maybe some day. But I'm afraid it might force him to make a choice and I might lose him for good. I catch him watching me sometimes, Father, and I can tell he still loves me. I know he does!"

"And you love him?"

"Yes, but..." She didn't know how to say it. "But at times I hate him, too, for punishing us the way he does. I know that's wicked, Father, but I can't help it."

"It's all right, cher. That just human. God understands. He forgives our weaknesses."

"Will He forgive Jacques, too, Father? I worry about that all the time. What if something would happen to him? He isn't a bad man, Father. If it hadn't been for the war..."

Listen to me, she thought, defending him!

"Adele," Father Sebastian said as if to a child, "didn't I baptize him? Don't you think I know? Whatever his sins, your Jacques is not a bad man."

It was such a relief to talk she lingered a while longer, although she needed to get back and had a lot to do. Before she left, Father Sebastian gave her his blessing and squeezed her hand. Nothing was solved, but she felt lighter, nevertheless.

That afternoon she was washing windows when Chris came running from the bus. The urgency in his voice made her stop in the middle of the song she was humming.

"Mom! Mom! Did you hear? President Roosevelt's dead!"

"No, Chris! Are you sure?"

"Yes ma'am. Sister Principal called us all to the gym to pray for him.

Adele made the sign of the cross and hurried to the radio.

It was true. All the stations were playing dirges interrupted by sporadic bulletins. An emotional reporter told how FDR had died suddenly of a cerebral hemorrhage at Warm Springs, Georgia. The body was being returned to Washington by train.

"Poor Mrs. Roosevelt," Adele said.

The broadcaster said Harry Truman was being sworn in immediately. Adele didn't know much about Truman. She couldn't picture anyone but Roosevelt as president. Like Father Sebastian, he seemed to have been there always.

She didn't think Papa would be home. He usually took the workers coffee and cigarettes in the middle of the afternoon. She tried to call anyway, but no one answered.

She'd just put back the receiver when the phone rang. Hannah's kids had brought home the news, too.

"Isn't it awful?" Hannah said.

"Yes," Adele said. "I can't believe it, can you?"

"With the war almost won, too."

"He sounded fine on the radio the other night."

"But he didn't look well. I told Carl that after we saw a newsreel at the Bijou Sunday when we took the kids to see Abbot and Costello. I told Carl the president looked haggard."

"How's Carl?"

"Chomping at the bit. Doc said at least one more week before he can get on a tractor. He's driving me crazy. Are y'all going to church tonight?"

"Chris and I are. Jacques didn't say. I took some flowers over this morning." After a pause, Adele added, "I had a good talk with Father." She knew Hannah would understand.

"Good," Hannah said.

"Let me go find Jacques and Papa. They'll want to know about President Roosevelt. I'll see you tonight."

That Saturday, when she and Chris went to Courville to get Chris's Easter shoes, the President was all anyone could talk about. Everywhere you went you heard the same unanswerable questions. What would happen to the meeting in San Francisco to start another world organization? Would it end up like the old League of Nations, doomed to fail? Could Truman get along with Churchill and Stalin? What kind of Commander in Chief would he be? People said his wife was shy, that they had only one child, a daughter, Margaret. Gossip had it that Truman was tied in with the Pendergast machine that was reputed to be more corrupt than the Longs.

Adele was shocked, waiting for Chris's hair to be cut, to hear a man in the other barber chair say he was glad Roosevelt was gone.

"Good riddance," if you ask me," he growled. "Never had any

use for him after he turned his back on Huey Long. The so-and-so wouldn't have been elected without old Huey's support. And as for that nigger-lovin' wife of his, that woman ought to be locked up somewhere, where she can't stir up any more trouble."

The other customers protested, and Adele could tell the argument was good for an hour, at least. She paged through a fishing magazine till Chris was ready, keeping herself aloof.

They walked all over town looking for shoes. It was too bad the pair her mother sent were too small. She just didn't realize how fast the boy grew. Jacques said Chris could use his ration stamps, which solved the problem, but Adele hated it that Jacques still refused to wear civilian clothes.

In the last shoe store they watched a young woman trying on a pair of patent leather high heels. Like a lot of others hit by the stocking shortage, the woman wore makeup the color of café au lait on her legs. She'd drawn a black line up her calves to look like a seam. It's better than nothing, I guess, Adele thought. She wondered what would happen, though, if the girl got caught in the rain. What a luxury it was going to be when the war was over and they could get stockings again, nice ones, not those ugly rayon things.

"What do you think, honey-bun?" the girl, preening at the mirror, asked the soldier who was with her.

"They're right purty," the soldier answered. "You like 'em? If they don't pinch, let's take 'em and git."

He looked uncomfortable, probably embarrassed about shopping with his wife. Adele recognized him and smiled. He was the guard who used to come to the house now and then with Papa, the one with the Texas drawl.

His wife couldn't make up her mind and told the long- suffering clerk she believed she'd look around. When you just got two pairs a year, you'd better be sure. The sergeant tipped his cap to Adele as they left.

"Now can we go to Ortigue's and get our banana split?" Chris said when the clerk produced some oxfords that fit. Adele smiled. His hair was still sparkling with oil, a pale border of scalp edging it. He smelled of talcum and his face shone. How could she resist?

"Okay, fella, let's go. The fast ended at noon. You deserve a treat after giving up sweets for Lent. That was a tough penance for somebody with a sweet tooth like yours."

"Yeah, but I offered it up for Daddy. Do you think it did any good?"

"I'm sure it did," she answered, wanting to cry.

At the drugstore they debated the battered cardboard menu while Mr. Ortigue finished waiting on customers.

"Hi there, Mrs. Viator, Chris," he said when their turn came. "Don't see enough of y'all. Your husband comes in pretty regular. Too bad about his leg, wasn't it? What'll it be today? Say, how'd you like those chocolates? I was glad to let y'all have them, it being Christmas and him being a veteran and all."

"Chocolates?" Adele said blankly.

Mr. Ortigue's face turned red.

"Oh, uh...my mistake. I must have got you mixed up with somebody else. Getting forgetful in my old age. Now what'll you folks have today?"

Chris said, "What's the matter, Mom? He's ready to take our order."

"What? Oh, nothing. Chris wants a banana split, Mr. Ortigue. With extra cherries."

"One banana split coming up. How about making it two?"

"Not today, thanks. I'm not very hungry."

Chapter 20

It suddenly dawned on Jacques, while he was hosing down the dairy stalls, that Adele was acting peculiarly. He'd been extra busy, keeping the water level even on the established fields and building up levees on the new. On top of that, every time he turned around another cow was dropping her calf and had to be watched.

Looking back, he realized Adele hadn't said ten words to him all week. Half the time she stayed over at Papa's, and if she wasn't gone or working, she had her nose in a book. Come to think of it, he hadn't even heard the piano except when Josephine and Kurt were there.

"Hmm," he said out loud. He had an uneasy feeling in his gut.

Water spilled off the concrete floor and snaked across the dirt. He rinsed the milking stool and set it out to dry.

That noon, at dinner, he tested her.

"Nice day," he said.

"Yes," Adele answered, but in a tone that suggested she hadn't noticed.

It wasn't his imagination. Something was eating her. He weighed the odds she'd found out about Betty, but he didn't think that was it. He'd been pretty careful, at least most of the time. It must be something else. Maybe she was in her period.

"You feeling all right?" he asked her.

"Yes," she said stiffly. "How's your leg?"

"My barometer? Now I know what Mr. Max meant about his

arthritis. I can tell when the weather is changing, just like he could. But it's not bad unless I'm on it too long."

"That's good," she said and fell silent, picking at the black eyed peas on her plate.

They were so unused to making conversation any more that their words seem to bounce off the wall and echo afterwards, the way sound does in an empty room.

"Chris has done a good job of bottle feeding that calf I gave him."

"I know," she said.

"Do you think he can use it for his 4-H project?"

"I imagine so."

He tried again.

"What's new with your folks?"

"Nothing much. The usual rationing problems. Not enough meat. Mother has to make fricasseed chicken every Sunday for the servicemen they have over."

"I'll bet they don't mind that a bit. I'd have given a month's pay for one of your mother's meals."

He helped himself to more rice and gravy and tried another tack.

"The dandelions are taking over your garden. Aren't you going to set out the tomato plants?"

"I guess."

Well, shit, he thought, I give up. Her indifference was galling. He hurried to finish eating and get away.

Later on, he remembered he needed oil for the tractor. He'd meant to ask Adele to borrow some from Papa. He groaned, disgusted with himself and decided he'd better stop what he was doing and go get a couple of quarts.

Driving to the filling station he came across old man Olivier's beat up Packard broken down on the side of the road. Jacques parked behind and got out to help.

"Bon jour, Mr. Olivier. Having trouble?"

The old farmer nodded, hat askew, mopping his face with a red handkerchief. The weather had been mild for days now, but Mr. Olivier still had on long johns.

"Mais yeah, Jacques. Damn thing just conked out on me. How you been?"

"Pretty good, Mr. Olivier. Let's take a look. Maybe I can

help."

"I'd appreciate it, son. Never was much good at fixin' cars. Our Joey always kept things up when he was home. We sure miss that boy."

It seemed to Jacques someone had said Joey Olivier was missing in action. He was scared to ask.

"Why don't you try to start it and let me see what happens?"

The engine didn't turn over.

Jacques lifted the hood and peered inside. He could hardly tell one part from another, they all were so covered with grease and grime. Steam poured from the radiator. Jacques poked around and came up with a piece of frayed rubber.

"You've got a busted coil wire," he said. "Hop in my truck. I'll take you to town to get one."

"Sure you don't mind?"

"No trouble. I have to get some motor oil, anyway."

Henri Olivier had onion breath and smelled of liniment. Jacques lit a cigarette and offered him one.

"The wife don't like me to smoke, her," Mr. Olivier said, accepting with undisguised pleasure. "Thinks it's bad for the health. I tell her my old man lived to ninety-seven and puffed his pipe every day of his life, but you know how womenfolks are. Always tellin' you what's best for you."

"What do you think of our new president?" Jacques asked him, to make conversation.

"I don't know much about him, but he seems like a regular fella. Men the likes of Franklin Roosevelt don't come along every day."

The mission turned out to be harder than Jacques expected. They had to go six places before they finally found a coil wire that would fit with a little modification.

"Count your blessings," the man at the garage told them. "That's my last one. Anything rubber, forget it. The war had better be over soon, or we'll be back on horses."

Jacques had a time making the connection, but he finally got the old car rolling again. Mr. Olivier tried to give him a couple of dollars for his trouble.

"No indeed," Jacques told him. "I might need a favor from you sometime. Give my regards to the missus."

"Well, merci, then. I sure thank you. Etienne's lucky, he's got a boy like you home safe from the war."

"I hope you'll get some good news soon," Jacques said. "You never know."

He wished the words didn't sound so hollow.

Heading back, he passed a couple of POWs clearing vines from the fence on the land that Jeanette inherited. Papa's horse was tied to a chinaball tree under which a guard lay sleeping. Jacques couldn't tell which soldier it was, with the guy's cap over his face.

"Some guard you are, you lazy idiot," Jacques muttered.

It didn't seem to make any difference to the Germans, though. They kept right on working. You had to hand it to them for that. Papa sure knew how to get work out of them, Jacques thought grudgingly.

Adele had signed another contract recently. She'd left a copy on the kitchen table where he couldn't miss it, and a note saying the POWs would be working Jeanette's share of the land now that he was strong enough to handle his own. It griped his ass, but he decided to ignore it rather than stir up another commotion.

He didn't like to admit how tired he got walking the levees every day. When no one was around to see, he leaned on a stick. The damn hip boots weighed a ton, even without a layer of mud.

"You birds better watch your step," he told the guards at Jo Jo's that night. "Those POWs working for my dad today could have been half way to Mexico before your man woke up. Haven't any of them tried to escape lately?"

"Naw," Carver said. "Them Krauts ain't stupid. They know when they're well off."

"I guess so," Jacques said with a snort. "They've got it a helluva lot better than we did. Beer twice a week, and no Spam!"

"Not any more," the M.P. said.

He was the only one drinking Coke, so Jacques figured he must be going on duty.

They were cracking peanuts and shooting the bull. Soon the green glass ashtrays were overflowing with shells.

"Hey, Lila Mae," the pockmarked Yankee called. "How about bringing another round and cleaning up this mess?"

Tex cocked his head.

"Say, Viator. I saw your wife and kid in Melancon's Department Store the other day. You did all right for yourself."

"Yeah," was all the response Jacques gave.

He didn't want to talk about Adele.

"What was that you were saying about the POWs?" he asked them. "What'd you mean, not any more?"

He shook salt in his beer.

"Haven't you heard? Orders from the top brass. No movies. No beer. Minimum rations. I mean they pulled the rug out from under the POWs, but good."

"Why the switch?"

"Cripes, after the concentration camps, are you kidding?"

Jacques thought to himself it took them long enough to get smart.

"That ain't the way I heard it," Tex said. "I heard it was 'cause the Nazis captured some of our guys and mowed them down like they was ducks."

He made machine gun noises for emphasis.

"Well, the POWs are sure as hell payin' for something, whatever it is," the redheaded guard next to Jacques said.

"Yeah, some of those boys are gettin' gaunt as Gary Cooper," Tex said. "Did y'all see Fritz when they was playin' soccer today? He ain't nothin' but skin and bones."

"I feel kind of sorry for them," Yank said. "Why take it out on these guys?"

"They ain't near as bony as them Jews!" Lila Mae butted in. "If I was you, I'd save my pity for them that deserve it."

The M.P. said, "I ain't got much use for Jews, but cripes, they're people! Women and children, for god's sake."

Tex turned and spat a piece of peanut shell on the floor.

"Right, but there ain't nothin' we can do to help them here, and them Jews ain't the ones supposed to be growin' rice and hoein' sweet taters to feed Uncle Sam's army. How the hell am I supposed to get them peckerwoods to work if they're too damn weak to hold a shovel?"

"Aw, you know the farmers are giving them food on the sly," Lila Mae said. "I heard some folks serve them regular meals. You guys going to report them?"

"I don't get what folks have got against Jews," Yank said. "Look at all the great people that were Jews. Einstein's a Jew. Hell, Jesus was a Jew!"

The M.P. shrugged. "Tell Viator about the picture show the other night. I bet the Krauts won't want to see a movie any time soon."

"How come?" Jacques said.

"Jesus Christ, it gave me the willies!" said Red. "And didn't I have to be on duty? I've got the lousiest damn luck. You reckon it was that shaving mirror I broke in boot camp?"

"Tell Viator," the M.P. insisted.

"Well, they sent us this film from Headquarters, see, and orders were to make all the POWs watch it from start to finish, no excuses accepted." He took a deep breath. "So we marched 'em to the mess hall and when they saw the screen set up, they thought, 'whoopee-doo, we're having us a treat'. Jesus!"

He took another deep breath and shuddered.

"You seen the newsreels of the concentration camps, Viator? That's what was on that film. It'd turn your hair gray, I swear. All them bug-eyed skeletons in striped suits, their mouths hangin' open. And they was the live ones!"

Red gulped some beer. He wiped his mouth with the back of his hand.

"Some of the guys had already started to puke before the worst stuff came on. You know what I'm talkin' about; those ovens, and the bones piled up like haystacks. Goddam, it was awful! We had to get out pistols out to make them stay and watch. Captain Bentley told their spokesman to order them to stay put or else. I never saw the Germans get so excited. They kept hollerin' 'Nein! Nein!' and all kinds of stuff I didn't understand."

"Not all of them," the M.P. said. "A bunch on my side sat there like zombies, especially that guy, Rolf. He's hard as nails. You know that young kid, Werner? He hasn't said a word since. It's like he's in shock. A couple of the others, too."

"They swear up and down they didn't know about the concentration camps," Carver said.

"I asked Rudi," said Tex, "the guy that translates the paper for the others every day. He claims there was a camp near Munich for so-called political prisoners, but he didn't know nothin' about no gas chambers. I like old Rudi, but I don't know as I believe him."

"What gets me," Carver said, "is how anybody could have it in for little kids. How can you hate kids, for cryin' out loud?"

The M.P. said, "One thing about it, pals, we won't have to worry about a birthday celebration for Hitler this year. I don't imagine he's anybody's Fuhrer now."

"You didn't expect a squawk, anyway, did you?" Red asked. "Not after you shipped those guys off to Oklahoma last year. I hear they've got some mean bastards in those Nazi camps. One word out of line and..." He carved an imaginary slice across his neck.

"I'm telling you, they ain't stupid," Carver insisted. They know when they're well off, out of the bombing and all."

Jacques paid for a round and said goodnight, stopping at the cigarette machine on his way out. He didn't care what was bothering Adele. Just because he'd let her get by with renewing the contract, she didn't need to think he was getting soft. She'd better not be giving Viator food to those murderers!

Chapter 21

Until then Adele had never understood how women could think of leaving their husbands, but on her knees, yanking weeds from a row of radishes, she found herself doing exactly that. Every few feet she had to stop and scrape tears from her cheek with a mud-streaked arm.

"Betty Hebert can have you!" she sputtered, attacking a clump of grass so vehemently that dirt flew in her mouth. Frustrated, still crying, she spat and rested on her heels.

If only I could go home for a while, she thought. Maybe if I could talk to Mother I could think straighter. Maybe if I stayed gone long enough Jacques would come to his senses. Maybe, maybe, maybe. Her mind reeled with maybes. Ache to as she might, though, she had to face the fact that running away was out of the question. Chris couldn't afford to miss school, not with only a few weeks to go before summer vacation, and she wasn't about to leave him alone with Jacques. She groaned and began to weed the next row.

Even if she didn't love Jacques, and she wasn't sure of that any longer, she knew she couldn't leave for good because she didn't believe in divorce. Sometimes she wished she did. Making a fool out of her over Betty Hebert was one thing, but this business about not feeding the Germans was the last straw. He'd come home from town last night ranting and raving about making them pay. There were times when she thought Jacques actually had gone a little crazy.

In the distance she heard the faint ring of the phone. She ran to answer, peeling off her work gloves on the way.

"Hello," she said, a little out of breath.

"Adele, it's me, Papa. Jacques there?"

"No. Do you want me to have him call you?"

Papa's "non!" was so emphatic she almost jumped.

"I thought that was him that passed. Where he went?"

"To pick up a tire Eddie patched. Why? What did you need?" The urgency in his voice worried her.

"I can come over, then?"

"Sure, Papa. Come on. I need to talk to you about something, anyway."

She barely had time to wash up and he was there, pacing back and forth in the kitchen. She was afraid he'd have something to say about how puffy and red her eyes were, but he must have been too preoccupied to notice.

"Sit down," she said. "It's not Jeanette, is it? What's wrong?"

For Papa not to be in the fields this time of day, something really serious must have come up.

"Non," he said, shaking his head. "It ain't Jeanette. We got to talk about Werner."

"What about him? Is he still not speaking? The guards told me he's been awfully depressed."

"Not talking and not eating, either. Me and Jeanette try to get some food down him, but he thanks us politely and goes back to work. It's like he's got the weight of the world on his shoulders. I swear, Adele, the boy's makin' himself sick."

"But he'll be going home soon, Papa. Surely he's glad about that."

"That's just what I'm telling you. He don't want to. There ain't nothin' to go back to."

"But Papa, he's got to go. He doesn't have any choice. And what about his family?"

"They're at the grandpere's since the Communists taken over, them and two other families. Sixteen people livin' in a cow barn, waitin' to see what comes next. Not enough food for themselves, even, much less one more. He's got no place to go, Adele. We got to help him. He ain't much older than Christophe. There must be somethin' we can do."

She walked to the window, trying to think. It seemed to Adele there'd been nothing but problems lately. She was worn out, trying to solve them all. The sun, filtered through a canopy of dogwood blossoms, dappled the linoleum in that part of the room. How can it look so peaceful here, she felt like screaming, when people are shooting each other right this minute on two sides of the world?

"Maybe you could write Senator Ellender," Papa was saying, "or even the president."

"I could try, Papa, but I don't think it would do any good. On the news they said there wouldn't be any exceptions."

"Well, how about we find him a place to hide? Maybe me and Chris could fix him a place in the woods till the soldiers is gone. Non," he said, shaking his head. "That wouldn't work. They got bloodhounds."

"I'll tell you what," Adele said after mulling it over. "I have to go in tomorrow to help out at school. Suppose I go talk to Captain Bentley? Maybe there's a loophole, some way we can get around the rules. I doubt it, but we can try."

"Oui," Papa said, ready to leap at any hope. "C'est bon. You do that, cher. Tell him we got to figure out somethin'."

She promised to pass on what she found out as soon as she could.

The next morning she left an hour early and drove straight to the camp. The guards on gate duty, usually so casual and friendly, opened up briskly and stood at attention. Through the open windows came the crisp syncopation of typewriter keys. It seemed to Adele every phone in the place must be ringing at once.

Two PFCs and a corporal were wearing a path across the hall between the cubbyhole offices, their arms loaded with files. The corporal noticed her standing there.

"Help you, ma'am?"

"I need to have a few words with Captain Bentley, but I seem to have come at a bad time."

"Yes, ma'am, it's pretty hectic around here today, but I'll see if the captain can spare a few minutes. Have a seat there," he said, pointing to a rickety looking pine chair. "What's the name?"

"Viator. Mrs. Jacques Viator."

The corporal's eyes widened. "Oh!" he said, and look embarrassed. "That is, just a moment, please."

His reaction made her self-conscious, but she tried to convince herself her imagination was working overtime.

She had to wait quite a while. She crossed and uncrossed her legs, and stared at the fly-specked picture of Lincoln hanging crookedly on the board wall opposite. There wasn't anything to read. The commotion was baffling. She'd had occasion to come to headquarters once before when Papa was down with a bad cold, and things hadn't been anything like this. The soldiers then had been joking and taking it easy. According to Papa, most of the time they didn't have anything better to do than sit around flying paper airplanes. Maybe there was some kind of maneuver going on.

At last Captain Bentley stepped out in the hall and showed her in. His was the corner office with windows on two sides half obscured by blackout shades. An ink-stained desk that had seen better days took up most of the room. Its scars were partially covered by a green blotter on which a stack of papers were neatly centered. A globe on one corner looked new, as did a set of sleek fountain pens perched on a marble base. Beside the telephone stood a rack of rubber stamps and a metal mail bin with its 'outgoing' tray full to overflowing. The only personal touch in the room was a photograph in a silver frame on top of the file cabinet. Adele felt sure the young Marine in the picture was Captain Bentley's son. The resemblance was strong, especially about the mouth.

In the adjoining office a private was pounding furiously on an Underwood typewriter that looked like it belonged in a museum. Captain Bentley closed the doors.

"What can I do for you, Mrs. Viator?"

"I'm sorry to bother you, Captain. I must have picked your busiest day to come. Is there an inspection or something?"

"No," he said, pushing up his glasses and rubbing the indentations they left on the bridge of his nose. "I guess you haven't heard. One of the POWs committed suicide last night. Hanged himself in the shower while the others were sleeping."

"Dear God!" she exclaimed. Her blood ran cold. All she could think was: don't let it be Werner, please don't let it be Werner.

"I'm so sorry, Captain," she heard herself saying. "How terrible!"

She had to know, even if it killed her.

"It wasn't Werner Meyer, was it?"

"No, another of the young ones. His name was Ernst. Ernst von Hildebrand. It's a crying shame. Why do you ask? Is something wrong with Meyer?"

"That's what I wanted to speak with you about, but perhaps I ought to come back."

If she'd been sure her legs would hold her, she'd have risen.

"It's all right." He motioned her to stay. "I've finished making out the reports and arranging the service. The investigators from the base camp won't get here for another hour or two. What about Meyer?"

She explained the reasons for Werner's hopelessness, his fear of the Russians and his dream of rescuing his family.

"Isn't there some loophole, Captain Bentley, some way to get around the Geneva Convention in special cases? Werner would be willing to do anything, work for the government, even serve extra time if he could be free and stay in America."

They were interrupted by Captain Bentley's orderly.

"Excuse me, sir, but Washington's on Line One, and there's a reporter here from the local paper wants to speak to you."

"Tell the reporter no comment till we complete the investigation. They'll get their press release then." Into the phone he said, "Captain Bentley here."

Adele rose to leave, but he signaled that she should wait. With the phone resting in his lap he swiveled around so that he had a view of the modest parade ground as he spoke. The conversation consisted mostly of "yes sir" and "no sir" with an occasional "right!".

The back of Captain Bentley's neck was a web of wrinkles. His close-cropped hair contained more silver than brown. Adele guessed he must have been close to retirement when the war broke out.

"Where were we?" he asked wearily, when he'd hung up the phone. "Oh, yes, Meyer. Believe me, Mrs. Viator, I'm truly sorry. I like the boy, myself. We get him in here sometimes when we need a reliable translator. He has a good record. Nevertheless, we've got strict orders that there aren't to be any exceptions whatsoever. The brass is afraid the other side might play fast and loose with some of our men if we can't account for all of theirs, and God knows our boys are having a hard enough time in the enemy camps without our doing anything to make it worse."

"Then Werner has to go back, too?" Adele said, but it was less a question than an acknowledgment of fate.

"I'm afraid so, ma'am. You can't run an army without rules. I'm sure you and your husband can appreciate that."

Adele didn't tell him her husband had nothing to do with her being there and would be furious if he knew.

She thanked him as graciously as the knot in her stomach would permit and left quickly, so shaken that she had to get the list out of her purse to remember what else she needed to do.

She was at the dime store trying to match some embroidery floss she'd promised to get for Jeanette when she heard someone call her name.

"Oh, hello, Miss Eula," she said.

Eula and Henri Olivier had been the first neighbors to welcome Adele when Jacques brought her home from their honeymoon. The kindness had endeared them to her forever.

"I'm so glad to see you," Miss Eula said. "My, though, you're looking wan." She leaned over to whisper, "Another little one on the way?"

Adele blushed. "No, I'm a little bit tired, that's all. But how are you? Is there still no news of Joey?"

Miss Eula's face fell.

"No. But maybe tomorrow," she said, brightening. "I just know our Joey's alive somewhere. I can feel it in my bones, and the Sisters are making a novena."

"We're praying, too," Adele told her. "I don't see how you hold up like you do."

"Well, you just have to keep on," Miss Eula said with a plaintive shrug. "What else can you do?"

Adele patted her arm. "Would you help me match these threads?" she said. "It's hard to tell, under these fluorescent lights. Do you think this shade is the closest, or the lighter one?"

"The lighter one, I'd say. What are you making?"

"It's not for me. Jeanette's embroidering some pillow cases for the church fair."

"That's nice. I'm working on a crocheted tablecloth. It's almost finished."

"You and Jeanette put me to shame," Adele said. "It's all I can do to make dish towels out of feedsacks."

"But you have other talents, dear. I'd give anything to be musical like you, and I can't even carry a tune."

"Speaking of that," Adele said, "I have to run. I need to pick up some sheet music and get to school by ten thirty. You and Mr. Henri come by and visit with us."

"We'll do that. I can't tell you how much we appreciate Jacques' fixing the car the other day. You know how helpless Henri is. I don't know what he'd have done if Jacques hadn't come by."

"I didn't know," Adele said, turning to pay the clerk at the sewing counter. "He must have forgotten to mention it."

"He surely is a fine man," Miss Eula said. "I'm always telling Henri, 'That Jacques and Adele make a perfect couple. Just perfect.'"

If you only knew, Adele thought.

Miss Bergeron at the piano store asked if something were wrong.

"No, no, I'm in a hurry, that's all," Adele said. Would you mind calling me, please, when those other pieces come in?"

Back in the pickup, she freshened her lipstick in hopes people would stop telling her how pale she was.

It was rush time in the cafeteria at school. They put her to work right away buttering bread and making cole slaw. From eleven thirty to one she loaded mashed potatoes on the plates of a steady stream of students.

Chris came through the line, grinned and said 'hi' which pleased her. Some of the other kids were embarrassed when their mothers served.

Kurt came back for seconds, and all the children from the Junction gave her a big smile, raising her spirits a few notches for the first time that day. She was relieved, nonetheless, when the last pot was scrubbed and she could slip off the bibbed apron to go home.

She dreaded reporting to Papa, and didn't get a chance to, till the following day.

"No good, huh?" Papa said. "We can't do nothin'? Werner's kinfolks said he could work for them."

"I'm afraid not, Papa. The government can't make exceptions for fear our boys will pay for it. Captain Bentley says it's final."

"What you think'll happen to Werner?"

"Oh, Papa, I don't know!"

She rubbed her forehead with the fingertips of both hands, unable to stop imagining the body in the shower, discolored and dangling from a looped leather belt, its slack feet turned pigeon-toed.

"Tell Werner not to give up," she said with a shiver. "Tell him we'll think of something."

Chapter 22

The idea came to her three nights later. She'd been too worried to sleep, and besides, Jacques kept gritting his teeth like he did when he was tense. She wondered sourly if Betty knew that. At least I have him at night, she thought with a little surge of triumph. Jacques had been home early every night since planting started. Maybe Father Sebastian was right. Maybe when the war ended, if she didn't push too hard, she and Jacques could start over. There were times when she wasn't even sure that was what she wanted. Some days she got so tired of hurting that she wondered if he was worth it, but then she'd hear him whistle, or see him shooting basketball with Chris, and she'd want to run throw her arms around him like she used to.

With Jacques right there next to her, his weight sinking the mattress, she had a hard time concentrating. He moved and his foot grazed her leg, making her tingle, but she forced her thoughts to work on the plan.

In the matter of Werner, she'd have to be very careful, for all their sakes. It gave her cold chills to think what could happen if Jacques found out what she was planning to do. He'd never understand, not in a million years.

Pondering the problem, more and more examples of the young German's kindness came back to her, some of which she'd barely noted at the time. There was the day the brush fire almost got out of hand, and the time Werner found Caspar whimpering in a trap and nursed him back to health. Jacques had never seen how Jeanette lit up with the way Werner had of describing sounds to her. It was almost as if she could hear again. Oh, God, help me to do the right thing, Adele prayed, almost, in her intensity, saying it out loud.

She couldn't get away to the other farm till mid-morning. Driving over, she noticed that the unplanted fields, the ones being rotated, were yellow blanketed with mustard flowers. You could feel the pulse of Spring in the country, unlike the city where you had to watch for every little sign. Surely it couldn't be wrong to give Werner a chance for a new life when even the flowers got theirs.

The POW named Rolf was on Papa's front lawn digging out crab grass with a hoe. He told her Werner was in the tool shed.

She parked on the far side of the garage, out of view of the kitchen windows. Before she got Jeanette involved, she needed to talk to Werner.

Papa's toolshed, which doubled as a workshop, was full of old fashioned equipment no longer needed but too good to throw away; things like the hand plow Jacques' grandfather had used, crusted over now with blisters of rust. Bamboo fishing poles idled against the walls, and harness, dark with age, hung from the rafters.

Werner had cleared some space around a sawhorse for stacks of bean poles and tomato stakes he was splitting from old lumber. Although it wasn't noon yet, the sun on the little building's tin roof had the temperature soaring, and Werner's bare skinny back was shiny with sweat. Never very heavy, he'd lost quite a bit of weight. When he saw Adele, he reached for his shirt, apologizing.

"I did not hear you, Frau Viator. The saw."

She pointed to the neatly piled stakes, wanting to put him at ease.

"We'll have our hands full this summer if everything comes up. It's a good thing you're making plenty."

Jeanette was going all out, encouraged by the "Grow for Victory" promotion that was advertised everywhere you looked. It was going to mean a lot of extra work, but Adele didn't have the heart to object. Jeanette was happiest when she was busy, as if having a lot to do filled some of the emptiness in her life.

Outside, two blue jays quarreled noisily. Adele cleared a barrel to sit on.

"I regret not to be here to see the harvest," Werner said.

She took a deep breath.

"Werner, we...Papa and I...we want to help you."

He looked puzzled.

"You do, Frau Viator, many times. My family, I write to them every week how good you are to me." A shadow crossed his face. "Whether my letters reach them now, since the Russians came, who knows?"

"You don't understand," Adele said. "We want to help you stay in America."

"But that cannot be, can it? They say every POW must be re... re-pa-tri-ated." He said the unfamiliar word in slow, careful syllables.

"I know what they say. Believe me, Papa and I have investigated. We can't see any way but one." She rose and looked around outside to make sure no one was within earshot. "We're going to help you escape."

"Escape! Frau Viator, that's madness. You could go to jail. Is crime. Nein, I must not consider it. Besides, there is no way. In my bunk all night, I think and think."

His agitation gave way to despair.

"Listen to me, Werner. I have a plan."

She took a small notebook and pencil stub from her pocket.

"Here. Write down the name and address of your relatives in New Orleans."

Werner shook his head.

"It is too far, across your great river. Already I looked on the map. I would be caught. I have no clothes, no money."

"We'll get you clothes, loan you some money. Later, when you've brought your family over, you can pay us back."

"You would do that?"

She saw hope flicker and just as quickly be snuffed out.

"My speech," he said. "It would give me away."

"Yes," she told him. "That was my biggest worry. I couldn't figure out a solution for the life of me until late last night. You mustn't say anything until you're safe, not a word to anyone."

"But..."

"You must pretend to be deaf, like Jeanette, and mute, too!"

He look aghast. "Deaf?"

"Don't you see? Then if you don't understand something, no one will think anything of it. And no one will expect you to talk!"

He sat on an apple crate, looking off into the distance. A

kaleidoscope of emotions crossed his face; consternation, fear, excitement, hope. She gave him time to grasp what she was propos-
ing. The enormity of it was overwhelming, she knew, but working
out the details had given her confidence.

His eyes were moist when he asked her, "Do you really think it
may succeed?"

"I do, Werner. I honestly do! I wouldn't ask you to risk it if I
didn't. The main thing," she said, "is to determine the best time.
Everything will depend on the right timing."

"Ja," he nodded. "I mean, yes. When I get excited, I forget
myself."

"You must practice and practice how to seem deaf," Adele told
him. "Until it's safe, that's the one thing you must never forget!"

"Whatever you say I will do."

"Good. Now tell me if there's anything that isn't clear. First of
all, no one, not even your best friend, must know. I can't impress on
you how important that is. Next, listen to the guards every chance
you get and tell me if there's any talk of moving the POWs. Hannah
says as soon as the war's over, the camp will be closed. I wish we
knew how long we have."

"By summer, I think, if the reports are correct," Werner said.
"Every day the Russians and the Americans get closer to Berlin."

"Then we've got to hurry, haven't we? Right after lunch you
go to Papa's house and work with Jeanette. You and Jeanette must
work every day for as long as you can."

"Work?"

"She will teach you to Sign, talk with your fingers. But only
in English, now, remember. That way, if you run across someone
who knows deaf language you can get by and it will give you cred-
ibility."

"But the guards, they will maybe be suspicious?"

"I can fix that, don't worry."

At the doorway she looked back.

"You believe in God, don't you, Werner?"

"Yes, certainly."

"Then practice being deaf. And pray!"

She didn't notice Rolf watching when she came out, a sneer on
his face.

From then on, Monday through Saturday, Werner went to
Papa's house every morning carrying a brush and paint can. His

uniforms when he returned to camp were spattered, and he made a point of cleaning his fingernails on the ride back. Rudi made sarcastic remarks calling him the Viators' pet, but neither the Germans nor the guards thought it strange since they were accustomed to his doing the handy work at the house.

As often as she could, Adele went to see how the lessons progressed. She did Jeanette's cooking, washed dishes and ironed while Jeanette coached Werner.

Jeanette got a kick out of teaching. "Chair," she would say, making the word with her hands and then showing him the Sign for 'sit'. Hopping about the room, pointing and Signing furiously, she'd call out things like "table", "window", "radio" until Werner could repeat the words with his hands automatically.

They made good headway at first, but the strain began to show on Werner and one day Adele found them near tears.

"What's wrong?" she said.

Werner put his head in his hands.

"I just don't know if I can do it, Frau Viator. Miss Jeanette says I will give myself away. By the time I think of the word in English and then the Sign, ach, I am all mixed up."

"Jeanette only says that because she's afraid for you, Werner," Adele said, patting both of them on the shoulder. "You mustn't let her get you down. You can do it. I know you can!"

He'd been writing in a Big Chief tablet when she arrived.

"What's that for?" Adele asked him.

"I'm making a little dictionary," he said. "Maybe that will help."

He sounded uncertain.

"Come on, you two," Adele said. "Back to work while I fix a tray. I brought a coconut pie for our coffee break."

In addition to the exercises in Sign language, Werner studied Jeanette's mannerisms and made notes. He began to cultivate a bland look, a tilt of the head that was surprisingly convincing. He also practiced not acknowledging anything said unless he could see the speaker. One day he asked Adele for some cotton. She got some from the medicine cabinet and he used it to stop up his ears.

Papa happened to come in to wash his hands one afternoon during a lesson. He walked in just as Adele clapped a paper bag to make it explode.

"Mon dieu, what was that?" Papa yelled.

He'd been working on the tractor engine and smelled of gasoline.

Adele had to laugh at his expression.

"Sorry, Papa. I didn't go to scare you. I'm testing Werner."

"Mais, I hope he pass!" Papa said.

It was good to hear Jeanette's crackly laugh.

"We have to make certain nothing takes him off guard. If he
reacts to a sudden noise it could be a catastrophe. Whenever you
can, see if you can surprise him. He mustn't act as though he hears
a thing."

"How's he comin' with the hand talk?" Papa asked.

"Good," Jeanette said, bobbing her head. She added with a
frown, "But he still needs more practice."

"Maybe I can do some more after lights out," Werner said,
"once the others are asleep."

Adele was wary.

"If you can, but be careful," she cautioned him. "If someone
saw you, he might get curious and spoil everything."

Chapter 23

Boogie showed up the following Tuesday, en route to Houston, and called from town. Jacques could hardly believe it. There was Boogie, big as you please, sitting in the grimy Courville bus station jawing with the shoeshine boy.

"I'll be damned, you're really here! I thought maybe you were playing a practical joke. Why didn't you tell us you were coming?"

Boogie ambled toward him with a grin like the proverbial cat's.

"Surprised you, huh, Frenchy?"

"Surprised, hell. Shocked is more like it. Welcome to God's country!"

They slapped each other on the back and looked each other over. Seeing Boogie in anything but hospital and army garb seemed strange. His plaid shirt looked brand new, as did the bright blue pants.

"What's with the uniform?" Boogie asked him. "You playin' hero or something? I couldn't wait to shuck mine."

Jacques shrugged. "Some people have to be reminded there's a war on."

"Come again?"

"Never mind. Give me that suitcase. I'll throw your gear in the truck."

Adele was waiting to take Chris to a birthday party, so they went straight home, talking a mile a minute.

Jacques introduced Boogie to Adele and Chris and stowed Boogie's gear in Chris's room.

"I sure am glad to finally meet Frenchy's family," Boogie said. "He talked about you all the time."

Adele gave him a big smile.

"I hate to run off when you just got here," she said, "but the kids have been planning this for weeks."

"Think nothing of it," Boogie told her. "It's my fault for popping in on you like this. I'll pester the farmer here while you're gone."

"Please make yourself at home," Adele said. "Jacques, I think we have some beer in the refrigerator, and there's meatloaf if Boogie's hungry."

"Mr. Chatham," Chris put in, "will you do Donald Duck for me when I get back? My dad says you do it good."

Boogie laughed, and to Chris's delight, quacked, "Okay, but drop that Mr. Chatham stuff. It's Boogie to you."

After Adele and Chris left, Boogie said, "You weren't kidding, Frenchy. She really is a dish. I'd like to do her portrait."

Jacques was digging for a pair of boots in the pile on the back porch.

"Here, Rembrandt, put these on and I'll give you a tour."

He got a charge out of showing Boogie the farm, because there wasn't anything Boogie wasn't interested in. He asked questions about the darndest things. The only rice he'd ever seen had come from a package at the grocery store. He wanted to know how tall the plants got and how deep the water was and whether there were any alligators around. People who came to Louisiana for the first time expected to find an alligator under every porch.

"You ask more questions than Chris," Jacques told him, "and that's going some."

"That's how come we're so smart," Boogie retorted. "He looks like a good kid, that boy of yours. You can sure tell he's a Viator."

"Yeah, he's all right. We got along real well before the war. He's too young to understand."

"I don't want to put him out of his room," Boogie said.

"Chris wouldn't think of anything else," Jacques told him. "We've got a rollaway Adele puts up in the living room when her folks come. He thinks it's a treat, like camping out. How long can you stay?"

"Have to be in Houston Monday morning. Got an interview for a job there."

"Yeah? Anything promising?"

"Sounds good. The Post is looking for someone to draw political cartoons. My uncle knows a sportswriter there, and he showed them some of my work. They want to talk about it."

"Hey, that's great, pal. Good luck."

"Well, if that falls through, I figure the size of Houston, I can always find something to pay the rent, advertising or something."

That evening was more fun than any of them had had in a long time. Boogie hit it off with Adele and Chris, charming them the way he did everybody. The nurses in Maryland used to say Boogie would make friends in Siberia. When he did his Groucho Marx routine, Jacques thought Adele and Chris would never stop laughing.

Boogie talked Adele into playing the piano and sang harmony to her melody, with Chris standing by to turn the music. A twinge of jealousy took Jacques by surprise. This was the Adele he remembered, her fingers dancing on the keys, smiling as she sang, only not for him, but at his freckle-faced buddy.

The following night he took Boogie into town. They shot some pool at Murphy's and had a couple of beers. Boogie couldn't get over the way the Cajuns talked, and he egged them on, just to hear them.

One of the old timers asked Boogie, "You mean you didn't never rode a tractor?"

"Tractor? Where I come from we live so close together the next door neighbors say 'gesundheit' if you sneeze."

That brought down the house.

"All the yard we have," Boogie went on, "you could cut with a pair of scissors. Now tell me again. How'd you say the name of that hot sausage with rice in it?"

"Boudin, mon ami. You say it like boo-dan."

Boogie had them eating out of his hand. Jacques wanted him to meet Betty, but when he started to tell Boogie about her the words got stuck behind his Adam's apple.

They stayed busy all week. Boogie said he wanted to see what farming was like, so Jacques gave him as much of a sample as he could. They dug a drainage ditch and butchered a yearling. Boogie rode the tractor and walked the levees. He even tried his hand at milking. If they had a little slack time between chores, Boogie got out his sketch pad and found something to draw; the barn, a twisted tree or Silver, indolently swatting flies with a flick of his tail.

When Friday came, they took off and went crabbing, but they kept close to the truck so they could turn on the radio every so often to listen to news bulletins. There were reports that Himmler was trying to make a deal with the Allies. The Nazis were said to be surrendering by the thousands, wounded, hungry and out of ammunition. It sounded as if things could break loose any minute.

Saturday afternoon Jacques was planning to take Boogie to visit Jeanette, but there were some POWs mending fence at Papa's place and when he saw them he drove on to town.

They went to the feed store first and picked up some fertilizer. Jacques tried to keep Boogie from lifting the heavy sacks, but Boogie insisted.

"I'm okay," he said, patting his stomach. "My embroidery's all healed up."

They got a cold drink afterward and Jacques drove around slowly, showing Boogie the town. They went by the big rice mills and the old court house with its fat columns on all four sides. On the way out to the battlefield where the Civil War monument was, Jacques took him to see the ante bellum homes and the mansion where a famous actress once lived.

Courville High School was a two story red brick building with stone lions flanking its front steps. Jacques pulled in at the curb and they got out and walked around. The old building was weekend-empty, but there were some kids about Chris's age on the playing field. He and Boogie threw some passes with the kids and then sat on the steps, smoking.

"My leg gets me after a while," Jacques explained. He was too proud to complain to anyone else, but he didn't mind admitting it to Boogie.

They made themselves comfortable, idly watching the kids, the occasional traffic and the woman across the street sweeping her porch while her baby shook the red and blue bars of a play pen.

"Did things change a lot at your house?" Jacques asked Boogie. "I mean, was it different when you got back?"

"Well, sure, Frenchy. Everything's changed a lot. We expected that." He locked his hands behind his head. "It felt strange at first. I couldn't get used to being in the house alone all day. Mom has a job now. She works on an assembly line, making parachutes, so she's not home much."

"No kidding," Jacques said.

Boogie said, "It's good for her, though. She didn't know what to do with herself after Dad died, and then with my sister married and me gone."

"What have you been doing since you got back?"

"Oh, visiting. Going to the show. There weren't too many of my friends around. Looking for a job, mostly. I could have gone back to the Post Office - they even offered me a better route - but I'd always wanted to try cartooning, and I thought, now's my chance."

Jacques shifted positions. "Y'all have any POWs up there?"

"Not close. My brother-in-law was working with some Italians for a while in a shoe factory, but they all got sent back when Italy surrendered."

"Did you see those workers at my dad's farm?"

"Yeah, why?"

"They're Germans. I made them get off my land."

"German POWs? Why?"

"Papa and Adele hired them while I was gone. We fight about it all the time."

"I could tell there was a fly in the ointment somewhere," Boogie said, "but I figured if you wanted to talk about it, you would."

Jacques ground out his cigarette with the heel of his boot.

"What's the use talking? We both think we're right."

"Hey, Frenchy. One war's enough to fight. Don't lose your happy home over it."

Jacques didn't answer. He scuffed the powdery dirt, making ripples and smoothing them out. The 'Keep Off the Grass' sign had never done much good. He leaned back on his elbows.

"It's funny, isn't it," he said. "You can't wait to get out of high school, and then, after a few years you start thinking what a good time you had. All I ever dreamed about then was going to Ag school and getting my own farm. I didn't even know where Normandy was."

"Me either."

"You got a girl yet, Boogie?"

"Nobody special. Suzanne married that sailor."

"Sorry, pal."

"It's okay. I don't know if I was really in love with her. I think maybe I just wanted somebody to come home to." After a pause he brightened. "They tell me those Texas gals are pin-up material."

Jacques wished him luck and then blurted, "There's a girl I used to go to school here with. I've been seeing her. I want you two to meet. Her name's Betty."

Boogie frowned and drew in the dust with a stick.

"The plot thickens," he said. "I thought you were a one woman man."

"I thought so, too. I didn't mean for it to happen this way."

"Does Adele know?"

"I think she suspects. We haven't been getting along, anyway, on account of the Nazis, so it's hard to tell."

"What became of the perfect marriage? You used to be the envy of the platoon with all her letters and packages?"

"I don't know. You'd think after all we've been through..."

"Where'd this Betty come in?"

"I ran into her at Jo Jo's one night after I got into a fight with my best friend over the POWs. She's a widow. Anzio. At first it was just friendly, but she understands me, how I feel and all."

"That's what they all say," was Boogie's laconic response.

Jacques flushed. "Well, it's true."

"Okay, pal. It's none of my business. I just hope nobody gets hurt."

They stood and dusted off their pants.

"Let's go gas up the truck," Jacques said. "We can call from the station and see if Betty's home. I told Adele not to expect us for supper."

Chapter 24

The windows at Betty's apartment were open, and through the
screen the scent from a bowl of gardenias poured like a potion. Her
radio was playing that silly "A Tisket, A Tasket" people whistled
everywhere you went. She had it turned up so loud they could hear
it plainly before she opened the door.

"Come in, come in," she said. "Let me take your jackets."

"Betty, this is Boogie."

"So I gathered." She put out her hand and gave him a twenty-
four carat smile. "Hi, Boogie. Betty Hebert. Jacques has told me a
lot about you, most of it good."

"I hope you believe the good part," Boogie bantered back.
"Nice place you have here. You like art?" He'd noticed the prints
over the sofa, some shimmery Mary Cassat paintings of rosy cheeked
children.

"I don't know much about it, I just know what I like." She
glanced at Jacques. "Can I get you something to drink? What have
y'all been up to?"

"I've been showing him around Courville," Jacques said. "Chris
took him fishing this morning. We'll make a Cajun out of him yet.
How about a beer, Boogie?"

"Sounds good to me," Boogie said.

"Catch anything?" Betty asked him.

Boogie feigned indignation. "Did we catch! How do you say it,
Frenchy? Mais, yeah, cher. We got us three catfish, two baby crabs

and an old bicycle tire."

"He learns fast, doesn't he?" Jacques said.

"Haven't you ever been down here before?" Betty asked.

"No, but I sure do like it, especially the weather. We still had snow on the ground at home."

"How does it feel to be a civilian again?" Betty asked while she opened a bag of pretzels.

"Any better, it'd be illegal," Boogie told her.

"You should see the arm on this guy, Betty," Jacques said. "We were over at the high school a while ago passing the pigskin with some kids. You must have been pretty good, buddy. You never told me that."

Boogie said, "Hey, I've got talents you haven't even thought of yet, Frenchy."

"So you got to see the old alma mater, did you," Betty said with a smile.

"Ah, yes. Frenchy here tells me he used to carry your books or something."

"Not exactly. Want to see what he looked like in the olden days?" She dug a year book from the bottom desk drawer and flipped through some pages. "Here it is," she said, handing the book to Boogie. "Get a load of Mr. Student Council President."

"Aw, Betty," Jacques said. "Put that up."

"Is that you, Frenchy? I'll be damned."

"Quit laughing, you joker. I'll bet you had a haircut like that, too."

With Betty looking over his shoulder, Boogie held the book in his lap, chuckling over the photographs and the class prophecy. Jacques enjoyed watching them. They were about the same height, Boogie and Betty. Bending over to see, Boogie's sandy head and her blonde one practically touched.

Boogie pointed to a picture of Mr. Guidry, the shop teacher.

"This one reminds me of my old art professor," he said. "I ever tell you about him, Frenchy? The old guy that used to paint with his shirt on backwards so that the front wouldn't get messed up? Came time to go home, he'd turn it around and put on his coat. What a character. I think he had delusions of being Gauguin in the islands. Kept a pot of water with cloves in it on the radiator. Said it inspired him. Place smelled like a dentist's office!"

They laughed, encouraging Boogie to new heights.

"His wife was pretty odd, too," he said. "She had this mynah bird and a Dalmatian like so, and she used to swear that bird and the dog could talk to each other."

"Cut it out," Betty said, wiping her eyes. "You're ruining my mascara."

"Oh, wow, look at lover boy," Boogie crowed, pointing to a page where Jacques and Sissy Fontenot posed as king and queen of the sweetheart dance. "Who's the cute gal?"

"Sissy? She's a nurse now. Who'd Sissy marry, Betty?"

"You know, Jacques, that guy from Edgarville. The one with the big nose."

"Oh, yeah, the sugar farmer."

Boogie turned some more pages. "I still don't see you, Miss Betty."

"Count your blessings," Betty said. "You wouldn't have wanted to see me in those days. Ask Jacques. He didn't even know I existed."

"I did, too."

She put away the book and gave the drawer a firm push.

"Enough of that foolishness. How about I fix up some spaghetti? Do you like avocados, Boogie? I make a mean tossed salad."

"What say we take the lady out, Frenchy? Dinner's on me. Is that okay with you?"

The invitation took Jacques off guard and he couldn't think of a way to refuse.

"Whatever you two want to do," he said. "Betty?"

"Just give me a minute to powder my nose."

They had the seafood special at a rustic little place on the bayou with the best oyster bar this side of New Orleans. After dinner Betty wanted to take Boogie to the Oleander Club to hear Raoul Theriot and his Cajun Band play at nine. When they arrived, the jukebox was going full blast and they had to wait a few seconds before they could see through the smoke enough to find a table. Jacques ordered a round of drinks.

"You've got to try some Southern Comfort," he told Boogie.

"Speaking of liquors," Betty said, "did Jacques ever tell you about Rustlin' Sam, our local celebrity?"

There wasn't much more light in the Oleander Club than a picture show had, but even in the dark her eyes were bright and happy looking.

"Who?" Boogie said.

"Didn't I ever tell you about Rustlin' Sam?" Jacques said. "No? Well, during Prohibition, Rustlin' Sam was the local bootlegger. He got to be a real legend around here. In his younger days he'd rustled cattle, but he discovered bootlegging was easier. He had himself a liquor store built on wheels, kind of a wagon-like deal. Kept it right at the boundary between two parishes - what y'all call counties. He had connections in the sheriff's office in one parish, see, and kinfolks lining the road of the other."

The barmaid interrupted with their drinks. Jacques paid her and continued his story.

"Where was I? Oh, yeah, well naturally, the police had to make a raid every so often to keep the preachers happy, so what they would do is a deputy would give old Sam a phone call, or the kinfolks would see the cops coming, and Sam would just roll his hootch into the other parish. They never did catch him."

"A man after my own heart," Boogie said. He raised his high-ball glass. "To Rustlin' Sam!"

The jukebox blared a snappy Glenn Miller tune. Boogie turned to watch the couples on the dance floor going to town.

"Come on, Betty," he said suddenly, "let's us dance. My toes are tappin'. You don't mind, do you, Frenchy?"

"I couldn't dance like you when I had two good legs," Jacques said. "Y'all go on and enjoy yourselves."

"Aw, Frenchy, I forgot. I didn't mean to rub it in."

Betty bit her lip.

"No offense," Jacques said. "Go on and dance."

They came back after the number and sat down.

"She's got great timing," Boogie said.

The band members trickled in then and started tuning up; three fiddlers and a guy with a squeeze box. Theriot, the leader, was so old they practically had to help him on stage. For that matter, none of the shirt-sleeved performers was a day under sixty, but once they began to play you'd never have known it. A feeble spotlight shone on one old fiddle player's bald head and bounced off the purple side of the accordion. The musicians held their instruments stiffly in cal-lused big-knuckled hands. Their faces were grim, and the way they kept their lips shut tight made them look like they were breaking in their first dentures. At last they finished adjusting their instruments, the squawking stopped and Theriot stepped to the mike to launch the first number.

Saturday night being the big night at the Oleander Club, there was a rush to the dance floor and it filled up fast.

"Come on," Betty said, taking Boogie by the hand. "I'll teach you the Cajun Two Step. All you do is put your right..."

Jacques went to the men's room and then the bar, where he ran into Carver with a little gal from the telephone office.

"How you doin', Viator? You know Marcia?"

"Hi," she said over the rim of a green drink that looked like hair tonic.

Jacques told her hi.

"It's lookin' good over in Europe, ain't it?" Carver said. "Now if we can just knock the shit out of those Japs. Christ, those so and so's are flyin' those suicide planes right into our ships!"

"You promised," Marcia pouted. "You said if I went out with you, you wouldn't say one word about the war. That's all you guys think about, I swear!"

"Okay, honey," Carver said, kissing the girl on the neck and making her giggle. "We won't talk about the war no more tonight."

That suited Jacques fine. He didn't want to talk about it anyway.

Carver said, "Who's that dancing with your girl, Viator?" and Marcia moved to get a better view.

"She's not my girl," Jacques snapped. "We're just old friends."

Damn you, Carver, he thought, and went back to the table before he was tempted to wipe the silly grin off Carver's face.

The question ate at him all the same. Betty and Boogie were oblivious, two-stepping around the room while the ice in their drinks melted.

Jacques made his way outside and walked around. Some kids piled out of a Model T and went inside, letting out strains of "The Tennessee Waltz" when they opened the door. Then it was quiet in the parking lot except for the crunch of Jacques' boots. The sky was so clear every star seemed to have been polished. It would have been a good night to break out the telescope Chris got for Christmas.

Jacques was restless. The noise in the club made him tired. I guess I'm getting old, he said to himself. When they were in college, he and

Adele could dance all night and go to the Tiger Café for breakfast afterward. He wondered what she was doing. Sleeping, probably. She and Chris had been disappointed about him going off
with Boogie instead of staying to eat fish. I wish we'd stayed home,
Jacques thought. He lit one cigarette after another, but they burned
his tongue and tasted like sawdust and he ground them out half-
smoked.

When he didn't return, Betty and Boogie came looking for
him.

"Are you all right, Jacques?" Betty asked.

"What's the matter, Frenchy?"

"Nothing. I'm fine. I just needed some air, that's all. Are y'all
about ready to go?"

Betty got her things and they drove her home. She invited them
in for a nightcap, but Jacques begged off.

"I've got to get up early tomorrow to spread fertilizer," he
said.

"Well, so long, Boogie," Betty said. "It's been fun. Thanks for
the dinner and dancing, and don't forget the two step."

"I won't, pretty gal. I had a swell time. Take care of yourself,
now."

"I can see why you like her," Boogie said as they climbed back
in the truck. "She's a sharp little cookie. Nice, too."

"Yeah," Jacques said. "That's what makes it rough."

He was so quiet driving home that Boogie asked him again if
something was wrong.

"Lots," Jacques said, "but nothing to do with you. Turn on the
radio, will you, and see if we can get the eleven o'clock news."

Chapter 25

Adele arranged her china and pink crystal on the tea-stained Sunday table cloth so the spots wouldn't show. It had been a long time since they'd had company, and she found herself humming a Broadway tune. Boogie's being there had made all the difference. Chris was having fun, and Jacques was almost normal.

She was at the stove stirring lemon custard when Boogie joined her in the kitchen.

"Morning!" he said. "Didn't mean to sleep so late. Where are the guys?"

"Good morning, yourself. Jacques had some work to do, and Chris is feeding the stock. How'd you sleep?"

"Like a log. I see where they get all that propaganda about country air. It seems funny, though, not to hear any traffic. At home the trolley goes by every fifteen minutes and shakes my whole room."

"When I was first married," Adele said, "I couldn't get used to it, either, but now when I go to New Orleans, I can't get used to the noise."

She turned down the fire a little.

"This is almost done. I'll cook some eggs for you in a minute. Your orange juice is in the refrigerator, and there are cinnamon rolls on the table."

"That's plenty. You're spoiling me. I'm not used to being waited on."

He got his orange juice, yawned and sat down. She felt him watching her, but wasn't uncomfortable. Boogie was the kind of person you relaxed with, like Father Sebastian.

"What did you fellows do yesterday?" she asked him.

"Oh, Frenchy showed me some of the local sights. Boy, those rice mills are huge! We played a little ball, went out to eat, had a few drinks."

Adele thought he hesitated a little.

"Ended up at some place called the Oleander Club, listening to Cajun music."

"He took you to hear chank-a-chank? How'd you like it?"

"A little was fun, but I don't think my ears could take a whole heck of a lot of it. The natives were sure gettin' into it, though, even the old folks. Some of them looked like they could barely walk till they got on that dance floor. You'd think they'd found the fountain of youth!"

"I know what you mean," Adele said. Out of the corner of her eye she saw him pick up the bulletin lying on the table.

"Don't tell me somebody's been to church already," he said.

"Chris and I went to the early Mass," she explained. "They call it the Fisherman's Mass."

"That was one thing about Frenchy I really admired. Whenever a Catholic chaplain would come, Frenchy was right there. He put some of us Protestants to shame, him and the Baptists."

"He quit going after he came home," Adele said. Her voice was pinched sounding.

"Oh." Boogie took in the implications of that. "Sorry, Adele."

She poured the custard into pie shells and began whipping meringue, grateful for the noise of the mixer. Boogie washed his dishes and watched appreciatively as she mounded the pies.

"Mmm, that looks good! I do love lemon pie."

"Jacques told me."

"Son of a gun. He doesn't miss a thing, does he? And you're a sweetheart."

Adele gave him a rueful smile.

"Come to think of it," Boogie said, "I guess he does. Things have been pretty tough, haven't they?"

She measured an answer.

"Did Jacques tell you?"

"A little. Not much."

"I guess it shows pretty badly, doesn't it? I hope it hasn't spoiled your visit."

"Don't worry about me. I've had a ball."

"Boogie," she said, "what's wrong with Jacques? You went through the same things he did, didn't you? How come he's so bitter and you're not?"

He folded the dishtowel as if it were a flag.

"I don't know, Adele. We saw an awful lot of good men die. It takes some guys longer to let go. I'm lucky, I guess. I never could stay mad very long."

"It's like he can't stop fighting," she said, "like he's got to keep on and on. But that won't bring people back, Boogie, so what's the use?"

They heard Chris coming up the barn pathway singing the Dwarfs' song from "Snow White". Boogie put his hand on her shoulder and gave it a quick squeeze.

"Keep your chin up, honey. Frenchy'll get over it. Now show me where the paring knife is and I'll peel those spuds for you. You see before you the potato peeling champ of Company D. Boogie Chatham, Master of the K.P., that's me."

Half a dozen times that day, beneath the jokes and the foolishness, Adele realized Boogie was cheering her on.

Papa and Jeanette joined them for Sunday dinner and Boogie had them laughing, too.

After the meal, Adele and Jeanette were in the kitchen getting ready the coffee and rinsing the good demitasse cups.

"He's funny," Jeanette said.

"Nice, too," Adele replied. She skimmed cream into a silver pitcher.

"Did you see Jacques? He was actually laughing."

"Yes, isn't it wonderful?" Adele said. "Bring the pies, will you?"

Papa was explaining to Boogie why the rice was kept standing in water.

"It's on account of the weeds," Papa said. "The water kills the weeds; alligator weed and watercress and them other weeds - we call 'em duck salad. They ruin your rice for sure."

"In the old days," Jacques explained, "the farmers had to depend on rain. Windmills help some, but they aren't dependable. It's just since you could pump water from the bayous and the canals that you could make any money on rice."

They sat around the table talking until time for Boogie to leave.

Jeanette had a hard time keeping up when that many people were speaking back and forth, but Boogie was so animated he was easy for her to read. Now and then Jacques would stop and repeat something for her in Sign.

When Boogie excused himself to pack, Jeanette got Papa to take her home. She returned a few minutes later with two of the clothes pin dolls she was making for the church bazaar, some jam and a jar of tomato relish.

"The dolls are for your nieces," she told Boogie in her sing-song voice. "I think they're the best ones I've made. And here," she said, handing him the jars, "I hope you like strawberry jam. Adele and I made it ourselves."

Adele could tell Boogie was touched by the offering.

"My favorite," he said, giving her a hug. "Thanks!"

He held the little dolls up to the light, full of admiration. The little enameled faces with Betty Boop eyes and cupid bow mouths were as perfectly traced as if they were fine porcelain, and the dimity dresses might have come from a lawn party in "Gone With the Wind." Adele didn't see how Jeanette could sew such tiny ribbons and lace.

"Where'd you learn to make dolls like this?" Boogie asked Jeanette. "They're beautiful!"

"I saw a picture in a magazine. Do you really like them?"

"Like them? They're wonderful! Norma and Alice will go out of their minds. Do you have a box I can use, Adele? I don't want them to get messed up in my suitcase."

"We'd better be going," Jacques said. "The bus will probably be late - they always are, these days - but you never know."

The house felt empty when they were gone. Adele wandered around emptying ashtrays, putting up the rollaway, straightening the Sunday paper scattered across the floor.

She realized with a shock the radio hadn't been on all day. It was as though they'd taken time out from the war. Some day it will be like that for good, she thought. Please, God.

When the house was tidy, she forced herself to get out the ledgers. With company there, she'd fallen behind in her paper work. The county agent wanted a report on the new strain of rice Papa was trying out on Jeanette's land. Papa was optimistic. She'd heard him say at dinner it might be hardier than the Edith brand or the Longchamps they'd been planting.

"But will it yield?" Jacques said. "That's the thing."

Time would tell. She posted the fertilizer for it to Jeanette's account and figured out the cost to date per acre.

Papa's bank statement gave her fits, but she was almost finished balancing it when Jacques and Chris came back from the bus station. They changed clothes and left again; Jacques to check the cattle, and Chris, to ride Silver over to Kurt's.

While she had the paper out, Adele decided to write her parents, telling them about Boogie's visit.

'It did us good,' she told them. 'Part of the time Jacques was his old self, and I don't know when I've laughed so much. Boogie could be another Red Skelton. I wish you could meet him.

Did Mrs. Anderson hear from her son? I hope he was just at sea and couldn't send mail. What about the Charpentier's boy?

What do people there think of Mr. Truman? I can't get used to the way he talks. He's so different from FDR, isn't he?

I'm sending you our extra ration coupons for canned goods. If you don't need them, give them to Weezie for her family.

Thanks again for the Easter clothes. Jeanette took my dress in at the waist and it looks fine now. Funny, what a difference five pounds can make. I'll send you some snapshots as soon as we get them developed so you can see us modeling and you'll get to see Boogie, too. He looks sort of like Van Johnson. Chris said you could draw dot-to-dot on his freckles.

Take care, dears. I'm lonesome. Love, Adele'.

In a separate note to her mother, Adele wrote: 'Don't worry. I'm doing all right. Jacques hasn't been gone as much and he comes home early, so I guess things are better. Boogie told me to be patient. Keep praying. I love you, A.'

Chapter 26

"What are you doing, Mama?" Chris asked.

Adele put her fingers to her lips. "Shh."

She'd brought the kitchen radio into her bedroom and plugged it in on the night table so she could hear the news as she worked. The closet was empty and there were boxes and piles of clothes everywhere.

The radio crackled with static.

"It is difficult to sort out the rumors," an excited correspondent said. "Berlin has been under continuous heavy shelling by the Russians for the past ten days. The capital of the Third Reich lies in rubble, surrounded by the Allies. In the chaotic streets there are pockets of resistance and hand-to-hand fighting. Although night has fallen, raging fires give the sky the brightness of many neon lights."

The correspondent's voice faded out but came back a second later in a burst of static.

"There continue to be unofficial reports that Heinrich Himmler has made an offer of surrender. We have no word tonight on the fate of Adolph Hitler. Whether he has indeed committed suicide is not known, but rumors persist that he has been flown out of the city. Some claim that he has escaped in disguise through enemy lines. Whatever the truth of the matter, the days of the self-styled Master Race are fast coming to an end. Stay tuned for news from the Pacific front after station identification."

Chris sat on the dressing stool swinging his legs.

"What does it mean, Mama? Is the war over?"

"Not quite, but it's getting close. Soon, please God."

"Where's Dad?"

Adele noticed he didn't say Daddy any more.

"He went to see Mr. LaBauve about buying some calves. There wasn't much else to do in this weather."

A slow rain had fallen with monotonous regularity since the day before.

"Did you get your feet wet?" she said.

"Not bad." Chris looked at his shoes and shrugged. "What are you doing?"

"Just sorting out clothes. I need to put the winter things in mothballs."

"P.u.! Do you have to? I hate that smell."

"Unless you'd rather have holes in your heavy coat. Speaking of smells, did you trap that skunk yet? If it decides to spray under the house we'll have to move."

"I set it, don't worry."

"Well, keep Caspar tied up. He's liable to spook your tuxedoed friend."

Chris laughed. "That's funny, Caspar, spook it!"

"It's called a pun. That skunk is no joke, though, son."

She started packing blankets in the cedar chest.

"Bring me your quilt off the line on the back porch and I'll put it away. Did you get your snack yet? How about homework?"

"I did it at school. We couldn't go out for recess."

While he was in the kitchen eating, Adele hurried to make packages of two stacks of clothes and slip them under the blankets. She'd meant to be finished before Chris got home, but deciding what to pack was a quandary. Werner had given her his measurements in centimeters and she'd had to figure them out to determine his sizes. Jacques' shirts would be all right, a little big across the shoulders, maybe, but his pants would be too long. She could hem them if there was time, but she never knew when Jacques might be in or out. She had to be careful and she was getting nervous. They needed to have everything ready, just in case.

She wished she'd hear from New Orleans.

"Chris," she called. "Go see if we got any mail. My umbrella's by the back door."

Between news broadcasts the radio station played music, mostly Nat King Cole. Adele listened carefully to each bulletin, but there was nothing new. The announcers just kept repeating the earlier reports. She wished they could give the weather forecast, but the government had forbidden those for the duration, lest U-boats in the Gulf pick them up and use them to advantage.

Chris returned, shedding raindrops like a puppy, and handed her the mail. Nothing but a feed bill and the Times Picayune.

"Heck," he said. "I thought sure my invisible ink would come today."

He was always waiting for something he'd ordered off a cereal box.

"Get the phone, will you?" she said. She was on a chair, stacking hatboxes on the top shelf.

"Mama," Chris yelled. "it's Grandma!"

Adele's heart raced. How was she going to talk? She couldn't send him back outside. She went to the phone and asked her mother to hold on.

"Chris, why don't you go in the living room and play the Victrola? Just be careful you don't crank it too hard."

"All right!"

He dashed up the hall and in a moment she heard the grinding of "Sugar Blues". Ordinarily it set her teeth on edge, but for once it came in handy.

"Sorry, Mother," she said into the receiver. "I wanted to get Chris out of the way. Little pitchers. Are y'all all right?"

"We're fine. You've got me curious, though."

"I know. Sorry to be so mysterious. Did you mail the letter like I asked you to?"

"Yes, and Mr. Faber from the bakery just called me. He said... wait, let me get my glasses. I wrote it down. He said to tell you the recipe you sent is very good and he will be waiting with all the ingredients you need.

"Is that all?"

"Yes. He said you would understand. Do you? What in the world are you making, Adele? Is it a surprise?"

"Sort of. I'll explain when I see you, Mother. Thanks for the help. How's Daddy's cold?"

"Lots better. He's putting up window displays, getting ready for the victory celebration. Isn't the news wonderful? But are you sure you're all right, dear? You're acting strangely."

"I'm fine, Mother, honest. Don't worry. I'll write again soon. Give Daddy my love."

"All right, bye, bye."

Adele hung up. "Darn the rain," she said under her breath. She could hardly wait to tell Werner.

Jacques came home in time to milk. She had their room back in order by then and was ironing the summer curtains to put up once the weather cleared and she could get the windows washed.

They stayed close to the radio all evening, hoping to hear what had happened to Hitler. It was terrible to wish someone dead, but Adele couldn't help it. The man was a monster, starting the war and killing all those innocent people, those poor Jews, like that. She simply couldn't fathom how the Germans could follow such a maniac. Werner said it was because they were demoralized after the First War and because of the Depression. He said Hitler seemed like a savior when he got the country going again. It still didn't make sense to Adele.

"What do you think, Jacques?" she said after another report of the situation in Berlin. "Do you think he's really dead?"

"I don't know. A war zone's a madhouse. Anything's possible."

Chris got tired of listening and went to his room. Adele knitted, watched Jacques hunched over the radio and wondered what it would be like when peace came. No one, in the beginning, had thought the war would last this long, but now they were so used to it that peace was hard to imagine.

Jacques gave up, finally, and went to bed. Adele listened till after midnight, too keyed up to read, much less sleep, torn between excitement that the war was ending and fear that Werner wouldn't be ready.

The following morning she and Papa went out in the pasture to talk things over. The German surrender was expected at any time. No one knew how quickly the POWs would be shipped back after that. Adele showed him a bus timetable she'd tucked inside a McCall's pattern leaflet.

"See, Papa, there's a bus to New Orleans leaving Acadia at nine-twenty every morning. That means Werner will be in New Orleans hiding by the time you have to report him missing. If Jacques is using the pickup I'll have to borrow yours. Okay?"

"You going to take him all the way to Acadia?"

"I think it's best, Papa, don't you? Any place around here would be too risky."

"Mais, yeah, I s'pose so," he agreed.

"What are we going to do if it's raining like this and the men aren't working?"

"I'll think of somethin', me, to get a crew. You 'bout got everything ready?"

"Almost. I don't know about shoes, though. He'll look funny in the city in those boots, but Jacques' shoes are way too big."

"Werner can have mine," Papa said. "They a lot smaller than Jacques', and I don't never wear them pointy toe things anyhow, if I can help it."

"How are the deaf lessons going?"

"Pretty good. Jeanette says the boy picks up that finger talk real good, and I been makin' noises behind his back like you did, but he don't budge. I never saw anybody could concentrate like that."

"He's got a lot at stake, Papa. Keep the truck on standby, all right?"

"Oui, cher. Sure thing."

"I have to go into town for a few things," Adele said. "Do you need anything?"

"Not that I know of. You best check with Jeanette. She said something about a package at that catalogue place."

"It's probably those dishes she ordered." She gave him a peck on the cheek. "See you later."

Adele returned some library books first, picked up Jeanette's package and traded in her savings stamps for a bond. She went to Woolworth's then, and gathered up some shoe laces and gift wrap and odds and ends they didn't need but could use later, hoping that way the salesclerk wouldn't remember the razor and men's toiletries - the things she'd really come to buy.

She was so preoccupied with her errand and trying to be inconspicuous that she'd completely forgotten the Hebert Brothers Insurance Agency was across the street. Coming out of the dimestore, she saw Betty over there. Butterflies did didos in her stomach.

The sight of Betty typing by the plate glass window, her blonde hair done up in a fashionable pompadour, made Adele acutely aware of her own baggy sweater and faded house dress. She watched as Betty made an erasure and lit a cigarette, every movement of her manicured hands a study in grace. No wonder Jacques was taken with her. How could he resist glamour like that? Adele felt like Tugboat Annie by comparison.

"I wish I could put you on a bus," she said through her teeth. She threw the packages in the truck and slammed the door.

Chapter 27

While he waited for Eddie at the Satisfaction Garage to fix a flat, Jacques strolled over to the pool hall down the block. Mid-afternoon there wasn't much happening, just a couple of high school boys playing hooky, and the old timers hunkered over the dominoes. Bubba, who ran the place, was on the phone taking bets on the cock fights they had every week out at Tee Frere Patout's place.

I should have taken Boogie to see that, Jacques thought. Bet he wouldn't believe his eyes. Jacques hadn't had much stomach for it, himself, though, since coming back.

He went across to Ortigue's to get something to read.

The Boudreaux sisters, Miss Bertha and Miss Lucy, were in the rear of the store getting a prescription filled. They never changed. You saw Miss Bertha in starched shirtwaists summer and winter, but Miss Lucy favored floral prints that stuck to her behind in hot weather. Jacques and Jeanette used to speculate the two old maids bought Blue Waltz perfume by the gallon. The smell, mixed with Dr. Tichenor's, was a combination that as a child Jacques dreaded worse than the incense in church.

After Jacques' mama died, the Boudreaux sisters had made pests of themselves, marching over daily with gluey casseroles, like crusaders out to rescue the grail. Miss Lucy would hug Jacques and Jeanette to her flowered bosom, moaning on and on about "their poor dear mother" and "this vale of tears" while Miss Bertha snooped around looking for signs of disorder to prove their services were indispensable. To the relief of Jacques and Jeanette, Papa soon got a bellyful and sent the Boudreaux sisters packing.

I'll bet they've never forgiven him, Jacques thought. He picked up the new Liberty magazine and flipped through it.

"Why hello, Jacques," Miss Lucy said with raised eyebrows. "We haven't seen you in a long time."

From the look they gave him, you'd have thought he was Jack the Ripper.

"Hello, Miss Lucy. Miss Bertha. How have you been?"

"Pretty well," Miss Bertha sniffed, "except for poor Lucy's rheumatiz."

"It's the weather, you know," Miss Lucy complained. "All that rain."

"That's too bad," Jacques said and turned his attention back to the magazine rack.

"I must say you're looking well," Miss Bertha continued.

She never had been one to let up.

"I mean, we didn't know," she ran on. "We haven't seen you at Mass."

Mr. Ortigue intervened. "What else can I do for you ladies this afternoon?" He peered at them over rimless glasses that seemed to grow from the middle of his nose. "Need any mosquito repellent? Vitamins? We got some fancy new stationery in, the other day."

"That'll be all," Miss Lucy told him, and counted out two dollars and thirty cents as though she were teaching first grade.

Jacques pretended to be reading when they passed, Miss Lucy fluttering after her sister like one of Adele's hens.

"Goodbye, ladies," he mumbled.

Mr. Ortigue came from behind the counter and offered Jacques a cigar from a box adorned with a picture of a red-skirted flamenco dancer.

"Have one," he said.

"Thanks. I'd better stick to my Camels."

The pharmacist was in a chatty mood. He clipped the end of a cigar and lit up.

"You're from the Junction, Jacques. What's this I hear about that priest of yours sending short wave messages to enemy U-boats?"

"Fr. Sebastian? Who told you that? That's the silliest thing I ever heard."

"Maybe not. One of the customers got it from his wife. You

never can tell, can you? A man of the cloth. I never even knew he was German."

"Oh, for Pete's sake. Sebastian's been here a hundred years. His mother was an immigrant, but hell, that doesn't make him a spy!"

"Oh well, you know how folks talk. Somebody said he'd been reported to the F.B.I., but I guess you'd know if there was anything to it."

"People talk too damn much, if you ask me."

"You're right about that. Like I told my missus, it looks like our boys'll be coming home most any day now, so we won't have to worry about spies anyhow."

"How much do I owe you?" Jacques said, cutting him short.

"Four bits. You want a bag?"

"No thanks," Jacques said. He paid and left.

It's a wonder, he thought irritably, walking back to the garage, that the neighbors don't complain about Eddie's radio. You could hear it playing Hank Williams a block away. Between the garage noises and the radio, Jacques had to shout so Eddie could hear him.

"Is that tire ready?"

"Almost!" Eddie shouted back. "Everybody and his brother needs a patch job today! I swear, if the war don't end soon, we're gonna have to use horses and buggies."

While they were talking a truckload of POWs passed, returning to camp. Eddie stopped what he was doing to wave.

"Why'd you do that?" Jacques asked him.

Eddie shrugged. "Why not? There you go," he said, rolling the tire to Jacques. "She's ready for a few more miles."

Jacques was getting more disgusted by the minute. He drove to Betty's, but to cap things off, she wasn't home. He wandered restlessly about the apartment, watching for her though the lace curtains, but there was no sign of the gray Studebaker. There were cards on the table where she'd been playing Solitaire, but he couldn't sit still. He read part of a week-old Courville Courier, opened a bottle of orange pop and lit cigarettes as fast as he put them out.

Betty sure kept the place nice, he had to give her that. The thought had occurred to him more than once that she'd make some guy a wife to be proud of, but today, somehow, it had the force of a fresh idea.

He held her perfume atomizer to his nose, an action which left

him feeling even more melancholy and ill at ease. He tensed at the
sound of traffic noises, thinking he heard her car, but it was only
a delivery truck at the neighbors'. He squirmed inside, wondering
what to do if anyone came. For some reason, he'd never thought of
that prospect before.

"I don't belong here," he said under his breath, but something
made him stay.

Betty breezed in a few minutes later, kicking off her high heels
at the door.

He took the grocery sack from her arms and she started unbut-
toning a snug fitting jacket.

"You look mighty sharp," he said. "New suit?"

"Like it? It's my career girl look. I've been using my wiles on
crusty old men of wealth."

"You have?"

"And," she said with a stage bow, "I got them to buy four
thousand dollars worth of Liberty bonds. I had to work Main Street
for the drive."

"Not bad."

"Not bad, my foot! Darn good. But how could they refuse a
poor old widow lady? Let me change into something comfortable
and I'll put some supper on."

"No supper for me. I could use a cup of coffee, though."

She returned wearing a seersucker housecoat with stripes the
color of Easter eggs. After fixing their coffee she curled up on the
sofa where light from the end table lamp shone on her hair.

"Guess what I got today," she said. "A letter from your pal
Boogie with a drawing of us dancing at the Oleander Club. He's a
riot, isn't he?"

"Yeah. We got a letter, too. Did he tell you he got the newspaper job?"

"Uh huh. Sounds exciting."

"I guess. If you like city life. I don't know about living at the
"Y", though. Too much like the army."

"Boogie says he likes it. They have a gym, and it's only six
blocks from the paper."

"Aren't you going to show me the picture?"

Betty handed him the manila envelope next to her purse.
Jacques pulled out the drawing and whistled.

"Damn, he's good, isn't he?"

Betty settled back on the cushions with a self-deprecatory shrug.

"It's flattering."

She was blushing, but he could tell she was pleased.

"You ought to get it framed," he said, sliding the picture carefully back into the envelope.

"I will."

The room got quiet. He fiddled with the ashtray, twirling it on the arm of the easy chair.

"You look nervous," she said. "Anything wrong?"

"Not 'specially. I just have a lot on my mind."

"The farm? How's the early crop looking?"

"Pretty good so far. It's too soon to tell much. A lot will depend on the weather. It always does."

Betty stretched.

"Did you hear about Bill Dautrieve? He was reported missing, but it was all a mistake. He's back in San Diego and Mary Ann's on her way to meet him."

"That's great. Any news of your cousin Scott?"

"Not so far. All they know is that he was wounded and is being shipped home. Aunt Marge would sleep at the Post Office if they'd let her. The suspense is killing them. Captain Bentley's son got shot up in the Phillipines, too, did you hear?"

"Who?"

"The C.O. at the POW camp, Captain Bentley."

"Oh. I never met him. Too bad. Is the kid going to make it?"

"They don't know yet."

"Seems like all you hear about."

"I know. Remember Laurette Jackson, the gal who had the beauty shop on Second Street? She's about to go to pieces worrying about her brother. He's on a submarine and they don't hear from him for months at a time."

"That reminds me. Have you heard any talk about Father Sebastian?"

"The priest out at the Junction? No, why?"

"Oh, just some bull Mr. Ortigue came out with. Some fool started a rumor that Father Sebastian's a spy."

"That old man? You're joking."

"It's no joke. You know how people are. They'll believe anything. Once something like that gets started, it spreads like wildfire."

"Why would anybody suspect him?"

"I guess because he speaks a little German, just enough to talk to the old timers and hear their confessions when he has to. When we were kids, he and Mr. Max used to talk German when they didn't want us to understand. They were big chess pals."

"That doesn't make him a spy. My Dad studied German in high school."

"Of course not, but old man Ortigue's got two and two added up already. Father Sebastian's a ham radio operator."

"He is?"

"It's just his hobby. He's been playing with radios all his life. He used to let us kids put on his ear phones and listen in. Some nut told Ortigue Father Sebastian was transmitting signals from the church steeple."

"Is that possible?"

"Hell, I don't know, but Father Sebastian couldn't climb up there if he had to! It's preposterous."

"Are you sure? Just because he's a priest doesn't make him perfect."

"Betty, for crying out loud, I've known him all my life."

"That's what you said about Carl."

"Come on, you know it's not the same thing. That's just stupidity with Carl, letting those Nazis soft soap him. They're accusing Father Sebastian of treason!"

"Okay, okay. Don't get sore at me."

Jacques took his empty cup to the kitchen.

"I'd better be going," he said.

"What's your hurry?"

"I told Chris I'd go with him to a Boy Scout meeting, some kind of father-son deal."

"Oh."

"I'll be in touch," he said and moved to leave without going near her. He felt clumsy and wished he hadn't come. Betty had a funny look on her face.

"I saw your wife today," she said.

He froze.

"Where?"

"She was coming out of Woolworth's."

"What did she say?"

"Nothing. I just saw her out the window as she was getting into the truck."

    Neither of them said anything for a minute.

    "Do you think she knows, Jacques, about us?"

    "God, I hope not!" he said without thinking.

    Betty's face fell.

    "Oh, hell, Betty, I'm sorry. It's just no damn good!"

Chapter 28

You'd have thought it was New Year's Eve, the way people on the radio were carrying on, shouting and singing themselves hoarse, blowing horns and whistles. Adele reveled in the happy racket while she iced a chocolate cake. President Truman had declared it V-E Day. The Germans had finally surrendered.

Thank God, Adele kept repeating to herself. Thank God. At least that half of it's over.

Chris came in from the yard.

"Boy, that smells good! What's cooking?"

"This and light bread and cinnamon rolls."

She gave him the spoon to lick.

"Mmm, mmm!"

"Where have you been?" she asked him.

"I rode over to see Jeanette. Did you know Werner can talk Sign language?"

"Oh?" she said, working at keeping a blank face. "What makes you say that?"

"Werner and her were talking Sign when I got there. I wonder why? Jeanette understands him good. She says he's easy to lip read 'cause he talks so careful."

"She and Werner," Adele corrected absently while she wondered how to handle Chris's discovery. She was already on edge, and the threat of a slip tied knots in her stomach. "I tell you what," she said. "Maybe it's supposed to be a surprise. Let's not mention it to anyone else."

"Okay," Chris said. "Anyway, I got to talk to Werner. Don't tell Daddy, though. I don't want to get him mad again."

"How is Werner?" Adele said, glad to change the conversation's direction.

"Okay. He said he's glad the war's over, but he seemed kind of sad."

"That's understandable. He worries a lot about his family. Here, you can have the bowl now. Did you ask Jeanette if she wants to go to the parade with us?"

"No, 'cause she said she was busy. She gave me some cookies and told me to come home."

"That's all right. We can check with her on our way to town. Your dad or Papa might want to go, too."

"I don't think Papa will. He has the POWs today. They're vaccinating cattle."

"What's your daddy doing?"

"He was seeding the back pasture. Do I have time to mow the yard before we go?"

"If you hurry. I guess you're going to want your allowance before we go to town."

"You betcha," he said. He planted a chocolatey kiss on her cheek and ran out.

She'd been tempted to tell him Werner's plans, but decided the less he knew, the better. That way, he wouldn't have anything to cover up. It was going to be hard enough for Papa and Jeanette and her to stay calm and keep the secret. She doubted that anyone would suspect Jeanette.

Adele tried not to think about the terrible consequences of what they were about to do, for fear she would lose her nerve. She was more afraid of Jacques' reaction than the government's. Time after time she racked her brain looking for flaws in their plan, anything that might incriminate them or jeopardize Werner.

Around one, when they got to Courville, street dancing had already started. Rowdy, exuberant people streamed in from every direction. The downtown had been roped off by police, and push-carts were doing a rapid business selling sno-balls and syrup pies, hot dogs and beer. The smell of popcorn wafted toward them from a glass walled wagon parked at the corner of Franklin and Main. Some of the more considerate merchants had set out chairs and boxes for the older people to rest on. Swaths of bunting, puffing in the breeze, scalloped the roofs with red, white and blue. Gustave Guilbeau's trio was on the bandstand, playing away, and Adele's foot automatically picked up the beat.

She let Chris run to meet his friends down at the end of Main Street where the coach from the high school was organizing sack races.

Nearly all the Junction people were there, more than on a Saturday night, when most of the farmers brought their families to town. Adele saw Father Sebastian, the Ardoins, the Fontenots and the Boudreaux sisters. Tee Broos waved to her from the barber shop. She spotted Hannah and Carl buying po-boy sandwiches for the kids, and steered Jeanette over to where they were.

"Can you believe it's finally over?" Hannah cried, hugging them happily.

Carl threw his arm around them, too, and when Adele said in his ear, "I'm so sorry about everything," he squeezed her, hard.

"Things are going to get better, now," he promised. "I miss those card games!"

Adele had to get out a clean handkerchief, her third for the day.

Mr. Ardoin came over to shake her hand and ask where Jacques was. If people only knew, Adele thought, how tired she was of making excuses.

"He was in the middle of something and couldn't get away," she said, knowing how lame the words sounded.

"Mais, that's too bad," Mr. Ardoin said. "He ought to be up there on the platform with them other veterans gettin' the glory. He done a whole lot more for victory than them fat-cat politicians, for sure."

A smiling Mayor Daigle stood up then and made a speech promising to do everything he could to help returning G.I.s.

"Every service man and woman from this fine community will get a certificate of honor personally signed by me," he said, "for they are indeed our most honored citizens. We celebrate today, but then we must redouble our efforts till the ones in the Pacific can come home, too."

The crowd cheered and clapped. Men whistled and threw their hats in the air. A small toothless woman wearing a sun bonnet sat on the Post Office steps and wept. Nearby, a cap pistol popped, making Adele jump. I must try that on Werner, she thought.

Sometime during the parade she became aware of a conversation going on behind her. Mr. Fontenot was shaking hands with some guards from the camp.

"When you boys fixin' to leave Courville?" she heard him ask them.

"Not till next month," one of them replied. "We'll start shutting her down the fifteenth, Captain Bentley says."

"What y'all going to do with the Germans?" Mr. Fontentot said. He moved to the curb to spit tobacco juice in a thin brown practiced arc.

"We have to take them back to the base camp first," the guard told him. "I don't know what happens after that. You know how the army is. Nobody tells you nothin' till they give you an order, and then they want it done day before yesterday."

"Sure wish you fellas would keep 'em here till after harvest. How're we supposed to cut and thresh all that rice we done planted, without no help?"

"I don't know, sir. You'd have to talk to the captain. Us guys, we just follow orders. I'm surprised they told us that much."

The band from Willow Grove High School passed by just then and drowned out the men's voices. Adele took Jeanette's arm and nodded toward the pickup.

"But the parade!" Jeanette protested. "It's not over!"

Adele frowned. "Hurry," she mouthed, moving her lips without making a sound. "I have to talk to you!"

At times like that she wished she'd learned Sign herself. She looked around for Chris and was satisfied that he was still with Coach Pellerin and the boys.

"Come on," she said.

The parking lot back of Ortigue's was empty, but they got in the pickup anyway, to make sure no one could overhear.

Jeanette was alarmed. "What's the matter?" she said.

"I didn't mean to scare you," Adele said, patting her hand, "but I had to talk to you before Chris came back. I heard the guard tell Mr. Fontenot they're closing Camp Courville on the fifteenth."

Jeanette made a choking sound.

"You have to tell Papa as soon as we get back," Adele went on, "and Werner, too, if he's still there. What's he doing this afternoon, do you know?"

"He's painting the kitchen for real. Papa said that way, if anybody looks, they won't get suspicious."

"Good idea," Adele said.

Jeanette was pale. Her bottom lip quivered when she spoke. "That means Werner has to leave soon, doesn't it?"

"I'm afraid so. But some day I hope he can come back."

"Then the war's not really over, is it?"

Adele sighed.

"I guess not. Not completely."

She had a mental picture of Jacques walking the levee, his right leg as stiff as the handle of his shovel. It won't ever be completely over, she realized, for some people.

"Adele," Jeanette said plaintively, "what's today? Tuesday the what?"

"The eighth. May the eighth."

Jeanette was trying not to cry.

"That's not much time," she said.

"I know. And I'll have to depend on you to warn Papa, in case there's anyone around when I take you home. Tell Papa Saturday will be best. Some of the soldiers will be off for the weekend and there'll be a lot of people on the street in New Orleans."

"This Saturday?"

"Right. We haven't any time to lose."

Jeanette nodded solemnly. "Saturday," she repeated.

Adele hated to have to say anything else, with Jeanette already so upset, but they couldn't take chances.

"Tell Werner to be extra careful. Chris saw him signing with you this morning. He didn't think anything of it, but someone else might."

"Can we go to the dime store before we go home?" Jeanette asked her. "I want to buy him a going away present."

"What kind of present?"

"He loves those blue bandannas like Papa uses. I don't know why, but he does. I want to get him one to keep."

"I think that's a lovely idea," Adele said. She didn't feel like going near Betty Hebert's office, though. "I tell you what, why don't you go on over to Woolworth's when the parade's over and I'll find Chris. Here's a quarter. Get a roll of caps while you're there."

"Caps?"

"For Chris's cap pistol. Meet us in front of Ortigue's and we'll have a banana split or something before we go home."

"I'm not very hungry," Jeanette said, and Adele's heart went out to her.

"I'm not, either, but we have to try to act normal for Werner's sake. We'd better put on smiles and get back before Chris or somebody starts wondering where we are."

They walked slowly back to the crowd and headed home as soon as they could decently tear Chris away. They stopped at St. Isidore's to light candles in thanksgiving, but every single votive light in the two wrought iron racks was already twinkling, the rows of red glasses aglow.

Adele genuflected and knelt in a back pew, but Jeanette went right up to the altar rail. Chris lasted a few minutes, then started to fidget.

"Can I wait outside, Mom?" he whispered.

She let him go, but even without the distraction of his wiggling, she couldn't pray. A calf somewhere was bawling and she could hear Jeanette mumbling. Dust motes traveled shafts of amber, crimson and blue light as the afternoon sun brushed the windows. Adele took out the mother-of-pearl rosary she carried in her purse, but even that didn't help. She couldn't get through a whole Hail Mary without thinking of Saturday and what would happen if Jacques found out. Doubts and fears washed over her in waves. She felt sure it would mean the end of their already foundering marriage.

"Please, please," she begged God silently. "Don't let anything go wrong."

Father Sebastian drove up as they were leaving and invited them to the rectory for tea.

"Some other time, Father," Adele told him. "Thanks, anyway. We're in kind of a hurry to get home, but could I ask you a favor?"

"You know you can. What's that?"

"Would you say a Mass for a special intention?"

"Any particular day?" the old priest asked.

"As soon as possible, please."

Chapter 29

When Saturday morning arrived, everything was working out fine. Papa came to get her as soon as the work details were assigned.

"I've got the rest of the crew choppin' weeds as far away from the house as possible," Papa told Adele. "Where's Jacques at?"

"He left right after Chris. He said he had to take care of something in town. How's Werner?"

"Scared."

"That makes two of us, Papa. Just a second and I'll be right with you."

She'd hidden the bus ticket in the big red leather family Bible. No one had paid any attention when she bought it a few days earlier, and anyone who knew her would simply think she was going to see her folks. They might have found it curious that she would leave from Acadia, but she could always have explained that it was cheaper.

Papa handed her his old billfold.

"Here. Put his ticket in there. I'd let him have the one I got for Christmas, but it don't do for him to look flashy."

There was twenty dollars inside.

"Jeanette put the rest of the cash in his suitcase," he said.

"Good. Do you think Werner can manage the money all right? I'm so afraid some little something will give him away."

"He does pretty good. Him and Jeanette, they done played

store enough. You 'bout ready?"

"I wonder if I should leave a note."

"Sayin' what?"

"I guess not. I'll be back in plenty of time to finish dinner by noon."

She took out the holy water jar she kept for emergencies, blessed herself and said, "Let's go."

It was a warm day, though overcast, so muggy the trees drooped and even the scolding of the bluejays was muted. The thick fragrance of magnolias and honeysuckle made the moist air heavier yet. Adele noticed Papa's shirt already had wet circles under the arms. Her dirndl skirt would be wrinkled in no time, not that she cared. It was comfortable to drive in, and the peasant blouse was cool.

Jeanette and Werner were watching for them. The change in Werner's appearance took Adele aback. Wearing Jacques' clothes, he might easily have been a senior at Courville High with nothing more serious on his mind than which girl to take to the prom.

"Doesn't he look wonderful?" Jeanette prodded.

"Mais, yeah," Papa said.

"You really do, Werner," Adele told him. "Turn around and let me see."

She made a critical inspection, checking every detail for natural-ness. Jeanette, bless her, had hemmed the pants. The clothes were just right, neat, but slightly worn. Inconspicuous.

Werner shuffled his feet, blushing under the scrutiny.

"Here," Papa said gruffly, taking the POW clothes from his hands. "Give me them things. Jeanette, what you did with that pa-per bag? Give me it and I'll burn trash when I get back."

They went over the plan together one last time. Werner kept swallowing, and Jeanette's handkerchief was twisted into rope. Papa looked out the window.

"...and whatever you do," Adele finished, "remember, you can't hear a thing."

She checked her watch.

"We'd better start," she said.

For a long moment they exchanged looks.

"Oh," Adele said, "I almost forgot."

She gave Werner a small piece of cardboard on which Jeanette had lettered I AM A DEAF MUTE.

"If you run into any questions, just show people this."

Werner shook her hand. He could hardly speak.

"Tell Chris I shall miss him."

"I will," she promised. "We'll miss you, too, but someday when all this is behind, who knows? Maybe we can be together again."

"Herr Viator," Werner said to Papa, "I don't know how…"

"Aw, go on, boy. Take care of yourself."

Jeanette started to cry.

"Auf wiedersehen, mein Freund," Werner told her gently. His eyes were glistening.

"Come on, now!" Papa said. "I want you to see what I rigged up for you to ride in."

An old refrigerator crate stood in the back of Papa's pickup truck.

"See?" he showed Werner, "I cut a door in the box on the cab side so you can get in and out easy. This way, can't nobody see you, and you can sit down."

"Papa, you're a genius," Adele said. "Let's get going, Werner. When we get to Acadia, don't come out till I give you the signal."

With one last nod he took the suitcase and disappeared inside the crate.

"Be careful, cher," Papa told Adele. "Hurry back. I don't like the looks of the sky, non. The air smells like a storm coming."

Papa's truck was easy to drive, and Saturday mornings, traffic in the country was light. Old Mr. Ardoin passed and waved. The dust in his wake settled quietly on the blackberry brambles and Burma Shave signs lining the road.

Adele maneuvered the ruts and took the bumps as easily as she could, and checked the rear view mirror often. So far, so good. She tried to get some music on the radio, but there was too much static. The static reminded her of the weather. She hated to think of more rain so soon, but maybe it would be a blessing. It might slow down the soldiers' search for Werner. That they would question and search she had no doubt. She tried to prepare herself for that.

Approaching town, she drove slowly. The Acadia police were famous for giving tickets to outsiders, and she certainly couldn't afford any souvenirs of her visit.

Main Street was only six blocks long. She parked at the far end, in front of a dentist's office that wasn't open on weekends.

They were a little early. Adele powdered her nose and put on lipstick, studying their surroundings in the rear view mirror. Her hand shook a little, causing her lipstick to go outside the line and smear. She fished for a tissue to repair the damage. Satisfied that from all sides no one was looking, she kicked the panel under her seat three times and got out.

She brushed at the wrinkles in her skirt and started walking toward town, wondering if anybody would be suspicious. Once again she racked her brain to think of anything they might have overlooked. She made up speeches in case Captain Bentley called her in for questioning. The pounding of her heart felt louder than her footsteps.

Acadia looked Saturday morning sleepy, off to a slow start, and Adele was glad of that. She felt as if there were a million eyes on them as it was, although hardly anyone was out that early. At the Handy Hardware Store she paused and acted like she was considering the set of ivy garlanded dishes on display. Out of the corner of her eye she could see Werner coming a half block behind on the other side of the street, Jeanette's old suitcase in his left hand.

Slowly they made their way to the center of town, with Adele stopping every little way to assure herself all was well. The smell of bacon from the Downtown Café reminded her she hadn't eaten breakfast. She hoped Werner had. He needed his strength. She'd been too nervous for anything but coffee.

The department store wasn't open yet. Adele stood in front of it, pretending to window shop. She could see Werner, reflected in the plate glass, put his suitcase on the curb in front of the bus station, directly across. Everything was going just right. Now if only the bus would be on time.

But it wasn't. Adele tapped her watch and listened, to make sure it was ticking. The manager inside the department store thought she was waiting to get in and came to unlock the door, but she told him she was just looking. She tried to appear interested in a jewelry display that revolved fitfully. A Grapette truck came to deliver soda pop to the café. The elderly postman making his way along the street tipped his hat to her and wiped his forehead with a rumpled handkerchief. Above the pink groove left by the hat his skin was pale and smooth. Adele smiled back at him and stepped aside to let two little girls in matching sundresses skip by.

When she looked again, some other passengers had joined Werner; a sailor and an ancient looking colored woman in runover shoes. The woman clutched a bedraggled shopping bag and a big red pocketbook as if she expected someone might snatch them from her any moment. Neither newcomer paid a bit of attention to Werner. The ticket agent came out with a dolly and deposited a stack of freight alongside the baggage on the sidewalk.

Adele was looking at her watch again when she heard her name.

"Adele! What are you doing here?"

"Aunt Geneva! How are you?" Of all people to run into, Hannah's Aunt Geneva. Adele kissed the tiny gray-haired lady on the cheek, trying to act nonchalant.

"I just made a quick trip over to get some material. They didn't have what I want in Courville."

"Have you tried Levine's?"

"Not yet. I thought I'd go here, first."

"Well, if you don't find what you want, you might try over there. Tell me, how's that handsome Jacques, and how is Hannah's bunch? I haven't seen them in ages."

"They're all fine. Working, of course. You know how it is, this time of year."

"Did Carl get his cast off?"

"I think he has another week to go. It's about to drive him crazy."

"Well, if you ask me, he's lucky that's all he broke, a grown man like him climbing trees!"

"I guess you're right."

Adele had to think of some way to get loose. Hannah's aunt had always reminded her of a parakeet hopping furtively around, not missing a thing. Adele didn't want her to linger there, across the street from the Greyhound bus station. She steered Aunt Geneva to a showcase in the foyer so their backs were turned to Werner, and pointed to a hat.

"See that pretty lavender pillbox with the satin piping? I need a new hat for church and I've been wanting one with a veil ever since I saw Bette Davis in 'Now Voyager'. Wasn't she gorgeous?"

"I don't know. Walter and I, we don't go to the show much. But I like the big straw with the daisies better, that one over there. You could get by with it, too, honey. I'd look like a toadstool. Why don't you go in and try them on?"

Just then the bus pulled up in front of the station. Adele smelled the exhaust and heard the doors suck open.

"I'd better not, Aunt Geneva," she said. "I need to see about the fabric and get home. Chris's pajamas are clear up to his knees."

"Well, let me get going, then. I'm on my way to the fish market. Walter's hungry for red snapper. Me, I'd rather have catfish, but not Walter. You know how men are."

"Tell Uncle Walter hello for me. Next time you two are at Hannah's, get her to bring you over."

"Why don't you pass at the house before you go home and have a cup of coffee?"

"Thanks, Aunt Geneva, but I really have to get back. I left a pot of red beans on the stove."

While she spoke, the bus pulled away from the curb and turned at the corner, leaving only a ragged shoeshine boy in front of the station.

Weak with relief, Adele ducked quickly into the store and located the fabric department. She handed a bolt of striped cotton, the first thing she picked up, to the sales girl.

"A yard and a half, please," she said.

While the girl measured the yardage, Adele dashed to the rest room and stood there, shaking. To regain her composure, she ran cold water over her wrists and dabbed some on her flushed cheeks. He's on his way, she kept thinking. We've done it! Her knees were shaking. You've got to act normal, she told herself. Don't mess things up now!

It was a long walk back to the pickup and an even longer drive home. She said the rosary prayers out loud, but couldn't keep her mind on the mysteries.

Even with the windows open, she was hot in the truck. Her blouse stuck to the seat and she could feel a rivulet of perspiration trickle between her breasts to her navel.

Papa was waiting by the roadside in front of his house. She pulled over and slid to the passenger side.

"How'd it go?" he asked anxiously, climbing in.

"All right," she told him. "He's on his way."

"Bon," Papa said and put the truck into gear. "I'll tell Jeanette as soon as I take you home. She's been boo-hooin' her eyes out all morning. You'd best get back quick. For sure we're in for a storm!"

"I hope we did the right thing, Papa. I sure am scared."

"The boy deserved a chance, cher. I just hope he don't get caught, nor us, neither!"

Chapter 30

All the way to town Jacques practiced a speech. He was anxious to get it over with before he got cold feet again. If only Betty would see that it was best for them both. If only they hadn't let themselves get carried away. If only. They should have known it wouldn't be any good. He'd miss her, he knew, and he wished there were some way they could stay friends, but he guessed it was too late for that. She had her life ahead of her, and he had to figure out some way to patch his.

The insurance office was closed and her car wasn't at the apartment. Nuts! He went up anyway. He decided to wait fifteen minutes. If she wasn't back by then, he'd leave a note. Maybe that would be best, anyhow, he thought and immediately rebuked himself for being a coward.

From the east window he could see a little girl desultorily jumping rope in the yard next door. Her pigtails swatted her shoulders with each stroke. The landlady's laundry hung on the line, limp as noodles. Damn, it was muggy out. He got himself a glass of iced tea.

The kitchen faucet dripped. He looked in the toolbox for a washer and fixed it, glad to have something to use up the time. Every few minutes he checked his watch. A note would have to do. He didn't like the idea of putting anything in writing, but what the hell. A man did what he had to do.

In the middle desk drawer he found some insurance agency

stationery. He looked around for a pen. Betty usually kept some handy to work the crossword puzzles in the Picayune. Damnedest thing he'd ever seen, the way she could zip through those things without an erasure.

He was still looking for something to write with when he noticed Betty's appointment book lying open. On Saturday's page she'd posted the words, 'Dr. Del - 8:30'. He stared at the flowery turquoise script, baffled. She'd looked okay Wednesday. Maybe she was getting that mole on the back of her neck taken off. It bothered her sometimes, when she brushed her hair.

He frowned, then hunted some more for a pen. The one he found turned out to be empty, so he had to get the ink bottle and fill it, and by that time his palms were sweaty.

"Just say what you have to say and get the hell out of here," he muttered.

He didn't want her to think it was her fault. He scratched away, one, two, three pages. When he finished, he read it over once, stuck it in an envelope and sealed the flap. He wrote her name and propped the envelope between some books where she'd be sure to see it. He was getting her key from his billfold, about to leave, when he heard her on the steps.

"Well, hi," she said. "Life's little surprises. What brings you to town on a big Saturday morning?"

She kicked off her shoes.

"Want some coffee? It won't take a minute."

"I'd better not. I've got to get back as soon as I get some medicine from Doc Harvey for one of the cows."

"Oh," she said, the disappointment showing. She tamped a cigarette on a silver case and offered it to him.

"Speaking of Docs, are you all right?"

"Sure, don't I look it?"

"I thought you went to see Dr. Del."

"Who told you about that?"

"I saw it on your date book."

"Oh," she said again, with a funny look on her face.

"You sure you're all right?"

"Yes," she answered, "but you might not be."

She took a deep drag off her cigarette.

"I think I'm pregnant."

"Oh, god! No!" It was like being hit by artillery again. His knees buckled so badly he had to hold onto a chair. "I thought we were careful! What do you mean, you think?"

"Dr. Del says it's too soon to tell for sure. I took the rabbit test, but we won't know till next week."

Jacques groaned. "Oh, god, Betty, I'm sorry! I ought to be shot!"

"Don't be that way!" she said, her eyes bright with excitement. "I wasn't going to tell you till I found out for sure, but just think, Jacques, our very own child! Wouldn't that be wonderful?"

"Wonderful? What are you saying?"

She blanched.

"I know it's a shock," she said, getting control, "but it can be worked out. I've had time to think, you haven't. There are several possibilities."

"Such as?" he said in a daze.

"I could go off somewhere where nobody knows me and say my husband got killed in the war, which is true. People wouldn't ask questions. I have Armand's insurance money put away. I could live off that."

He couldn't believe this was happening.

"Or I could go to my folks. I think they'd be all right once they got used to the idea. They always wanted a grandchild."

Jacques stared at her, speechless.

"Or..." she said softly, "You could get a divorce and make an honest woman out of me." It was like he was paralyzed, frozen. Betty didn't say any more, either, after that.

Thunder rumbled in the distance. The sky had taken on a yellowish, malignant cast.

"Listen, Betty," he said urgently. "I've got to get home. Give me a chance to think, and for god's sake, please don't do anything rash, okay?"

"Don't leave," she said plaintively.

"I shouldn't have stayed this long. We're in for some rough weather, I can feel it."

"Dr. Del said a hurricane hit Bermuda two days ago. You don't suppose it's coming here?"

"Oh, shit! It's probably been out there building up in the Gulf. Listen, Betty, I've really got to go, but what are you going to do? You can't stay here. It's not safe."

"Don't worry. I always go to my sister-in-law's when it storms.

I help her keep the kids calmed down."

"Okay, but don't wait too long. And don't say anything about the baby, whatever you do! I'll see you as soon as I can. We'll figure out something."

Just then a gust of wind blew the door open and sent the newspaper on the coffee table flying all over the place. While Betty bent to pick it up, Jacques retrieved the letter he had written and stuck it in his pocket. He hesitated in the doorway.

"You haven't told anyone else, have you?"

"No," she said, shaking her head. "Don't worry, our secret's safe."

"I'm really sorry," he told her helplessly.

"I'm not," Betty said. "Go on, Jacques, and be careful."

By now the wind was making the smaller trees flap as if they were on springs. Low thunderclouds gathered. Squawking birds zigzagged beneath them, spreading the alert. The wind parted the bright green rice fields like some great comb. Jacques had to keep a firm grip on the steering wheel to hold the truck on the road.

Adele ran out to meet him, grabbing at the skirt that billowed around her like a parachute.

"Carl called," she told him breathlessly. "He said to tell you they think it's a hurricane!"

"I know. Where's Chris?"

"He went fishing about two hours ago. He's not back yet."

Chris rounded the corner, his pole over his shoulder and a disgusted look on his face.

"Oh, there he is!"

"Nothing's biting in this mess," he grumbled.

"Hurry up and put away your tackle," Jacques told him. "We've got to get the animals to high ground and see about the house."

"It's a hurricane," Adele explained to the bewildered boy. "We don't know how bad."

"Wow!" said Chris. "What to do first, Daddy?"

"Get all the loose stuff hanging around and put it in the barn or the tool shed, anything the wind can sail through a window. We don't want any flying glass."

While he was talking, a pot of geraniums tipped over and broke.

"See what I mean? Adele, get the damn flowerpots in the house! Chris, when you're finished, round up all the lumber you can find and I'll be back to help you board up."

Adele had gone to get Chris's wagon and was already gathering up the plants.

"I'm sorry I yelled at you," Jacques said.

She gave him a look that made him even more sheepish.

"You know what needs to be done," he told her. "You'd better draw as much water as you can, in case the power goes off and we can't use the electric pump. We might have to water the yard animals, too, if the salt water backs up."

"All right, Jacques."

She had to put up a hand to keep her hair out of her eyes.

"Do we have kerosene?" Jacques asked.

"Yes. I'll get the lanterns out. There's a flashlight in the truck."

"Right. Keep an eye on Chris. I'll see about the equipment and move the cattle. Call Papa, will you, and find out if things are under control there?"

He got his hip boots and slicker and headed for the west pasture as fast as he could. The first rain hit his windshield in a fine spray. He had to get some rope and tie open the pasture gate. It would have ripped off its hinges if he hadn't. The cows were restless and suspicious. Their leader took a while to convince. Jacques wished he'd brought Chris and Caspar along to help count and corral them. It was a job, working alone.

"Come on, you stupid animals!" he yelled. "Do you want to stay here and drown? You won't have anything to graze on when this is under water! Come on, Bossy...move it! This way!"

Every time a clap of thunder growled, they stalled. The calves howled for their mamas. It was pandemonium. If he'd counted right, there were two missing. He fastened the gate and went looking but realized he wouldn't have time to do that and move the other herd. Damn, he wished he'd started sooner. If only there'd been some warning!

The sky was getting dark as sundown. The wind slapped his coattails, and the rain was starting to come down in earnest. He wished to God he'd taken care of the house first, even if it meant losing some cattle. There wasn't anything he could do about the rice, but he could have protected the house.

The second herd was going to be even harder to manage, with the ground already soggy and getting sloppier by the minute. To compound things, Jacques' bad leg was aching. In his rush he'd twisted it, and it was slowing him down.

Papa met him on the road and waved him over.

"I brought you some hands," he yelled. "For cryin' out loud, let 'em help you. Damn storm's comin' fast, yeah!"

Four faces peered from oilskin panchos in the back of Papa's truck. Jacques hesitated, his mind churning.

"They SURRENDERED, son. Take 'em. We're wastin' time!"

Not far away a pine tree doubled over, cracked in half.

"Get in!" Jacques said, motioning to the men. "Do any of you speak English?"

"I do," the tallest one answered.

"What's your name?" said Jacques.

"Johann."

"Then you get in front," Jacques ordered. "I'll explain what we need to do."

Chapter 31

'Something's happened to Papa,' was the first thing Adele thought when she saw the POWs with Jacques.

"Mama, look!" Chris cried out. "Look at Daddy!"

She and Chris were trying to board up the side windows. They stared in amazement. The wind jerked the piece of plywood out of her hand and blew rain in her eyes.

On the back porch Caspar barked and clawed at the screen, clamoring to get out.

Jacques came straight over and took her by the shoulders.

"Are you okay?"

Still in shock, she responded, "Yes, are you? Is Papa all right?"

He gave a quick nod and took the hammer from her hand.

"Here, give me that. It's going to be a bitch. You go on inside and get dry. Chris, bring the ladder over here!"

Jacques pointed to the round faced man. "You! Help the boy. Johann, quick, in the truck, the tool chest. Bring the hammers. You there! Take some of those boards to the next window and nail them like so, see?"

The men struggled to respond, though every move was a contest against the steadily increasing force of the elements.

Inside, toweling her hair, Adele could barely hear them hollering and hammering, the wind and rain made so much noise. A branch rattled overhead. Thank goodness, she thought, we don't have a tin roof. She hated to be at Jacques' Aunt Philomene's house in a storm, where the rain sounded like machine gun fire.

She went to the buffet to get the holy candle, praying as she lit it, and set it in a shallow dish of water on the dining room table.

The men would be hungry. She hurried to cook extra rice, added more smoked sausage to the beans and opened another jar of pickled beets. She was glad she'd done the baking yesterday, to keep from stewing over Werner. She wondered how far away he was now, and if he'd eaten the lunch Jeanette packed for him. The storm had eclipsed the morning's events, but even so she remembered to send up prayers for Werner every few minutes.

She simply couldn't believe the POWs were out there working alongside Jacques. Periodically, she tried to call Papa to see how it had come about and what was going on at the other farm, but the phone was dead. You might know, she said to herself. The least little sprinkle and service was liable to go out. Edna June, the telephone operator, was scared of lightning.

The electricity flickered but came back on. Adele wasn't worried. The kerosene lanterns were cleaned and filled, lined up on the dining room table. As Chris and the men boarded up the other windows, the house got darker and darker, so she turned on the rest of the lights. They might as well use them as long as they could.

Surely the men were almost finished. She fetched a stack of towels from the hall closet to have ready on the back porch. Caspar was on his hind legs, scratching the screen door, continuing to bark.

"Hush, boy," she said, patting his head. "Calm down, and I'll give you some sausage. Chris'll be in, in a minute."

By now she could scarcely see as far as the clothes line, but she caught a glimpse of two figures coming from the barn, leaning against the wind. The first man stumbled. The other helped him up. Rain was coming in curtains and she couldn't make out through the blur whether or not one of them was Jacques.

Just then the screen door flew open, straining the hinges, and Jacques was there, pushing Chris inside.

"Look after him, Adele," he shouted. "I'll be back as soon as I put the truck away. We've done as much as we can!"

She watched the tail lights disappear behind a waterfall, drowning red glimmers swiftly washed away.

A puddle as big as a throw rug spread out where Chris was standing, but he was hugging Caspar and didn't notice.

"You're safe!" he said. "I kept hearing you, but I didn't know where you were."

"Hurry, son," Adele told him. "Strip down to your shorts and run get dried out. I put some clothes on your bed."

The lights blinked, went off and stayed off this time.

Adele lit the lanterns, putting one or two in every room. The house had become as dark as if it were night instead of mid-afternoon. The holy candle burning in its moat made shadow tongues that licked the walls.

By the time Jacques hustled the POWs inside he had to struggle to fasten the screen door. Several times the wind took it clear out of his hands, causing it to bang madly against the house.

Adele helped the men out of their slickers and handed out towels, watching Jacques carefully as she did. Caspar ran between the men's legs, sniffing. One of the Germans said something about "der Hund" and two others laughed. To Adele's amazement, Jacques didn't seem to mind. He peeled off his sopping undershirt.

"Chris, show them where to wash up," he said. "Johann, y'all go with Chris."

"It looks like we're stuck with them," Jacques mumbled brusquely to Adele as he went past, adding, "till the storm's over."

When the men came back, they stood around in the kitchen looking awkward. All but Rolf, expressionless as usual, seemed shy, and Adele realized it must have been a long time since they'd been in a home.

"I know who you and Rolf are, Johann, but tell us the others' names."

"This is Claus," Johann said, of the man next to him, and pointing to the one with the big ears and the Jack-o-lantern smile, "That's Kurt."

"My best friend's named Kurt!" Chris said. "Kurt Kaufmann. How about that? He lives right over there, on the next farm."

Adele looked to see Jacques' reaction, but he was oblivious, tuned only to the storm.

Claus's fine brown hair had been neatly combed, and despite the wet yellow-stenciled fatigues, he gave the impression of being well groomed. He was scarcely an inch taller than she was, but the way he held himself made him seem taller. Johann, on the other hand, looked the way Adele pictured Germans: tall, blonde, with high cheekbones and Delft-blue eyes.

"You're the one who repaired the magneto, aren't you?" she

said to him. "We're much obliged."

"It was a pleasure, Frau Viator. I miss my work."

They were still standing around, waiting for Jacques to give orders.

"Help me pull out the table, Jacques," Adele said, breaking the heavy pause. She got them to sit down and filled their plates. Johann and Kurt bowed their heads awkwardly while Chris said grace. Adele noticed that Claus made the sign of the cross, too.

"There's plenty of food," she assured them. "Take as much as you want." As soon as the words were out she glanced at Jacques, but he wasn't paying any attention. He looked preoccupied, worried about storm damage, probably.

Indicating the rain whipping the house, Johann asked, "How long will it last?"

Adele had to nudge Jacques.

"Johann wants to know how long it will last."

"Huh? Oh, hours, depending on how big it is and how fast it's traveling. If we're close to the eye, it'll get a lot worse than this. Nothing to do now but wait."

Adele sliced another loaf of bread and opened a pint of strawberry jam. The POWs were noticeably hungry, and they all took second helpings. They must have been on really short rations, she thought, ever since the concentration camps were discovered. She didn't like to think about the atrocities. Those gruesome faces at Buchenwald haunted her. How could men like these have let such things happen?

She'd asked Father Sebastian that, once.

"Look at history, cher," he'd said. "Look at the crusades, and us and our lynchings."

She didn't like to think about those, either.

"Did you get the cattle moved?" she asked Jacques, hoping to make conversation.

"Most of them. We never did find two of the calves."

"Will the rest of the herd be all right?"

"I hope so. If the fences hold. I should have put up some new ones."

He nodded perfunctorily at the Germans. "They helped me shore up some weak spots."

He lit a cigarette and she saw him hesitate. Then he passed around the pack of Camels and threw it on the table with some kitchen matches.

"Help yourselves," he said curtly.

A prolonged thunderclap shook the house. Chris jumped.

"It sounds like the belch of a great giant, does it not?" Johann said. "In your school do you read the stories of our Brothers Grimm?"

Jacques went back out on the porch to watch the storm. Adele noticed Rolf's eyes following Jacques. Rolf made her uneasy. The others rose and helped her clean up the kitchen. Rolf only did what he was told. Afterwards, Adele led the POWs to the living room.

"You might as well make yourselves comfortable," she said. She pointed to the magazine rack and adjusted the wicks of the kerosene lamps to make them brighter.

Claus began fiddling with the jigsaw puzzle Chris had left half finished on the card table, a garish mosaic of the Grand Canyon with a thousand brown, orange, pink and blue pieces.

"Is it all right if I put?" Claus asked Chris.

"Sure," Chris said, and Claus pulled a chair up to the table.

"Good luck," Adele said with a smile. "Chris has been trying to get me to do the sky. Did you ever see so many pieces that look just alike?"

Claus didn't understand what she said, and Johann had to translate.

Kurt thumbed a Saturday Evening Post, and Chris recruited Johann to help sand the wings of a model B-29. Adele offered Rolf a magazine, but he shook his head scornfully.

"Don't mind him," Johann said. "Rolf thinks we should not fraternize."

Satisfied that everyone was settled, Adele went to see about Jacques.

He stood in the same spot, watching and smoking. Above them, water poured off the roof in a continuous stream. Sheets of rain marched past, one after another. Spray bathed the screened porch in gusts.

"Did you call Papa?" Jacques asked her.

They had to shout to be heard over the storm's roar.

"The phone's dead," she yelled back.

Lightning split open the sky for a moment, giving a glimpse of frenzied trees slashing wildly about. It reminded Adele of a scene from one of those South Sea island movies, except there weren't any volcanoes here. She gasped, and Jacques put his arm around her.

"That field I planted this week is going to wash out," he shouted.

"I know. At least you got the barn roof fixed."

The storm seemed to swallow their words.

"Let's go in," Adele shouted, clutching Jacques' arm, "before you get soaked again and catch cold."

After they dried off, he checked all the windows and came back to the kitchen where he could see through the back door. He got out the whetstone to begin sharpening her knives, something she'd asked him over a week ago to do. She thought he'd forgotten. From time to time, when Chris's voice and the sharp guttural sounds from the living room occasionally overrode the noise, Jacques would stop filing and listen to their conversation. His expression remained serious, but it seemed more thoughtful than harsh. More than once Adele caught him looking at her strangely.

To have something to do, she popped corn to pass around. The living room, on the back side of the wind, was quieter than the kitchen. Adele found Kurt asleep in the easy chair, snoring with a little whistle, his lower lip quivering loosely. Rolf's eyes were closed, but he seemed alert, even in repose. Claus and Johann acted skeptical about the popcorn, though they thanked her politely. She told them not to stand every time she came in the room, but they did it anyway.

While she was scrubbing the pot the storm died out like a wild stallion abruptly tamed. The POWs came looking for Jacques.

"We go back now?" Johann the spokesman said.

"Oh, no," Jacques told them. "It's the eye of the storm, very dangerous. There's more to come."

They didn't understand.

"Is not over?"

"Hurricanes are tricky," Jacques said. He took a memo pad and drew a rough diagram to illustrate. "They move in a kind of a circle, see, and right now we're in the middle. A lot of people get killed thinking it's safe to go out. Then the second half hits, and wham!"

Frowning, the Germans said, "Ach..."

Jacques said, "We have to sit tight and pray the damn thing doesn't set off some twisters."

"Twisters?" Johann said. "Sit tight?"

"Stay put," Jacques explained. "Tornadoes," he said, and drew a funnel. "There's nothing to do but wait."

"Oh," said Johann, comprehending. He explained in rapid German to his companions who nodded and shrugged.

Kurt took a battered deck of cards from his shirt pocket and said something to Johann.

"Kurt says perhaps we teach you to play Skat, a game we Germans enjoy. You like?"

Adele looked questioningly at Jacques.

"You go ahead," he said. "I can't sit still."

Chris caught on to the game faster than she did. She had difficulty keeping her mind on the cards. Watching Kurt deal she looked across the dining room table at the clock on the buffet and thought of Werner with a pang. If all went well, he was with his relatives now. Please, God, she prayed silently.

Jacques pulled a chair beside her and straddled it. After only a few minutes, however, he was back pacing the floor. The others, engrossed in the game, didn't seem to notice, but she saw the way he would pause every so often, rubbing his jaw, to study the Germans.

The score was close. Then, in the middle of a decisive hand, a crash of glass brought them jumping to their feet. A living room window had blown in where the hastily hammered boards had come loose. Through the jagged opening, in the next illumination of lightning, Adele saw that the pear tree in the front yard was toppled completely over, roots and all, as though it had meant to do a cartwheel. She ran to get the oilcloth from the kitchen table for Jacques to nail over the hole.

"Move the furniture to the side," Jacques directed the men. Chris helped her pick up the shards of glass and put down rags. A dark stain ran down the wallpaper, and in no time the rags were saturated. Adele went for a bucket, and Kurt took over wringing. She kept an anxious eye on the window nearest her piano. The panes in the dining room were buckling from the pressure of the wind. Jacques and Johann up-ended the table to deflect the glass in case it shattered.

The storm didn't begin to wear itself out till late that evening. Adele barely noticed the thunder diminishing to a distant rumble, but some time after supper she became aware of hearing ordinary sounds again. Rain was still falling, but dully now, its passion spent.

"There won't be a thing any of us can do till daylight," Jacques told Johann.

"They can have my room," offered Chris. "I can sleep on the floor."

"Oh no," Johann protested. "We already impose."

"It's okay," Jacques said. "Get the rollaway and make it up for them, will you, Adele? I'm going to hit the sack."

She expected him to be sleeping when she got to bed. Instead, she felt him stroke her hair, and she got under the covers silently, afraid to break the spell. He took her in his arms and held her, just held her, until finally fatigue and the drone of rain put her to sleep.

Chapter 32

As soon as daylight came, Jacques prepared to assess the damage.

"Go ahead and feed the men breakfast," he said to Adele, "and I'll be back for them as soon as I see what's what."

The way her eyes followed him while he dressed, he felt more naked instead of less. He would have liked to have kissed her good-bye, but it didn't seem right after the Betty business. It hurt him to see how scared of him Adele and Chris had become, made him feel like a monster. A fifty pound weight had parked itself inside his chest, a lump the size of a grapefruit in his throat. What was he going to do about Betty?

He hated to admit it, but the Germans weren't such bad guys after all. These last twenty-four hours had got his head spinning. 'Where the hell do we go from here?' he thought. For now the farm demanded attention, which was just as well. Worrying about Adele and Betty was driving him nuts.

The water had begun to drain off the yard except in a few low spots, but the ground was like a soaked sponge. The squish of his footsteps caused a flock of sparrows to skitter. They were reconnoitering, too.

Caspar ran ahead, poking and sniffing, pausing every so often to give himself a shake. The chickens, the animals, everything seemed more animated in the pure, thin, after-storm air.

The yard was a mess, though. You couldn't go two feet without stepping on branches and debris. Jacques sloshed his way slowly around the house appraising the damage. There were shingles missing from the roof, and a shutter on the west side was gone, but nothing had fallen on the house, and the place had held up pretty well considering the beating it took. The wind must have climbed to eighty miles at least. With a gale like that, they were lucky only a window had give way.

Jacques spotted the lid to the cistern way back in the barn lot.

"Shit!" There was no telling what might have landed in their reserve water supply.

He primed the old pump and cranked it till he worked up a sweat and the troughs for the yard animals were filled. It was going to be a damn nuisance, having to pump and haul water in all that mud. He wondered how long it would take the electric company to get things fixed. No telling.

Making his way back to the house, Jacques tripped over a hole in the driveway.

"Great!" he mumbled, nursing his wrenched leg.

He stuck his head in the back door and yelled, "Adele?"

"Yes?" she called back.

"It's okay for Chris to go milk. Just tell him not to touch any downed wires, whatever he does. And get him to gather the eggs for you. I don't want you out here yet. I'm going to check the fields."

It didn't take long to see what sorry shape the vegetable garden was in. The plants standing in low water looked as if they'd been stepped on. Only time would tell how many would recover. In the corn field you couldn't even determine where the rows were, the young stalks were so tangled and torn.

Still worse, he could see where the levees in the rice fields had washed out, making the water low on one side and high on the other. God only knew what the fields close to the bayou would be like.

It's a good thing we got the cattle moved, Jacques thought. He wondered how much fence damage there was. Considering the state of the posts and the force of the wind, he wasn't optimistic. These pastures sure wouldn't be any good for grazing for a while.

While Jacques was surveying the damage, Papa's truck crept toward him, easing cautiously under a snapped utility pole that dangled by wire threads. The truck barely moved, yet water splashed up to the door handle on either side. Jacques worked his way to the road.

"Made it!" Papa said. He wiped his face. He hadn't shaved and his eyes were bloodshot.

He looks haggard, Jacques realized, and felt a twinge of guilt.

"Is Jeanette all right?" he asked.

It was always his first question. He felt ashamed for avoiding her. She shouldn't have to pay for his problems.

"Yeah," Papa said. "How 'bout y'all?"

"We're okay. Nobody hurt. Did you stop at Carl's?"

"Oui, they high and dry. Carl, he lost part of his barn and his hay got wet, but they wasn't much left from the winter. Good thing."

"Damn, Papa, I thought we were going to blow away!"

"And me! You know that barometer thing of Max's? Carl said that sucker like to fell out the bottom."

"It was a hell of a storm, all right. I didn't expect one this early."

"Never can tell about them hurricanes. Joe Daigle claims it's all them bombs that's messin' up the weather."

"Could be," Jacques said with a shrug. "How are your fields? Don't you want to come to the house? Adele's fixing breakfast."

Papa shook his head, scratching his grizzled stubble.

"Better not. You want me to take Johann and them back with me?"

Jacques looked at the ground and swallowed hard.

"Not unless you need them. I can use the help."

"Naw, you keep 'em. They can't get back to camp, no how. Bridge is washed out. The guards don't act worried, them. We gave 'em your old room, and they like Jeanette's cookin'."

Jacques smiled.

"I'll bet. Tell sis I said hi. I'll try to get over later today."

When he got back, Chris and the Germans had nailed up the broken window and taken the boards off the others. Kurt and Johann were trying to right the pear tree. Claus was at the pump, cleaning the cistern lid.

"Be with you in a minute," Jacques told them.

Adele had kept his breakfast warm on the stove.

"Sorry to track up your kitchen," he said, taking the plate and eating quickly.

"Don't worry about that," she said.

Between bites, Jacques said, "I ran into Papa. He said to let the POWs stay and help."

"On Sunday?"

"He can't take them back, anyway. The bridge is out. You'd

better cook extra."

"All right. I was going to see if you could spare the truck long enough for us to go to Mass."

"I could, but you can't get through. Sorry, hon."

The endearment slipped out, taking them both by surprise. Like a fool, he felt himself blush. He avoided her eyes.

"Be careful," she said softly as he turned to leave. "Oh, Jacques, by the way. I told Johann to explain to the others about watching out for live wires, but maybe you ought to caution them again."

"Right," he said. "I'm taking Chris, too, okay?"

"Okay."

They filled their canteens, got the extra shovels and headed for the fields. Jacques showed the Germans how high he wanted the levees and how to pack the mud so it would hold up.

"Ja," they assured him, "Ja, Herr Viator," and went right to it.

The mud sucked at their boots, and the foreigners were amused that their feet kept slipping out from under them. Jacques had to laugh, himself, when Kurt broke out singing a barely recognizable version of "Don't Fence Me In". Sarge would have loved it. The men got the knack quickly, so Jacques left them repairing levees while he and Chris went to check the cattle.

He saw why Papa was driving so slowly. The water was deeper than he expected. His brakes got wet and he had to nurse the truck back to the house.

"What do you say we try that new pirogue of yours?" he said to Chris.

"Sure thing!" Chris said, and ran to get his paddle.

They waded through the pasture to the bayou. The sun was up over the trees now, glinting off the wet fields so brightly it made you blink. A squirrel the color of acorns was doing acrobatics in the trees.

"Shucks," Chris said, "I wish I'd brought my b-b-gun."

"That's all your mother would need, for us to bring home something to clean."

Jacques had his pistol along, just in case. With the high water, snakes were likely to be bad.

A plane passed over, and they tried to spot its markings, but the sun was too bright.

"Sounds like a Piper Cub," Chris said. "When I get big I'm going to join the Civil Air Patrol."

"Yeah?"

It struck Jacques there was a lot about his son he didn't know.

The bayou was up over the bank, full of leaves and branches roiling in the muddy waters. Nevertheless, they found Chris's pirogue undamaged. It bobbed securely under a cypress sapling.

"You must have done a good job tying it," Jacques said.

Chris beamed. "It's a good little boat. You get in. I'll hold her steady."

Jacques wished in passing he could swing his leg over the side the way Chris did. Damn, he hated having to move like an old man.

Chris untied the rope and shoved off, using his paddle to push against the cypress. The current was pretty swift from all the run-off. Jacques wondered how many inches of rain had fallen. A bunch, that's for sure.

Chris maneuvered skillfully past some stumps, pausing periodically to shake loose twigs and leaves that stuck to his paddle.

They came alongside the acreage Jacques had planted last and it wasn't as bad off as Jacques had expected. A stand of live oaks had probably taken the brunt of the storm. Most of the levees had held firm. He was glad he'd gone over them some extra times with the tractor.

"Pull up right here, son! There's a break. See it? That levee over there."

Chris grabbed hold of a muscadine vine and pulled the pirogue onto land.

"Give me the shovel," Jacques said. "You hold the pistol. But for God's sake, be careful. Make sure the safety's on."

By the time they'd repaired the levee, steam was rising from the fields and their shirts were sticking to them. The work wouldn't have been so bad if they'd had solid ground to stand on, but they had to stop all the time to scrape the shovels and knock the mud off their boots so they could move.

South of there, by the pond, the cattle were grazing. Jacques thought they were all there, but he couldn't tell for sure.

"Let's go a little farther before we turn back," he said. "You tired? Want me to paddle?"

"No, sir. I'm fine. Here's your gun."

Jacques leaned back and smoked a cigarette. The boy had good arms. A rainbow-winged mosquito hawk skimmed past, adding ripples to the current. The smell of wet manure was strong in the warm air.

Jacques studied his son.

"School will be out soon, won't it?" he said to start a conversation.

"Yes, sir. Two more weeks."

He's scared to talk to me, Jacques realized with a pang. He only speaks when I speak to him first.

"You doing okay in arithmetic now? Making better grades?"

"Yes, sir."

"We'll have to do some fishing this summer."

"Yes, sir. I guess so."

Jacques closed his eyes and tried to make some sense of things. He still didn't know what to do about Betty and he felt guilty as hell every time he thought about Adele. How could he have been so stupid? He shifted positions and made himself think about the crops instead. Surprised to realize he trusted the Germans, he wondered how they were coming with the levees on the other side. It all seemed unreal.

He was just about to tell Chris to turn around and head home when, a little beyond them, he saw something brown floating at the edge of the water.

"Paddle to your left," he said "and let's see what it is."

When they got close, Chris said, "Ugh!"

A dead calf lay half in, half out of the water. Its body had already begun to bloat, but from the way the head was twisted, Jacques figured it had slipped over the bank and broken its neck. Flies were going after it with a vengeance.

"Hell!" Jacques said. "We can't take a chance on disease. Let's get it out of the water and bury it the best way we can. I'm glad it's a small one."

They dug a hole up under the bank, got a log and rolled the carcass into it, covering the whole thing with mud and rocks. Chris gagged, the stink was so awful.

"Whew," Jacques said when they finished and were rinsing their arms in the bayou. "Let's head on home. It's lunch time."

The sun was straight over their heads now, white hot.

"I think I'm going to throw up," Chris said, gulping.

"Try not to think about the calf," Jacques told him. "Think about baseball or something. Who do you pick to win the pennants this season? I'll make you a bet."

By mid-afternoon they had the major problems under control. The phone and electricity were still out, but you had to expect that. Jacques thought he could keep the crop loss pretty low. Everything, in fact, seemed to be looking brighter until Carver drove up in a jeep. Adele had made lemonade and Jacques and the Germans were taking a break.

"Hi, Viator," he said. "I come to take a head count for the captain. You folks might not be able to get through yet. Where's Werner?"

"What do you mean?"

"You kidding me, Viator?"

"Hell, Carver, I never spoke to any of them till yesterday. I don't even know which one Werner is. Did you ask my dad?"

Carver jumped over the side of the jeep. "Johann, get your ass over here! Where the hell's that Meyer kid?"

Johann said, "I don't know, sir. Is he not with you?"

"Oh, shit," Carver fumed. He slapped his cap against his thigh. "Would I be asking you? See if those other peckerwoods know anything."

Johann and the Germans jabbered among themselves, getting more and more excited. Only Rolf stood removed, looking insolent. Jacques couldn't make out a word other than Werner's name. Johann turned back to Carver, wide-eyed, shaking his head.

"They also know nothing, Corporal."

"When was the last time you saw him?"

Johann discussed the question with Kurt and Claus.

"Yesterday, sir, on the way to work."

"What about him?" Carver asked, indicating Rolf.

Rolf just laughed.

"You reckon Werner escaped, Carver?" the jeep driver said with a drawl.

Chris gasped. "Escaped!"

The Germans got very stiff and watchful. Carver was beside himself.

"You'd like that, wouldn't you, you stupid bastards! Didn't he know we were about to send him home?"

"He no longer has a home," said Johann quietly.

"Well, he sure as hell can't live on berries in the woods the rest of his life. Damn jackass! In the middle of a hurricane, no less. Is your phone working, Viator? I gotta report this to the C.O."

"Not yet. It's still out."

"Shit! Just my luck. Make it snappy, L.J.," Carver barked at the driver. "Back to camp, on the double."

Jacques turned to say something to Chris, but Chris had disappeared.

Chapter 33

She'd been expecting it for the past twenty-four hours and bracing herself, but all the same, when Adele saw the jeep and heard the commotion outside, her heart rattled against her ribs. The next thing she knew, Chris came tearing into the house.

"Mama! Mama! Werner's gone! We gotta find Werner and help him!"

So he hadn't been captured. He must have gotten through! She didn't know whether to laugh or cry, but Chris looked so distraught, it sobered her.

"Wait, son," she said. "You know how smart Werner is. I'm sure he's all right. What did the soldiers say?"

"They thought he was at our house, with Johann and them. Nobody's seen him since yesterday morning."

"Where do they think he is?"

"In the woods, I guess. The man said something about Werner eating berries. Will they punish him, Mama? We've got to do something!"

This was what she'd been afraid of. In all her hours of planning she hadn't been able to solve what to tell Chris. She couldn't leave him in distress - it was too cruel - but what if she explained and the army questioned him?

"Listen to me, Christophe," she said, squatting in front of him and gripping his shoulders tightly. "It's going to be all right."

He ran out, unconvinced, before she could finish.

"Chris! Chris, wait!"

She smelled the beans scorching and hurried to the stove. By then Chris was out of sight.

Left by herself, Adele fingered her rosary and puttered about the house in a daze, her head scrambling with questions. Was Werner really safe? What if the army found out the truth? What would Jacques do? Just when things were getting better, she thought. She could hardly bear the suspense. Within the hour, three jeeps and a canvas covered truck passed, headed for Papa's.

Papa told her later that the army asked a lot of damfool questions and then fanned out over the farm. It was slow going, of course, with the mud like it was. Finding footsteps was out of the question. Sheriff Prudhomme had been out, too, but not for long. He was too busy handling emergencies caused by the storm.

Mid-afternoon, Tex and an interpreter showed up with orders to interrogate the Germans some more.

"Tell Viator to round 'em up," Tex said to Adele. "Send them over here one at a time."

She rang the big iron bell. Jacques came and spoke to the soldiers, then yelled for Johann to come. Johann whistled, bringing the others in from the fields.

From the kitchen window Adele watched the men being questioned alongside the jeep. She couldn't make out what was said, but their gestures were plain enough. One by one, Tex dismissed them and sent them back to the barn. He questioned Rolf last, then, looking thoroughly frustrated, motioned the driver to turn around. Plumes of muddy water almost swamped the departing jeep.

The phone rang, making Adele jump. It was just the lineman, checking to make sure service was restored. Adele hung up, relieved. Now her mother would be able to call when Werner's family sent the agreed-upon message that he'd made it. Adele returned to the kitchen to check the cake in the oven.

The sound of shouting drew her to the back porch. With horror and mounting foreboding she saw Jacques and Rolf scuffling in the dirt at the entrance to the barn. Johann and Kurt rushed over to pull Rolf off, all of them yelling at once. The next thing Adele knew, Jacques was astride Rolf, pummeling him until Rolf went limp. Jacques got up, spat and hollered, "Tie him up!"

Seconds later, he came brushing past her.

"You stupid woman. Don't you know it's a crime?"

"What...?"

The tendons of Jacques' neck were rigid. His voice was icy and mocking.

"'Too bad they didn't ask your wife or that dummy sister of yours. They could tell you where your darling Werner is.' The bastard! I had to beat it out of him. What were you thinking of, Adele? Aiding the enemy!"

Before she could respond he was jiggling the phone.

"Edna June...Edna June, can you hear me? Get me Captain Bentley - quick!"

Adele lunged for him. "Don't, Jacques. Don't! Give the boy a chance!"

He stiff-armed her, pushing her away.

"Jacques, stop!" She tried to grab the phone away from him, but he was too strong.

"Let me talk to Captain Bentley," he snapped at someone. "Never mind who it is, just give me the captain!"

"Don't, Jacques! You don't know what you're doing!"

Sobbing now, Adele continued to fight, but Jacques overpowered her.

"Captain," he said, "I have information that the escaped man may have gone by bus to New Orleans."

Heaving with all her strength, Adele pulled the cord from the wall. The phone went dead.

"Hello? Hello?" Jacques slammed down the receiver. "You fool!" he said. "You were in on it, weren't you?"

"Damn you, yes, I helped him! I helped him the way I'd want somebody to help if it were Chris. And I hope he gets away, too, in spite of you! Why did you have to ruin it?"

"We'll finish this later, when all this is over," Jacques said.

"No, Jacques, we're already finished. When this is over, I'm taking Chris and going home. I'll get a divorce. You and Betty Hebert can live bitterly ever after!"

How she got through the rest of the day she didn't know. It was as if someone else went through the motions of cooking and cleaning. She was beyond feeling anything but despair. That evening a truck came for the POWs. She saw Jacques talking to the guards, pointing angrily toward the barn. The guards nodded, and brought Rolf out, handcuffed.

Chris came home dirty and dejected.

"I'm not hungry, Mom. Can't I just go on to bed?"

"All right," she said, too drained to argue.

She was cleaning the kerosene lamps when Jacques finally came in the house. She turned away, felt him pause, then leave the room. He came back as she was putting the lamps away.

"Do you want to talk?" he said stiffly.

"No."

"It was my duty."

She gave him a withering look and went outside.

He followed her.

"I don't want a divorce."

"I do."

"I need you."

"No, Jacques. You've got your hate to keep you warm."

That night, she fell asleep on the kitchen table, sitting in the dark, and began to dream that Werner, dressed in a baker's tall cap and white apron, was planting raisins in cinnamon rolls, making little faces with them. A piece of masking tape covered Werner's mouth, but he didn't seem to mind. His eyes were merry, and he offered her a tray of gaily decorated petit fours. She was about to take one when someone began banging on the large double doors behind Werner. The doors were heavy looking and latched with a steel bar. Werner looked at her, beseeching her help. In her dream she kept crying to him to run, run, but he couldn't. His feet were tangled up in telephone wire.

"Jacques! Adele! Let me in!"

It took a moment for her to come to and separate the dream from consciousness, to realize that it was Papa, pounding on the back door.

"Coming," she said, and fumbled for the light pull. "What is it, Papa?"

"Cap'n Bentley. He wants to see me and you at once."

She sucked in her breath.

"I'll get my purse."

On the way, she looked in on Chris. He lay across the bed in his underwear, snoring. She sighed, and spread the quilt over his legs.

Jacques was sleeping, too, but she didn't try to be quiet. She didn't care any more. He heard her in the closet and shielded his eyes from the light.

"What are you doing?" he said.

"Captain Bentley wants to see Papa and me."

Jacques threw his legs over the side of the bed. The sudden movement made him flinch.

"I'll go with you."

"No! Stay with Chris and be a father, for once!"

She left before he could respond.

Papa had the engine running, ready to go. His hand trembled when he shifted gears.

"What you think they want?" he said.

"I don't know," Adele said, afraid to consider the possibilities. That had become her standard answer to everything lately: I don't know.

Papa tried to dodge the craters where the road had washed out, but even so, the truck kept bucking on potholes. To keep her head from hitting the roof, Adele kept a tight grip on the door handle. Their headlights shimmered on the full ditches. Water was backed up clear over the road in spots and spewed as they passed.

Adele rubbed her arms and wished she'd brought a sweater. The night air had a bite, but it was probably the prospect of what they were in for that made her shiver. Had Werner been caught? Had Captain Bentley found out what they'd done? She tried to make her mind go blank. It felt like they'd driven a thousand miles before they finally got to the camp.

Despite the hour, the entire compound was illuminated inside and out. The guards were unusually snappy.

"Go right in," the soldier at the gate told Papa. "Captain Bentley's order."

Adele tried not to show how nervous she was. Papa kept one hand on her shoulder and held his hat to his chest with the other like he was about to say the Pledge of Allegiance.

Captain Bentley, looking tired and unhappy, sat behind his desk. In front of him, with wrinkled yellow tags attached, were Jeanette's old suitcase and the black wingtip shoes Papa had given Werner.

Adele's hand flew to her mouth to cover an involuntary scream. Papa took a step back and stiffened. His fingernails dug into her arm. Tears of disappointment stung Adele's eyes. They'd captured Werner. It was all for nothing. Damn Jacques!

"Sit down," Captain Bentley ordered.

Footsteps thundered loudly in the wooden hallway, and in the next office a mimeograph machine was thumping out copies. Farther back in the building a burst of laughter was quickly squelched. Papa squirmed. Adele steeled herself, fighting panic. The captain eyed them over laced fingers.

"We have located Werner Meyer," he said wearily.

"Is he all right?" Adele asked in a whisper.

"I'm afraid not, Mrs. Viator. Meyer's dead."

"Dead? No!"

Everything in the room shifted and swayed. Through the ringing in her ears she heard Papa saying 'mon Dieu' over and over. Rage surged up in her like bile.

"You've killed him! Why did you have to kill him? He only wanted to stay!"

The captain shook his head, sighing, and answered as though he were speaking to a child.

"You don't understand, Mrs. Viator. No one shot him."

Adele and Papa were uncomprehending.

"He was run over," the captain said.

"No!" Adele and Papa cried together. They turned grief stricken faces to each other. Tears oozed from Papa's eyes and wet his wrinkled cheeks. Adele inhaled deeply, trying to clear her head. In a choked voice, she said, "What happened?"

"As near as we can figure," the captain said, "the bus he was on broke down. They had to wait out the storm for a replacement. Our men went to his cousin's bakery to bring him back. When Meyer got off the streetcar, he must have caught sight of them. He bolted and ran right smack in front of a florist truck."

"Dear God," Adele moaned.

"The driver's an older fellow," the captain went on. "Been with that company thirty years. They say he's pretty broken up, but there wasn't any way he could have stopped in time."

"Did the boy die instant?" Papa asked in a hoarse voice.

"On the way to the hospital, Mr. Viator. In the ambulance. The doctors say he never knew what hit him."

"Thank God."

Adele stared at her lap. Werner was dead. Not free, dead. What if he'd had a chance with the Russians?

Beside her, Papa shaped and re-shaped his hat. The captain was saying the police had investigated. The driver had not been cited. Adele, in shock, barely listened.

The captain cleared his throat. "Meyer was pretending to be a deaf mute. He gave the conductor a note to that effect, saying he wanted to get off on Napoleon Avenue. Clever plan. He looked American enough to get by with it, too."

"Werner was an honor student, Captain, before the war," Adele said.

"The only thing we haven't established for sure is how he got to Acadia. We know that's where he caught the bus."

Neither Adele nor Papa spoke, but stared fixedly at the dark, varnished floor.

There was a pause and then Adele heard the captain say quietly, "He would have been nineteen next month, same as my boy."

She wept, then, and Papa hunkered next to her, his head in his hands.

There was a scraping sound as the captain stood up.

"Go home," he told them heavily, "and take Meyer's things with you."

"But, Captain," stammered Adele.

"What's the point in pursuing the matter, Mrs. Viator? It's been a long war. Enough people have been hurt."

He closed the manila folder on which Werner's name was typed.

"Red Cross will notify his family. Let's leave it at that."

Papa took the suitcase and handed her the shoes. Adele grasped for words, but the captain had turned his back to them and was standing in front of the photograph in the silver frame. Adele would remember the sight of him as long as she lived.

Chapter 34

Toward dawn, Jacques heard Adele stir. He was waiting with coffee when she came out of the bathroom.

She'd fallen asleep, after hours of tears and recriminations, out of exhaustion and grief. She was still wearing yesterday's clothes. The night's crying showed. Her eyes were badly swollen and her face was pale. The cup, when she took it, rattled against the saucer until she steadied it with both hands.

"Is Chris awake?" she asked dully.

"Not yet," Jacques told her.

He dreaded it, too. Jacques had spent the rest of the night on the front porch in total confusion. Ever since Adele had cried herself to sleep he'd wrestled with what to do. He paced, he wept. He cursed Hitler, the war, himself. Killing a man in combat was one thing, but to be responsible for the death of an unarmed man - that was like murder. How could he expect Adele to forgive that? What if he lost her?

There in the dark he surveyed his life the way they say a drowning person does. He'd asked himself for the thousandth time how this could happen to people like them. The thought of Werner filled him with remorse. The thought of Betty filled him with shame.

Coming to terms with all that had happened meant thinking about France, something he'd tried his best all these months to avoid. He broke out in a sweat recalling the carnage at Normandy, the panic, and the Nazi snipers he'd gunned down with the blood of his sergeant still on his hands.

In the prelude to dawn, that first faint brightening of the sky, he'd cried for them all and for what the war had taken from them, cried like he hadn't cried since he was a boy.

Adele barely sipped her coffee and lay back down. She stared at the ceiling with lifeless eyes, all but her face under the cover.

Jacques sat on the dressing table stool staring at his bare feet, overcome with helplessness.

"I should have let him take his chances at home," Adele said. "Maybe it wouldn't have been as bad as he thought."

"Don't."

"You know that snakeskin belt Papa wears? Werner made that. He was always making little presents for us or bringing us something from the canteen."

"Please, Adele."

She shook her head and went on in a flat, faraway voice.

"You never saw a harder worker. If the other men finished early, Werner would find something else to do till time to go back to camp. He'd sharpen the shovels or hoe the corn, anything we needed."

"Stop it, Adele! Stop torturing yourself. I wish there were something I could do!"

"It's too late," she said, and went on remembering. "Werner and Chris built a tree house last summer in that farthest pecan tree. Did you see it?" She choked up again. "How am I going to tell Chris? Werner would still be alive if I hadn't helped him. How am I going to tell Chris?"

"It's not your fault, I told you, it's mine! I wish to God I'd never reported him. Damn that Rolf!"

He wanted to put his hands over his ears. He didn't think he could stand seeing her hurt so much. He got up and lit a cigarette to clear his head.

Adele's straw purse was on the bed. She fished in it for a tissue.

"You would have liked him, Jacques, if you'd given him a chance."

"Oh, God, Adele! I'm so sorry!"

Chris came in then, without knocking. He was rubbing sleep from his eyes and tugging at a pair of high water jeans that, without a belt, slid to his hips.

"Did they find him yet? Did they catch Werner?"

"Come here, son," Adele said, sitting up slowly and patting the bed. "Let me do the talking, Jacques."

Chris crawled in bed next to her, looking apprehensive.

"Can you be a real brave soldier?" Adele said. While she spoke, she rubbed the back of her fingers on Chris's cheek. "We got some bad news last night."

"About Werner? What's the matter? They caught him, didn't they?"

"No, dear. There was an accident. In New Orleans."

"New Orleans? How could Werner get to New Orleans? Is he hurt? Can we go get him?"

Adele's face was the color of ashes.

"I'm afraid not, son. Werner's dead. He got hit by a truck. They don't know exactly what happened. He was going to his relatives to hide till the war was over."

"No!" Chris screamed. "No, Mama! Maybe they made a mistake. Maybe it's not him."

He looked at them pleadingly and began to crack his knuckles.

"It's him," Jacques said, putting his hand on the boy's shoulder. "The army's sure. I'd give anything if it weren't true, son, but it is."

Chris yanked free.

"I'll bet you're glad!" he shouted at Jacques. "You got what you wanted, didn't you?" His voice broke and he was crying and yelling at the same time. "Now are you satisfied? He's dead, Daddy. He won't bother you any more. He's dead!"

Adele said, "Don't, Chris, please. It's my fault, too, really it is. I helped Werner escape. I should have gone with him, or got Grandma to meet him, or..."

Jacques interrupted her. "You did what you thought was right!"

"Daddy wanted him dead. You know he did, Mama. He ruins everything. I hate you, Daddy. I wish you'd never come back!"

Chris ran sobbing to his room and slammed the door.

Jacques started after him, but Adele stopped him. "Leave him alone," she said. "He needs to get it out."

Jacques fled outdoors and chopped firewood until his arms couldn't hold the ax any longer. About eight he went in. Adele was still in bed, unmoving.

"Where's Chris?" he said.

"I made him go to school." She spoke slowly, as if talking were an effort.

"Do you know when the funeral is?"

"Captain Bentley said they'd let us know. They were bringing the body back from New Orleans."

"I've got a couple of things to do in town," he said. "Will you be all right?"

She didn't respond.

He hadn't noticed till then the lines that time and worry were fixing, like tracings on a leaf, around her mouth and eyes.

"I won't be long," he told her. "Try to get some rest."

At the door he paused. He had to say it.

"You won't leave me, will you?"

She turned and faced the wall.

Chapter 35

Jacques went to the bank first, and then the POW camp. Other than a little activity by the motor pool, there wasn't much going on. It'd be a while before the playing fields could be used. Water stood under the barracks as high as six inches up the concrete blocks. You could see the stain marks where it had gone down some already. A couple of Germans on the roof cleaning pine straw from the gutters turned to look when Jacques' boots made a racket on the board walkway.

Shorty was on duty at the gate.

"Hey, Viator, what're you doin' here?"

"Business," Jacques said.

"You look like hell. Man, we had enough rain here to float Noah's ark. Storm do much damage out at your place?"

"Could have been worse."

"Sure scared the shit out of us here. Cripes, we thought the whole damn place was going to blow away. Know anything about the tornado south of town? I heard it tore up a row of houses."

"Anybody killed?"

"No, but don't ask me how. Say, did you hear about the German kid?"

"Look, Shorty, I'm in a hurry. Where's the captain's office?"

The sergeant on desk duty wasn't one of Jo Jo's clientele. In Jacques' experience, guys with prissy mustaches like that were usually a pain.

"I need to speak to Captain Bentley," Jacques said.

"He's over at the infirmary. Your name?"

"Viator."

"Spelled?"

"V-i-a-t-o-r."

The desk sergeant noted his watch and wrote in the day book in a cramped, vertical script. His pen scratched.

"Nature of visit?"

Jacques felt like saying it was none of his business.

"Personal," he said.

The sergeant said, "Oh," and gave him the once over.

"How long will he be?" Jacques said.

"No idea. You can have a seat, or you can go over there and see if he's busy. Suit yourself."

"I'll go. Where's the infirmary?"

"Barracks B, back door. Inside, on your right."

"Thanks for the hospitality," Jacques told him drily.

"Hey, corporal," the sergeant's voice stopped him. "If I were you I'd do something about that uniform. If there's one thing the captain gets the reds over, it's sloppy soldiers."

"The hell with it," Jacques mumbled under his breath. Who had time to think about clothes?

He found the infirmary using the snotty sergeant's directions, but he could just as well have followed his nose. The rear of B Barracks reeked of rubbing alcohol and the pine oil an orderly was using to mop the far end of the long room. Of the four cots the infirmary was equipped with, three were empty. A light-haired middle aged man holding a bandaged left arm sat on the fourth, the captain and a medic beside him.

"I took in the arm fifteen stitches," the medic said with a thick, gravelly accent. "Your doctor will look at it tonight when he makes his rounds."

"Will the hand be all right?" the captain asked.

"If there are no complications. I think yes. He has luck."

Jacques watched from the doorway. The captain clearly had a lot of mileage on him. He looked overdue a furlough. His uniform was first rate, obviously tailor made, and over the breast pocket were two battle ribbons and the Silver Star. He turned. Jacques saluted.

"Excuse my dress, sir," Jacques said. "The storm and all."

"At ease, corporal. Were you looking for someone?"

"You, sir. I'm Viator. Jacques Viator."

"I see. What is it, Viator?"

"A word, sir, when you're finished?"

"All right. We're almost through. Alfred here's done a good job. This man's a violinist. Hurt himself chopping some bamboo the storm flattened."

Shifting from one foot to the other, Jacques waited for the captain to finish and motion him out side.

"Now what?" the captain said.

"The dead man, sir. Werner Meyer."

"The matter's closed. Didn't your wife tell you?"

"I didn't mean that."

Before Jacques could explain, the captain's orderly approached them on the path between buildings.

"Excuse me, sir. The undertake just left. The body's ready for viewing."

"All right, sergeant. I'll check things out. Want to come along, Viator?"

Jacques took a deep breath.

"Yes, sir," he said.

They'd laid out Werner's body in the POW's day room. The ping pong tables had been pushed aside, the chairs lined at attention along the walls. Jacques was surprised at how bright the room was, colorful as a bazaar. It was a regular gallery of drawings and paintings - pinups and castles and mountain scenes. The Germans had covered one wall with red and orange paper flowers made from those tissues that apples and citrus fruit came wrapped in. On a card table in the corner sat a hand carved chess set with somebody's king in check.

Against such a background, the raw pine coffin seemed even more out of place. It sat in the room's center on four gray folding chairs, directly under a light shade made of glued and brightly lacquered popsicle sticks. A black cloth was draped over the light fixture, but you could still see the sticks, and they cast slatted shadows on the corpse.

Jacques swallowed hard and made himself look at the body of the man who'd been his family's friend. Without thinking, he made the sign of the cross.

"They did a good job, don't you think?" the captain was saying. "You can see the bruise on the side of his head, but it isn't real noticeable."

Jacques had never given any thought to what Werner would look like, and his first jolting reaction was to remember Carl at that age. The wide jaw was the same; the same far apart eyes and straight blonde hair. Werner's face was tanned, and probably hadn't needed shaving more than once a week. A boy's face, almost, like Adele said.

Jacques had seen many corpses, but none that affected him like the sight of this one.

"I didn't know him," he heard himself say. The words sounded remote, as if filtered through cotton.

The captain shook his head.

"Damn shame. Meyer was one of the best we had here. Never gave us any trouble. War is hell, Viator."

"Yes, sir," Jacques said. He couldn't take his eyes off the body.

"Hans says Meyer surrendered first chance he got. The boy's father told him not to get taken by the Russians. God knows what's become of the father. He got carted off to Dachau. At least Meyer never knew that. The censors brought me his sister's letter the same day he ran off."

Jacques had to sit down. He put his face in his hands.

"Sorry, sir," he said.

"It was you that called, wasn't it?" the captain said. "We'd have traced him sooner or later. You all right?"

"I'll be okay in a minute," Jacques said.

The captain sighed.

"It's such a stupid damn waste. Why'd they have to start it, Viator? If it hadn't been for Hitler, we could have stopped Japan."

"I don't know, sir. I just don't know."

"Well," the captain said, becoming official again, "everything seems to be in order. I'll see what I can do about some flowers."

Jacques opened his eyes and struggled to get a grip on himself.

"Captain...I...we wondered about the funeral, my wife and I. May I ask where you plan to bury him, sir?"

"Back by the woods, I guess. Some of the locals object to having him in the cemetery. There'll be a service tomorrow at ten. The German-speaking chaplain's coming over from St. Martinville."

"That's what I wanted to ask you about, Captain," Jacques said. "You see, we have our own little plot out there on the farm. It's consecrated and everything. My mother's buried there and the little girl we lost." He had to clear his throat to go on. "We'd like to have Werner there, too, with your permission. It'd be a comfort to my family."

The captain rubbed his chin and took his time answering.

"I don't see why not," he said at last, "as long as it's on record that way. We'll be breaking up camp soon, anyhow. I'll send a squad out to dig the grave this afternoon. You can show them where you want it."

"If you don't mind, sir, I'd like to take care of it myself."

"As you wish. Call if you need any help."

Chapter 36

The funeral wasn't anything like Adele expected.

She'd steeled herself to be strong for the sake of the others, but she nearly buckled when they arrived and saw the coffin, its starkness only slightly softened by some wilting carnations and several jars of day lilies. The smell of raw lumber hung in the damp air. The body - it didn't seem like Werner - lay waxy and stiff. You could see where the undertaker had tried to cover the injuries with makeup. The Germans had pooled what pieces of their old Wehrmacht uniforms they still had for Werner to be buried in. Adele cringed at the sight of the swastikas. She would have preferred to remember Werner in the familiar navy blue fatigues, or better still, the yellow and gray striped shirt of Jacques' he'd worn when he made his break for freedom.

Jeanette sobbed, and Adele was afraid for a minute that Chris was going to faint before Captain Bentley's orderly directed them to their seats. Places had been saved for the Viator family in the army section with the camp personnel. The POWs, some of them dressed for the special occasion in the remnants of their tattered uniforms sat, shabby and erect, across the room.

On the old piano in the corner, Claus was playing Bach. The music, "Jesus, Joy of Man's Desiring," was very nearly Adele's undoing, and she saw several of the POWs wipe their eyes. Looking at them face to face across Werner's remains, Adele wondered at their expressions. What were these defeated soldiers feeling on the verge of their long journey home, and what would they return to? What had they learned? Were their families and Werner's waiting and praying the way she'd prayed for Jacques? If only they hadn't listened to Hitler and his crowd.

An elderly minister rose, and after some introductory remarks addressed to the Americans, began conducting the service in German. He read something, apparently from the Bible, and then asked them, in German and English, to bow their heads in prayer.

During what Adele supposed was the eulogy, she glanced sideways at her family. Papa was clearly sweltering in his only suit. It was wool, but he'd insisted on wearing it, out of respect. She and Jeanette fanned him with the cardboard fans from Joubert's Mortuary, the ones with the garish copy of The Agony in the Garden on them. Jeanette kept looking around nervously, the way she always did in a crowd, trying to follow what was happening, unaware that her charm bracelet tinkled with each flick of the fan. Chris's head was lowered, his shoulders slumped. As for Jacques, he stared straight ahead, statue still.

The old chaplain droned on, and since she couldn't understand him anyway, Adele let her mind wander.

She'd been amazed the day before when Jacques returned with permission to bury Werner on the farm. It eased the pain, a little, to know that Werner wouldn't be stuck in an anonymous grave somewhere with no one to put flowers there on All Saints. She didn't know what had been said between Jacques and Chris, but after Jacques told her about his conversation with Captain Bentley, he went looking for Chris, and they'd come back an hour or so later with shovels, saying they'd be at the cemetery. Chris was still keeping his distance from Jacques, but more from grief now than anger, she felt.

Late afternoon, Captain Bentley had come out to make sure everything was done according to regulations. There were papers for Jacques to sign and a map to be made showing the grave's location. The map would be placed in the file, Captain Bentley said, for the benefit of next of kin. He'd stayed and had coffee, and Adele noticed his eyes following Chris.

Now the chaplain finished speaking, bringing her back to the present. The POWs filed by the body to pay their last respects, a rag-tag group in combination winter/summer, German/American clothing. Kurt and a young German Adele didn't know wept openly.

Returning to their places, the men picked up dog-eared hymnals. The pianist struck a chord on the chipped, yellowing keys. At the tone, the POWs proceeded to sing in excellent three part harmony, a capella. Adele recognized "Fairest Lord Jesus", but it sounded strange in German.

The chaplain stood, and the men again bowed their heads.

Chris whispered, "Is it over?"

"Almost, I think," she whispered back. "Are you all right?"

He nodded, but he was greenish looking and tight lipped. He'd begged off breakfast, saying his stomach was upset.

The men sang another hymn, one she didn't know, while the casket was closed. They folded the flag and laid it aside. Someone gave an order, and the Germans, as if in a single motion, extended their arms in silent salute. Then most of them marched solemnly out. The eight pallbearers loaded the coffin on the covered army truck waiting at the door, climbed aboard and stationed themselves four on each side, militarily erect.

The reporter from the Courville Courier, making notes on the back of an envelope, scrambled to get out of the way and got in beside the driver.

Captain Bentley asked Jacques to lead. It should have taken them only half an hour to get to the graveyard, but they had to drive slower than usual, with the roads in such bad shape.

Adele was too numb to talk, and Chris didn't say anything at all. He merely rested his head against the truck door and stared out the window.

They turned off the main road onto a lane where buttercups grew in mounds on the grassy strip between ruts. The flowers, nature's delicate survivors, were already recovering from the fury of the storm. A short distance farther and the procession came to the white picket fence that surrounded the cemetery, protecting it from the heedless hooves of cattle.

Chris got down and held the gate open for the little cortege to pass through; their truck first, then the makeshift hearse, the jeep with Captain Bentley and the chaplain in it, and Papa and Jeanette, bringing up the rear.

When Adele had first come to the Junction, it had seemed strange to find the gravesites underground and covered with grass. She was used to New Orleans, where the dead were buried in vaults above ground because of the sea level. Still, she'd fallen in love with the tiny private cemetery even before they'd buried their baby there. It was an island of peace in a sea of undulating rice. Papa kept the border of dwarf azaleas trimmed and the place immaculately tended whether his other work got done or not. Sometimes, when she needed to get away for a while, Adele came and sat under the pine trees near where their little girl lay. It wasn't far from there that Jacques and Chris had dug Werner's grave. Adele was glad. Werner had liked to hear the wind in the pines, too.

His made the fourth grave. Jacques' mother and Mr. Max's had large granite headstones. A small marble angel marked the grave of Jacques' and Adele's baby, as if to watch over her. Adele and Chris had discussed what kind of marker Werner should have. A simple cross would probably be best, she thought, like the ones you saw in pictures of Flanders Field.

In the bright May sun the geraniums Chris had brought over from the house were stunningly red. The freshly dug brown trench split the vivid grass like an open wound. They gathered beside it for the last, brief ceremony. Adele could feel her high heels sinking in the sodden ground. She became aware of sniffling, and of Jeanette's stranglehold on her hand.

With the end of the service, Adele looked helplessly at Jacques and put her arm around Chris. They exchanged a few words with the others and then rode home in aching, empty silence.

Hannah had come and left a basket full of food. Adele put an apron over her good dress and set the table. It was something to do.

She called Jacques and Chris to lunch, but none of them had much appetite. Chris chewed on a drumstick and picked at some rice dressing.

For his sake, she tried to keep up a front.

"It was a nice funeral, wasn't it?" she said. "I hope someone tells his family. If they're still alive," she added thoughtfully.

"Yes, it was." Jacques said. "As much as I could understand."

"I'm glad he's here with us."

Chris asked to be excused.

Jacques laid his napkin on the table.

"I need to get out to the field," he said.

"I know."

He moved more quickly now, but there was a jerk to his walk, the one leg slightly off beat. Adele watched him go till he was a dot in the distance. Then she turned to the sink and filled the dishpan with suds and the tears she'd been holding back all day.

"Why, God?" she cried. "Why?"

Chapter 37

The strain was killing him. There wasn't much time. Maybe, just maybe, if he could straighten things out with Betty, Adele might give him a second chance. He wouldn't have any peace till he tried. It was driving him nuts, the way Adele gave him the cold shoulder. She slept on the rollaway in the living room and she'd started packing. He had to find a way to make her stay.

He'd been tied to the farm ever since the funeral. Each time he thought he'd found a chance to see about Betty, he was thwarted by some new crisis. The irrigation pump was acting up, and a stretch of fence had given way. The damn snakes were playing hell with the levees, burrowing in the soft dirt like earthworms, shifting the water levels on the young rice. You expected an invasion after a hard rain, but he and Chris must have killed a dozen, easy, plus a slew of muskrats. The boy had been a godsend.

More than once, Jacques regretted planting the new field. It only meant more levees to look after. Between the morning and evening rounds he hardly had time to tend to the cattle, much less take care of personal business. He told himself it was worth it, though, that if it would help beat the Japs and get the other guys home, he shouldn't gripe. It was just that he desperately needed time to work things out with Betty.

Twice, when he'd been alone in the house, he'd started to call to see if she'd got the report, but he didn't dare. That nosy Edna June was liable to be listening, or somebody on the party line.

Jacques had even started a couple of times to pray, but he figured he wasn't in very good standing with the Man Upstairs, and he didn't know what to ask for, anyway. It didn't seem right to expect God to bail you out when you'd been thumbing your nose at the rules.

The evening he finally got a chance to go to town, Jacques broke a couple of speed records. By the time he reached Betty's apartment, he was as jumpy as if he were going into battle.

He couldn't bring himself to use the key, and knocked, instead.

"Who is it?" Betty called. "Come on in, the door's open."

He walked inside and stopped in his tracks. The green brocade sofa, the glass-topped desk, the mahogany end tables with the radio and brass lamps were all gone. Their absence made the tiny living room look smaller than ever, with nothing but a rolled up rug and some Campbell's soup cartons to hide the bare floor. Sticking out the top of one box were the Cassatt prints.

"Not you, too!" he said.

From the next room Betty called out "Hi" as nonchalantly as if he were the paper boy, and continued folding a ruffled petticoat.

A jumble of tissue – trailing hat boxes and open, partly filled suitcases covered the bed.

"What's...?" he heard himself ask in a voice that sounded more like a croak.

"What does it look like, Jacques? I'm packing. Have a seat, if you can find one."

He watched, stupefied, while, brisk and purposeful, she emptied her lingerie drawer.

He cleared his throat. "Can we talk? I wanted to come sooner, but I couldn't."

"I guess so, but I haven't much time. I've got some stuff to finish up at the office."

She led the way to the breakfast nook.

"Do you want a Coke or iced tea or something?"

"Yeah, sure. Anything."

She had on the red halter and striped shorts that could give Lana Turner competition. Jacques looked resolutely away.

Blushing like a fool, he said, "Are you all right?"

"Don't I look it?"

He hadn't expected her to be flippant.

"For God's sake, Betty, don't beat around the bush. You know what I mean. What did Doc say?"

"All right, Jacques. You can relax. I'm not pregnant. I'd have called you, but I didn't want to make trouble."

The relief he felt was akin to standing up in a foxhole after the strafing stopped. You wanted to jump and holler, but you were too weak and all you could say, over and over, was thank you, Jesus, thank you, Jesus. Jacques swallowed hard, and leaned back, a little woozy.

"Oh, God, Betty, I'm so glad."

She dabbed at a limp sprig of mint in her glass.

"You'd better let me have the key," she said. "I have to give it back to the landlady."

"I was going to," he said.

"I know. You dropped the note you were going to leave last time. I found it under the stairway."

"Oh," he said. "I didn't realize."

He'd been so upset he'd forgotten the note completely.

"We both knew it couldn't last," she said, but there was a catch of sadness in her voice.

He got the silver key from his billfold and laid it on the table between them. "But why the packing? Where are you going?"

She picked up an emery board and proceeded to file a crimson fingernail.

"Houston," she said. "I called Boogie and he thinks he can get me a job. He knows a big shot with one of the oil companies. Somebody he plays tennis with."

"You aren't going to move in with Boogie!"

"Don't be ridiculous! Not that it'd be any of your business," she snapped. "For your information, I've got a room at the Catholic Women's Club. Isn't that a joke? I'll really have to be good there, won't I? Do you suppose they'll let me smoke?"

"Betty, don't. I'm sorry. I shouldn't have said that. I hate it when you make yourself sound cheap."

"Guilty conscience, I guess." She looked at her nails. "I didn't set out to ruin your happy home, Jacques. I just couldn't help wanting you. Adele's a lucky lady."

"I don't know about that," he said, "but I'm flattered you cared, I really am. I'd give anything if I could take back what I've put us all through."

"You and I were pretty mixed up," Betty said. "What do you

say we just blame what happened on the war, okay? Temporary insanity or something."

"But you don't have to leave Courville. I won't bother you, I promise."

"It's not just you. Armand's brother came home. He pulled something in his back and got a medical discharge. How do you like that? He never even left Washington."

"That's still no reason for you to go. You could get another job, easy."

"I need a change, Jacques. Don't you see I need to start over?"

Her eyes, so blue that even the whites had a bluish tint, pleaded with him to understand.

"Can't you wish me luck?" she said.

"Sure," Jacques said. "All the luck in the world. You deserve it."

She walked him to the door.

"Isn't there anything I can do?" he said. He took out his billfold again. "I withdrew some savings in case you...uh...you know, the baby. Let me help with your expenses. It's the least I can do. Please!"

Betty shook her head in a way that forbade argument.

"No, thanks. I've got plenty. Armand saw to that."

"Are you sure?"

"Positive. Buy Adele a peace offering."

"Well," he said after an awkward silence, "I guess this is it, huh?"

She held out her hand.

"Goodbye, Jacques. Good luck."

"Tell Boogie to take good care of you," he said. "And tell him he owes me a letter!"

"I'll tell him."

"So long, Betty."

"So long, soldier," she said softly, and closed the door.

Jacques slipped off his khaki tie with one hand and loosened his collar. The air was fragrant with new-mown grass. He took deep, prolonged breaths of it, one after another. Crickets had set up their fierce, competitive rasping. He felt like hailing the stars that had sprouted like seed broadcast in the limpid twilight sky.

Thinking of Betty going off to Houston, of Betty and Boogie having good times together, threw him a little, but he was getting used to the idea already and feeling better about it all the time. He felt young again, and in a crazy kind of way, full and hollow at the same time. He just knew there was hope, now, for Adele and him.

The stores were open late on Thursdays. He went to Western Auto and bought the best ball and bat they had. After that, he made two more stops: one at Miss Libby's Flower Shop and another at St. Isidore's.

Father Sebastian was in the rectory, fixing supper.

"Pull up a chair," Father Sebastian said. "How about a bologna sandwich? Effie's off visiting her sister. That niece of theirs just had another baby. You know Effie. She had to go make sure it got baptized properly."

You'd have thought Jacques dropped in every day.

"I was on my way home and wondered if you could hear my confession."

"Of course," Father Sebastian said. "I'll get my stole."

"Eat your sandwich first. I'll go on over to church and make a visit."

"All right. I'll be there shortly."

The side door was left open for anyone who might want to pray. Inside, the musty smell of incense lingered in the air. Jacques' hand found the holy water font and he blessed himself. At first he couldn't see anything but the rosy blinking of the votive candles and the sanctuary lamp. He had to grope his way along the outside aisle to a back pew. The kneeler clattered when he lowered it, and creaked under his weight, sounding disproportionately loud in the empty church.

Stillness returned, settling around him again like dust, and when he looked up he could make out the splayed corpus on the crucifix above the altar.

"Forgive me," he whispered. The words were accompanied by tears, sudden and smarting. "Forgive me!"

Only a short while passed before Jacques heard the sacristy door open. He hastily blew his nose. A few of the lights came on, producing a mist the color of pollen. Jacques' throat tightened. He hid his face in his hands until he heard Father Sebastian pass and enter the confessional. Jacques rose, trembling, and approached the penitent's cubicle. He was more nervous than he'd been the first time, thirty years earlier. He fell with a thud to his knees.

The window slid open and Father Sebastians's profile became dimly visible, a gray silhouette behind the grille.

"Bless me, Father," Jacques said, "for I have sinned. It's been about eight months since my last confession." He stopped and gulped. "I...uh...haven't been to Mass since November. I've cussed a lot, and I've been taking the Lord's name in vain. It's a bad habit I got into, in the army."

He broke out in a sweat.

"I caused a man's death, I've hurt my family real bad and..."

He couldn't go on.

"Something else?" Father Sebastian prodded.

Jacques had put it off as long as he could.

"I committed...oh, God help me, Father, I broke the sixth commandment. A whole bunch of times! I cheated on my wife."

He was glad it was out.

The priest asked calmly, "With more than one person?"

Jacques winced. "Oh, no, Father. Just one!"

"You realize God gives us the strength to resist temptation, don't you? It's difficult at times, but it can be done."

"I know," Jacques told him. "I don't know what got into me. It won't happen again."

"Are you certain?"

"Yes, Father. It's all over, I promise. I came as soon as I was sure."

The rest was easy, even his grudge against the Germans. The more he talked, the lighter he felt.

When Jacques was through, Father Sebastian gave him a lecture on mending his ways, assigned a penance and told him to make a good act of contrition. After the absolution, the priest said, "Good. Go in peace, now, and God bless you."

Jacques could have shouted, the relief was so great.

Walking back from church, Father Sebastian put his arm around Jacques.

"Remember the time I caught you and Carl sampling the altar wine?" The old priest chuckled.

"Do I remember! We were so scared you'd tell our folks we nearly peed in our pants. How about the time I was chasing Jeanette and she fell in your goldfish pond? Whatever happened to that, by the way?"

"Oh, the fish got old and died and I got tired of fooling with it," Father Sebastian said. "It was a lot of trouble to keep clean."

They lingered by the driveway. Jacques thanked him again.

"When are you coming to listen in on my radio?" Father Sebastian said. "The one that stirred up the hornet's nest."

"So you heard about that."

"Oh, sure. It isn't every day you get a visit from the F.B.I. People jump to conclusions."

"People should have better sense," Jacques said.

"Rumors were a lot worse in the last war. You have to expect a little hysteria."

"I guess I'm not the only one who's been a little crazy. Listen, Father, how about if I come back next week for a real visit? I want to get home to Adele."

"Run along. Next time will be fine."

"Thanks, Father. Pray for us!"

Jacques felt as light as the white egrets looked, sailing over the fields with their long legs trailing like kite tails. He felt like he could fly the rest of the way home.

The house was quiet. Chris was already asleep. Jacques pulled a chair up close to the bed and put the bat and ball where Chris would see them as soon as he woke up.

Adele was sitting in the living room. She looked up anxiously, leaving a half finished argyle sock dangling from her knitting needles. Jacques started to squat down along side her, but a cramp locked his leg and he had to straighten up. His heart pounded a fusillade in his chest. What if she turned him away?

"Here," he said, and laid in her lap a green paper cone with a dozen roses in it.

She searched his face.

He bent in front of her, kissed her on the forehead and squeezed both her arms.

"Listen to me," he said. "I've just been to confession."

"You have?"

"I'll tell you anything you want to know, anything. But you've got to believe me." He looked her straight in the eye and said, "I'm sorry for everything that's happened and I'm all yours. If God can forgive me, can't you? I love you, Adele!"

Tears trickled down her cheeks.

"Oh, Jacques!"

"It can't be too late, Adele. It just can't!"

Adele looked down at the flowers.

"What about Betty?" she said.

"It's all over. It was all over before the storm. I wanted to tell you, but I just couldn't."

They hugged each other long and hard. Eventually, Adele got up, half-crying, and put the roses in a cut glass vase.

"Did you eat?" she said. "There's some gumbo left."

Jacques hadn't had time to think about food.

"Now that you mention it, I'm starving!"

They went to the kitchen arm in arm. When he had eaten, they sat on the porch in the dark, close together, until they could talk without so many hesitations. She took the pins from her hair and rested her head on his shoulder. The squeak of the glider made an accompaniment to the familiar night sounds. A cool breeze came up and made Adele shiver.

"Do you want a blanket?" Jacques asked her.

"No, let's go in."

They closed up the house together, reverting easily to their old way of doing things.

While Adele brushed her teeth, Jacques folded the bedspread and laid it on the cedar chest.

"Guess what I'm going to do first thing in the morning?" he called out.

"What?" came the answer, muffled by the sound of running water.

"I'm going to call Carl and see if he'll meet me at The Tree."

"I'm glad," she said.

He pulled down the shades.

Adele came out of the bathroom smiling shyly.

In seconds Jacques had skinned out of his uniform and tossed it in the corner.

Tomorrow, he said to himself as he turned off the lamp, I'm going to see if my jeans still fit.

The End

Made in the USA
Lexington, KY
17 May 2013